THE RANCHER'S SURRENDER

JILL SHALVIS

INTIMATE™MOMENTS®

Published by Silhouette Books

America's Publisher of Contemporary Romance

SILHOUETTE BOOKS

ISBN 0-373-07941-9

THE RANCHER'S SURRENDER

Visit us at www.romance.net

Printed in U.S.A.

Books by Jill Shalvis

Silhouette Intimate Moments

JILL SHALVIS

When pressed for an answer on why she writes romance, Jill Shalvis just smiles and says she didn't realize there was anything else. She's written over a dozen novels so far and doesn't plan on stopping. She lives in California, in a house filled with young children, too many animals and her hero/husband. Readers can write to Jill c/o Silhouette Books, 300 East 42nd Street, 6th floor, New York, NY 10017.

To Kelsey—
you may be my oldest,
but you'll still always be my baby.

Prologue

Zoe Martin squeezed her foster sisters' hands tightly, but only because she thought Delia or Maddie might be scared of the dark.

She wasn't scared, she was scared of nothing. Nothing at all.

A cricket burst into melody, and she nearly leaped out of her skin.

Delia and Maddie scooted closer, until they were practically in one another's laps, reminding Zoe she wasn't alone. They were all the same age: the quiet, withdrawn Maddie, the bossy Delia, and herself. And they were all very different. But the three of them had pledged to be sisters forever, and that was all that mattered now.

Cranking her neck back, Zoe stared at the city sky littered with fog and pollution, and forgot her six-year-old bravado. Forgot that her eyes burned from lack of sleep due to bad dreams, her cheek burned from where she'd been smacked by an older child in their group home, one of the bullies.

She forgot everything but what she and Delia and Maddie had crept out here for—their dream.

As they huddled on the damp grass, holding on to one another, she stared at the faint stars and offered up her one and only wish—that they would be kept together, forever.

One thousand miles away in Idaho, Constance Freeman hung up the phone and sighed deeply with painful regret. If her heart felt as though it were cracking open, she knew it was no one's fault but her own.

She'd let her son get away, though that wasn't what tore at her now, for he'd been mean, dishonest and selfish. A bad seed.

What she regretted with all her heart was that he'd gone without telling her the one thing she so desperately needed to know.

Where her young granddaughter had been taken.

For six years, since the birth of the child, Constance had been begging her son for information. Cruelly, he'd withheld it, saying only that his ex-girlfriend, the child's mother, had vanished. And so had the child. Tracing her was difficult, for her son hadn't married the girl's mother, and Constance had no idea what the mother's name was. Heaven only knew what name was on the birth certificate.

But Constance would find her, she vowed with renewed determination. She'd search everywhere if she had to, spend every last penny she had. It would be worth it.

She'd find that child and shower her with all the love and attention Constance was so certain she wasn't getting now.

She'd leave that child her legacy, though she knew others might not see it as a legacy so much as a burden. Certainly her own son had felt that way.

But Constance's ranch, Triple M, was her one true love, and she wouldn't be happy until she knew she'd taken care of both its future, and her granddaughter's.

Chapter 1

Twenty years later

In the dark night the mountains rose like giants. *Three* giants. And excitement ripped through Zoe so that she could barely contain herself as she parked.

"We're here!" she cried, leaping out of the car first. Not because she was the oldest; she wasn't. They were all close enough to the same age that it didn't matter.

But Maddie-the-Worrywart had pretended to fall asleep in the back seat on the long ride from the airport, and Delia-the-Know-It-All still couldn't believe what they'd done.

And Zoe was so thrilled to be at Triple M Ranch, she couldn't stand it. Her dreams were about to come true, after a lifetime of uncertainty and nowhere to belong, she was home.

Everyone that mattered to her was in the car. And she wanted them to be as happy. "Come on, you two," she whispered in the absolute darkness, her feet crunching in the dirt beneath her as she turned and peered back into the open rental car. "Let's go."

"It's...black out there" came Maddie's hushed reply. Her pale, sleepy face popped up from the back seat. Rumpled and tired as she was, her creamy skin glowed and her sable hair curled around her face, giving her the look of a precious china doll.

"Yes, night is usually pretty black," Zoe agreed with a little laugh. "Come on."

"Darker than Los Angeles," Delia decided, speaking from the front passenger seat and peering out into the night. She flipped back a blond tress. "I can't believe we've done this. I bet there's not a Thai takeout within three hundred miles."

"Well, it's not every day we just inherit a ranch," Zoe pointed out. "We couldn't *not* come."

"We could have waited for daylight." The face that usually inspired grown men to beg for attention now creased in stubbornness, a look that Zoe knew all too well. Delia wasn't budging for anything less than a shopping spree.

"Oh, and I suppose you have money for a hotel room." Suddenly willing to stall, Zoe clung to the side of the car, because after all, her sisters were right...it was pretty dark.

And the fact that they were here at all, in the middle of the Idaho wilderness, one thousand miles away from their comforting city of Los Angeles, was mostly her fault.

"We'll be fine," Maddie said, her voice quiet. "We're together, that's all that matters."

"We could have stayed together at the airport hotel until morning," Delia pointed out calmly. "Might have been a whole lot smarter than rushing out to the middle of the boondocks without even the moon for company. And I bet the hotel had a hot tub."

If there was something Zoe had a hard time with, it was taking the blame, especially when she was in the wrong.

Because their ranch supposedly came with two trucks, they had sold her car and Delia's. Maddie hadn't owned one. They'd flown into Boise from L.A., and then rented a car to take them to the ranch one hundred and fifty miles away, excited and hopeful about their future.

Zoe had always wanted a truck, but there hadn't been much reason for one in L.A., not to mention cost. Because of that, her secret fantasy of driving a truck and owning a horse had never materialized.

Until now.

"You know we're on a tight budget," she said with more defense than was necessary, but she was out on a limb and couldn't afford to fail. "And anyway, I don't see the difference between arriving at our new property now or in the morning."

"In the morning it would have been light."

An owl hooted, or at least it sounded like an owl. Zoe hugged the car door to her side, glancing warily over her shoulder. Man, the night was noisy here. Water rushed nearby, which she knew to be the Salmon River. Crickets blared. She could hear the sound of trees rustling in the wind.

Something howled.

"What was that?" Maddie whispered in terror, their bickering forgotten as they reached for one another through the open window.

"A coyote?" Zoe guessed.

"Let's hope coyotes don't eat city women for dessert," Delia said in her usual calm voice, but she squeezed Zoe's hand so hard the bones cracked.

The goose bumps that rose on her flesh had nothing to do with the late spring cool air.

"Sounds different from Los Angeles," Maddie whispered.

"Yeah," Delia whispered back. She wasn't a worrywart,

but she wasn't too tough to admit to a good, healthy fear. "Never thought I'd miss all the sirens."

"At least the land is ours," Zoe said. *"Ours."*

"Supposedly ours."

Zoe couldn't blame Delia for the doubt. After all, the whole inheritance thing was a bit spooky, considering the twist of fate that had left them unsure as to which of the three of them had actually inherited. Which in turn was due to the fact that since all three of them had been born out of wedlock, with birth certificates void of a father's name, not one of them knew any more about themselves except their mother's maiden names.

But a woman, Constance Freeman, had located them just before her death last month. Through her private investigator, Cade McKnight, who had matched the dates of their arrival at the group home to the approximate date of Constance's granddaughter's disappearance, Constance had been convinced that either Zoe, Maddie or Delia had been her long-lost granddaughter. The one she'd been looking for over the past twenty years. It was enough to boggle Zoe's mind. "We've come this far, right?"

"Right," Maddie agreed. Both she and Zoe looked at Delia.

"Right," Delia admitted warily.

"And we all agreed we wanted a new life together, no matter which of us is heir, right?" Zoe asked.

"Right."

"So stop whining." That said, Zoe straightened and glared into the dark toward the house. "Let's just do this. The faster we get inside, the faster we'll be able to flip on every light in the place."

"Good plan." Delia hopped out, looking city chic in her black pantsuit. She held the seat back for Maddie, whose long floral dress caught on the door.

Zoe rolled her eyes heavenward. Her foster sisters were

day and night, yet after hours and hours of traveling, they still looked incredibly beautiful. No one would ever guess that they were only one step ahead of the poverty line. That Delia designed and hand-sewed their clothes because that's all they could afford. That they depended tightly on one another for security, and had for twenty-odd years.

Zoe glanced down at herself, even though she knew what she would see—secondhand jeans and a T-shirt. Her shoulder-length auburn hair, full of natural curls that were the bane of her existence, had rioted. Compared to her lovely sisters, she was a disheveled mess, but that was nothing new. She'd been the ugly duckling for longer than she cared to remember, though she rarely obsessed over it since it was her own fault. Makeup and hairstyles had never been as important to her as survival.

Delia moaned theatrically. "Oh Lord, have you ever seen such a black night? Where's the flashing neon billboards? The floodlights? The—"

"Get over it, Delia. You're not in Kansas anymore."

"No kidding."

Zoe flipped on her flashlight. Turning, she aimed it down the road they'd just come from. *Road* being relative, of course. From the airport in Boise they'd driven north for hours, to Riggins. There they'd gone west, down narrow curvy roads that had eventually turned to dirt. Zoe considered it a miracle they'd even made it. Her meager light disappeared a few feet into the inky darkness. She shivered, wondering how they'd managed to find their way, but Cade had left excellent step-by-step directions.

Still, Zoe hadn't expected it to take so long, or to be so far from civilization. They were really isolated out here, and the thought brought an even mix of surging excitement and grim reality.

A whole new beginning.

"Triple M Ranch," she whispered reverently. Their home.

Maddie nodded, her eyes glued to the night and the shadows of the mountains so far above. "Fitting, isn't it? Three distinct mountains...three sisters."

Turning, Zoe lifted the light, accenting a long, circular drive. Three peaks for three sisters. She liked the sound of it.

They couldn't see it clearly now, but according to Cade, Constance's will had left them a large piece of property nestled between the base of the mountains and the Salmon River. Zoe knew the Salmon River was reputed to be as wild as the greatest imagination. Around them were the eighteen million, even wilder acres of Idaho. On their property sat a ranch house, two barns and a series of cottages, even a dock.

Zoe imagined the truck, the horses of her childhood dreams, maybe even a boat...and gave a hearty laugh.

Which died in her throat when she got her first look at the house.

"Damn," Delia said eloquently.

Maddie, in between the two of them, hugged their arms closer to her. She remained silent, though Zoe had no trouble detecting the anxiety running through her.

She understood the feeling as she flickered her light over the ranch house. It was old and falling apart at the seams.

"Not good," Delia said in a huge understatement. "Not good at all. Let's go back."

Zoe knew that was the city girl talking. But the truth was, they had nothing to go back to. They'd packed up their meager belongings, which would be delivered in the next few days, and given up their apartment and jobs.

And this...decrepit old place, for all it was worth, was theirs. All theirs. At the thought, a burst of territorial pride overcame Zoe. She hadn't had much in her life to feel territorial about, so she enjoyed the feeling. Nothing was going to get in the way of that, not even if the house blew over on the next wind. "We'll be okay." She'd make sure of it. "Come on."

Together they walked toward the house, which was nothing more than a large shadow looming over them. The wooden porch creaked warningly, making Zoe wonder just how safe it was. The front door, crooked on its hinges, looked as though a light kick could knock it in. She fumbled through her pockets for the keys she'd been given.

Her flashlight wavered and went out.

Maddie's breath caught, the only audible sound in the ensuing blackness.

Before Zoe could so much as form the swearwords coming to her brain, two headlights gleamed, wavering up and down in the rough road as they came closer and closer. A moment later she could hear the sound of a truck, and her heart lodged in her throat.

They were three women out in the middle of nowhere, sitting ducks, and here she stood, frozen in the oncoming headlights like a deer.

The truck stopped directly next to their rental car, and blinded by the glaring twin lights, Zoe threw a hand up in front of her face.

The driver left the headlights on—to torment them? Zoe wondered frantically—as he stepped out.

The crunching of the stranger's booted feet on the gravel of the driveway propelled Zoe into action. "Down," she whispered, pulling her sisters out of the path of the bright lights. They ducked low, tumbling into one another as they shifted to the side of the patio, only to find themselves cornered by the wooden railing.

"Hey," a deep male voice called out. "Who's there?"

"Don't move," Zoe instructed, holding on to her sisters' hands tightly. "Don't even breathe. Maybe he'll leave."

"He saw us," Maddie whispered frantically, her voice wavering, making Zoe hug her closer. "I know he did."

"Maybe it's just a neighbor?" Delia suggested hopefully.

Maybe, but Zoe didn't plan on taking any chances. Not with her sisters. She weighted the meaty flashlight in one hand, considering it a weapon now.

"Can't believe you didn't check your batteries," Delia hissed. "You *always* check them. You're anal-retentive about that stuff."

Zoe considered testing her weapon on her sister's pretty head, but changed her mind when the stranger called out again, much closer this time.

"Hello?"

For some reason, the husky, grainy voice tickled Zoe's tummy, and she clutched Maddie and Delia in a vise grip.

"I know you're here, I saw your headlights from my house."

When no one answered, the man's wide shoulders rose and fell sharply with a sigh, as if he were annoyed. "Cade sent me out to check on your arrival. I'm your neighbor, Ty Jackson."

Delia shot Zoe a triumphant glare, pulled her hands free, adjusted her still-perfect hair and stood, only to fall back down to the patio when Zoe yanked hard on her arm.

"Are you crazy?" Zoe demanded in a harsh whisper. "You can't just blindly trust him."

"But he knows Cade—"

"Honest to God, Delia, I have not a clue as to how you managed to survive in Los Angeles." Furious, Zoe clenched both sisters now with fisted hands. Fear did that to her, kicked up her temper.

Fear and regret, for if anything happened to either Delia or Maddie, it would be *her* fault because it had been *she* who had insisted they go on this crazy adventure. Crazy, *stupid* adventure.

The man stepped up onto the patio, looking larger than life with the yellow lights of his truck highlighting him from behind. He stood on the rickety old porch, his easy, loose-limbed stance revealing a tall, rangy body with legs and arms that seemed to stretch forever.

None of the women budged, or even breathed, but he turned unerringly toward them, allowing the light to fall over him.

"See?" He lifted his hands, apparently to show he meant no harm, but his irritation was unmistakable. In one of his hands was a heavy-duty flashlight, which he left off. "Just your friendly neighbor, not the boogeyman."

Zoe recognized his name, knew that he was the caretaker of this property, and due to the terms of Constance's will, he was to remain manager for one year. Still…her fingers dug into her sisters' arms, silently daring them to move.

When they didn't come forward, the man crouched low on the protesting wood planks, as if he instinctively understood how overwhelmingly male he seemed. His unbuttoned plaid shirt spread wide over a white T-shirt that revealed an expanse of well-muscled chest and shoulders. His faded jeans encased powerful legs that strained taut in his hunkered position. The light fell over his face, casting his dark, chiseled features in bold relief.

"Come on," he said. "It's late. Let's do this." He blinked into the darkness, his glittering eyes somehow landing directly on Zoe. "Maddie and Delia, right? And… Zophina?"

Delia snorted, and Zoe, masked in the dark patio, pinched her.

"Look, would I know your names if I wasn't telling the truth?" he asked, exasperation clear.

Good point, Zoe supposed, but she didn't move.

His head dropped between his shoulders for a moment, his frustration tangible. Then he tried again. "You know that I've been working part of this land with mine, leasing it from Constance for years. And you know who Constance was…your grandmother, or one of yours, anyway."

In the dark, the women looked at one another. Certainly he had to be who he said, for what stranger could know all this?

"Quite the mystery, isn't it?" He shook his head, then glanced over at them as if to make sure he had their attention.

He'd never had anything but.

At their lack of motion, he looked around him at the land. "Constance tried like crazy to find her granddaughter over the years. It's hard to believe she didn't live long enough to see it through."

Would a bad guy really show such insight? Zoe didn't know and refused to take a chance. But his voice mesmerized her as he continued to speak into the dark night.

"She didn't even know her granddaughter's name, only the month and year of birth and approximate last sighting of her son's girlfriend."

Los Angeles.

Emotions tumbled through Zoe, and she knew it was no less for her sisters, for each of them wanted to know more about Constance, more about where they had possibly come from. Delia nudged her, and even in the darkness, Zoe had no trouble deciphering Delia's glare.

Trust him.

She wasn't ready yet.

"You still there?" He craned his neck as he shifted, trying to see into the shadows where they huddled ridiculously together. "Well, what else can I tell you… Okay, from what I understand, you were all left in a group home at approximately the same time and age. Took poor Constance more than twenty years to get that much information, but she never gave up.''

The silence seemed to drown out the night noise, except for the ever-present rush of water. The crickets stopped. Even the owl went quiet. And there on the porch, surrounded by the only two people in the world who had ever cared about her, Zoe squeezed their hands tight and closed her eyes.

Each of them had been a deserted three-year-old. The remembering hurt, when that hurt should have long ago been healed. But now they knew that one of them *had* had someone searching for her, desperately.

That hurt, too, for Zoe could only imagine how different life would have been for the girl who might have been found by a loving, frantic grandmother.

They had no idea which of them it was—Maddie, Zoe or Delia—but it didn't matter now. They were sisters of the heart and soul, and they'd stick together until the end.

The ranch belonged to all of them, and together they'd learn more about their grandmother.

"I'm guessing you're hoping I'll talk myself out and disappear." Slowly, Ty Jackson shook his head. "No can do, ladies. Cade told me your plane had been delayed, and he was worried about you getting up here at night, which by the way was a stupid thing to do, drive up here in the dark.''

Delia and Maddie shot a look at Zoe, who bristled. It was one thing to be stupid, but it was entirely another thing to have it pointed out to her by a stranger. She had her sisters to do that.

"Cade wanted me to call him back." He shifted impatiently. "Can we get on with it now? It's late, and frankly, ladies, I'm tired of listening to myself talk.''

Zoe could feel her sisters' resistance melt away, but she held on to hers with all her might. Despite his obvious caring for Constance, he was big, he was a man, and he was barely managing to control his irritation at being bothered so late at night.

Trust was a big issue for Zoe, it had been for as long as she could remember. Alone in this world except for Maddie and Delia, she had managed to eke out a calm, quiet existence. And if her life was a little, well...*empty,* if she'd never learned to really have faith in another human being since the day her mother had dumped her at age three, failing to come back for her as promised, she could live with that.

Bottom line—Zoe rarely believed in another, especially a far-too-good-looking cowboy with a voice that could melt the Arctic.

In the beam of light, he quirked a dark, challenging brow and continued to speak in that rough-timbered voice, the one Zoe imagined could convince a less-hardened woman to give him the moon.

"You plan on sleeping there on the porch, that's just fine with me," he said with a shrug of those impressive shoulders. "But I wouldn't be neighborly if I didn't try to warn you...that wood there's littered with rats. Big, fat, *hungry* ones."

With a muffled shriek, Delia launched herself toward the light, brushing and swiping at her legs, for if there was one thing that could shatter Delia's calm, it was a rodent.

Maddie's mouth opened in a silent scream as she followed Delia in such a rush she nearly fell headlong into their "neighbor," who easily caught and uprighted her.

Both women continued to shiver and squeak, placing themselves behind the man, who slowly rose to his feet, a grin firmly in place.

Amid feet stomping and panting, huffy screams, Delia twirled in a circle, mindless, until the man reached out and touched her arm.

"Safe," he claimed, not bothering to hide his amusement. "Don't worry, I think you two managed to scare them all away."

Delia stopped screaming, and Maddie just gaped in surprise. Zoe knew why, for though it took Delia forever to get riled, it took just as long to calm her back down. No one, and most certainly not a man, had ever been so effective in quieting her.

In the startling silence, the man who caused it winked at Maddie, who brought a hand up to her mouth.

Still hidden by the darkness, Zoe stood quickly, for she knew Maddie's unease around strangers, especially men, but she stiffened in shock when she realized Maddie was holding back a *smile*.

In less than ten seconds, the man had completely tamed her sisters. Unbelievable.

"You okay now?" Ty Jackson asked.

Delia smoothed down her clothes and shot him an apologetic smile. "Yes, sorry, but rats just get to me."

"Understandable."

"Now, if you tell me you have batteries in that truck of yours," Delia said, her smile warming, "you'll really be my hero, Mr. Jackson."

"Ty." Any irritation at having been disturbed so late had apparently vanished, replaced by the pleasant surprise of a man who suddenly finds himself in the company of two beautiful women. He held out his hand. "And you are...?"

Delia offered him a perfectly manicured hand in return, the one she'd spent an annoying amount of time this morning doing herself, nearly making them late for the airport. "Delia Scanlon. And this is my sister, Maddie O'Brien."

He took each of their hands in turn as though they were at a tea party, not standing hundreds of miles away from nowhere on a battered, neglected ranch. From her perch in the corner, Zoe rolled her eyes.

"It's a pleasure," Ty said to Delia. "And I always carry spare batteries." He looked pleased with himself, as though he'd invented the darn things himself.

Zoe remained in place, thoroughly disgusted now. How could her sisters just cave like this? What had happened to their natural reserve of anyone and everyone?

They'd stuck together through thick and thin, mostly thin, but in all that time, Zoe had never, not once, seen either of them let down their natural distrust so fast.

Of course, none of them had ever been charmed by such a master, either.

Fine. If she was the only one with a thought left in her head, so be it. She'd keep them safe.

"I thought there were three of you," Ty said, squinting a bit as he searched through the darkness, easily focusing to meet Zoe's gaze again. "What happened to Zophina?"

"Zoe," Zoe snapped, stepping into the light, having no idea why she was letting him get under her skin like this. He was just a stranger. "The name is Zoe."

"Well, hello there. *Zoe.*" That damn grin flashed again, the one that made her somehow want to smack him and melt at the same time. He tucked his thumbs into his front pockets in a stance of confidence...not to mention how his hands pretty much outlined the vee of his jeans in a way that showed off his...big build. "Can we go inside now?"

"I'm sure we'll be just fine alone," she replied coolly.

"I'm sure you will." He didn't so much as blink, but Zoe could have sworn he was laughing at her. "Maybe you'd like me to check it out first."

"For more rats?" she inquired sweetly.

He didn't look in the least bit ashamed of himself. "You never know."

Before Zoe could suggest that there was a two-legged rat standing right in front of her, Delia firmly stepped between the two, her flattering, social smile in place. "You'll have to excuse Zoe, Ty. She's tired, and a tired Zoe is a grumpy one.''

Zoe turned away, piqued for no particular reason. It was her own fault, she reminded herself. They'd come here at *her* insistence, at *her* excitement at completely starting over.

Not that Delia and Maddie hadn't wanted to come, they had, but they just hadn't been quite as sold on the idea as she. Yet they'd given up their lives, anyway, *for her.* A pressure built in Zoe's chest, a familiar one. The pressure of their love, which she was eternally grateful for. But deep down, somewhere in a place she didn't like to go too often, were the same old doubts.

She didn't deserve all they gave to her, not when she didn't—couldn't—give it back. She had long ago locked up her heart from hurt.

As if she sensed her unease, Maddie slipped an arm around Zoe's waist, giving her a quick squeeze. She reached for Delia's hand, uniting them without a word. As always, at the caring, kind, accepting touch, Zoe immediately softened; she couldn't help it.

"Ready, ladies?" When they nodded, Ty took the keys from Zoe, and before she could analyze why the slight brushing of his work-roughened fingers against hers made her stomach tighten, he'd unlocked the front door. "This will have to be fixed," he said, easily maneuvering open the rickety screen.

Standing just behind him as she was, with her level of vision at his shoulders and his own truck headlights highlighting his every movement, Zoe had no choice but to stare at the way the muscles in his back flexed and bunched beneath his shirt. No choice at all. Nor could she help but smell him, all fresh and delicious male. That he smelled so good made her annoyed all over again.

Ty flipped on his flashlight and beamed it inside. "The door will have to be replaced, too."

"That's not all," Zoe said as she caught sight of the interior.

Ty hit a light switch on the wall and let out a low, heart-felt oath. The light illuminated what had been their hopes and dreams, and Zoe's stomach sank as they all crowded in. They hadn't gotten a good look at the outside in the dark, but she had gotten an image of a two-story sprawling ranch house in desperate need of repair.

The inside was worse, far worse.

The paint on the walls was peeling off in long strips. The wood floors were thick with dust. The light above them flickered warningly, but at the last second, somehow managed to hang in there. Standing in the midst of it, Zoe saw past the gloom and straight to the heart of the matter—this place was theirs. *Theirs.*

The thrill of that would never wear off, no matter what happened.

"But…how can this be?" Delia asked in a confused voice that didn't sound at all like her usual take-charge attitude. "I thought Constance lived here."

"She did, up until two years ago, when she had to move to a retirement home." Regret and sadness filled Ty's voice. "Had no idea it was this bad."

Silence fell at that, and sadness welled through Zoe, overcoming her strange protectiveness of the house. If only Constance had found them sooner, she thought, then nearly laughed because that wouldn't have changed much. They couldn't have helped her financially.

But they could have gotten to know Constance, and at the knowledge they'd just missed that opportunity, her throat tightened. For years she'd yearned for more information about her past. Since she'd been so young when she'd arrived at the foster home, she remembered next to nothing. Yes, there was every possibility Constance *hadn't* been her grandmother, that she'd been Maddie's or Delia's, but it didn't change Zoe's need.

All her life she'd been an outsider, without a background, always a burden, always dependent on the kindness of others. It had left scars.

She needed to know more about herself, needed to really *belong* somewhere. To someone.

She needed, with every fiber of her being, for this place to be hers. And she hated herself for the selfishness, because her sisters deserved it every bit as much as she did.

"She couldn't swing all the work by herself and she couldn't afford help." Ty's face was tight, and surprisingly full of compassion. "I did what I could, but I have a ranch, too, and between my land and hers, there aren't enough hours in the day. Constance wouldn't consider my offer...not until she'd located her granddaughter. And that, unfortunately, came too little, too late for her to enjoy."

"Offer?" Zoe narrowed her eyes as his words sunk in. "Wait a minute. Are you telling us...you wanted this place?"

His eyes, dark and full of a whole host of things she was sure she didn't want to know, met hers straight on. "Yes."

"No wonder you're being so neighborly," she said without thinking, a bad habit she had yet to learn to curb.

"What are you talking about?" Delia asked, coming closer.

Zoe's gaze didn't leave Ty's as everything fit into place. "He wants to buy the ranch."

Ty looked at her, his eyes cool and assessing.

"Don't you?" she pressed.

"Yes," he said, without a hint of apology.

"But..." Maddie looked at the mess in confusion. "Why?"

"Good question," Zoe said quietly, even as her possessive, protective feelings for the land continued to swamp her. This place was *theirs* now. *"Why?"*

Chapter 2

Ty hesitated, absorbing three women's gazes. He had to be careful, because not all those gazes were friendly.

Dammit, he *did* want this land. Badly. And he'd almost had it. "It's a little early—or late—to be discussing business, don't you think?" he asked.

Zoe's eyes, fascinating as all hell in their shade of mystic forest green, sharpened. "No," she said. "But I *do* think we can handle everything from here." She opened the door, inviting him to leave.

He spared a thought for the condition of the bedrooms upstairs. "But—"

"No buts." Her voice had chilled twenty degrees, if that was possible. She was the tough one, and he doubted anyone ever got anything past her. "Good night," she said.

Dismissed! The woman had a major attitude problem. Too bad he enjoyed baiting such a problem. Ignoring her, he crossed the room, reaching up to fiddle with the flickering light above them.

Immediately, it came back to life full force, illuminating the shabbiness of the room.

Delia shot a sharp look to Zoe, but spoke in a voice full of sweet honey. "We appreciate your help, Ty. Please…just ignore Zoe. She's—"

"Grumpy?" he interjected, giving in and letting his grin spread across his face. "I hadn't noticed. Can I help you with your things from the car?"

She smiled. "Oh, yes, please."

Zoe shook her head. "Didn't you hear him, Delia?" she demanded, hands on hips as she glared at her sister. "He wants to buy this place."

"Well, since we're not selling, this shouldn't be a problem for you, hon." Back in control after her initial shock, Delia took over, and Ty watched, enthralled at the silent hierarchy of these foster sisters. Clearly Delia thought herself in charge at all times. Just as clearly, Zoe believed *she* ran the roost. And sweet, quiet, shy Maddie just let them both go, acting as intermediary when required. With just a light touch or small smile, she could melt anyone.

He remembered the sight of them huddled pathetically in a small corner of the dirty, dark patio. Remembered the way his heart had stuttered at the realization it had been *him* who had inadvertently terrified them.

He'd be the first to admit he wanted them gone, but not by his own hand. And he certainly hadn't meant to scare them.

They'd been holding on to each other like…they belonged together, that was obvious. The tall, serene, sexy, in-control Delia. The smaller, hauntingly beautiful Maddie. And the rough-and-tough Zoe. She was every bit a looker as the other two, but he doubted she'd appreciate the compliment. She was different, far more unrefined. Her auburn hair was wild, not carefully groomed. She wore little to no makeup, and her clothes…well, she looked as if she'd fit into the hard ranch living just fine. Her jeans were faded and oh-so-snug in all the right places, showcasing a slim yet curvy body that for some reason he couldn't keep his eyes off of.

Three women; so different and yet obviously they lived together, loved and laughed together. They were a unit.

A small place inside him ached, a place he didn't visit often, because it only brought great pain. Once upon a time he'd belonged, too. But that had been ten years ago, before his brother Ben had died.

That part of his life was over.

No amount of standing around and staring at these women was going to change that. Nor was it going to change the unrelenting truth—he did want their land with a singular purpose. A purpose so personal and painful he had no intention of sharing it. He'd been only twenty-two when he'd promised Ben a huge ranch someday, and even though Ben was no longer on this earth to enjoy it, Ty never broke a promise. *Never.*

These three women had ruined Ben's dream sure as they were standing there staring back at him. Constance had cared for Ty deeply, deeply enough to want to leave her land to him *if* her granddaughter hadn't been found.

But Constance had indeed found an heir. *Three* of them.

No doubt, they were three of the loveliest heiresses he'd ever laid his eyes on, but "lovely" didn't count for much when he remembered what Cade had told him—this place was all these women had in the entire world, which made Ty's gut tighten just thinking about it.

He was busting out of his britches at his own place. He raised and trained quarter horses for ranches throughout the entire state, but his place was small and insufficient for his needs. He'd bought it long ago when money had been incredibly tight, just after Ben's death. It was a beautiful strip of land on the narrow end of the small valley between the river and the mountains. It was lush, green, fertile, and though Ty loved it with all his heart, it was far too small. There was only one way to expand—toward Constance's property.

Ty had a ten-year promise to fulfill; a painful, unrelenting promise, and to do it he needed more room. He wanted, indeed what he'd wanted since he'd been a little boy starving and struggling on the rough streets of Chicago with Ben, to raise horses. Train them. Sell them. Then do it some more.

He was amazingly successful, but he'd maxed out at his own place, and Ben's dream was just out of reach.

More land was crucial. Crucial to his promise to Ben, crucial to making sure he couldn't ever feel claustrophobic again.

Yet how was he supposed to wrangle his dream land away from these women who also needed it? It was all they had, and was he really cruel and selfish enough to get it away from them?

He stood there, wrestling with his deeply woven morals and innate courtesy, as they both reared up and bit him. Across the room, his gaze met Zoe's, and that strange electric current shot through him, the same one that he'd experienced when he'd accidentally touched her at the door. Looking at her only intensified the feeling.

Seemed he'd also been bitten by the lust bug, sharp and relentlessly. But why for the wildcat Zoe and not one of her infinitely more appealing and *nicer* sisters?

Delia swept across the room as if she'd lived there all her life instead of ten minutes. "Zoe, why don't you do me a favor and check out the bedrooms? Figure out the arrangements, will you?" She turned to Maddie. "Sweetie, maybe we should make sure the kitchen is functioning."

Maddie nodded.

When she was gone, Delia smiled at Ty. "The kitchen, any kitchen, is her favorite place in the world."

"Do you think he cares, Delia?"

Delia lifted a shoulder and sent Zoe a long look. "Hon, you're going to get some sleep and then feel bad about how you're acting."

"And then you'll owe me an apology," Ty added helpfully.

"Don't hold your breath," Zoe muttered, making him laugh, which earned him a glare.

"I'll direct the luggage shuffle with Ty," Delia said, wisely intervening. "Most of our things are coming by professional movers in a couple of days."

Ty turned to follow her outside. At the door he stopped and flicked a glance over his shoulder at Zoe.

She was still standing there watching him, and if looks were any measure, she hadn't taken to him much.

It wasn't often he managed to tick off such a beautiful woman so quickly. His mischievous streak reared and he winked at her.

Her glower deepened, and he laughed for some reason. Things looked bad, they had his land. But Ty just shook his head and went out into the night, looking forward to challenging Zoe.

"Move out of the way, Slim, it's pouring buckets."

Zoe stood firm in the doorway of the ranch house as though butterflies hadn't instantly ravaged her stomach at the sound of Ty's unexpected low, husky voice. "Why should I?"

Ty groaned and lifted his drenched head, shoving back his dark hair. His eyes, the color of the storm wreaking havoc behind him, pierced her. "Because if you don't," he said with silky promise, "I'm going to drag you out here so you can see for yourself how icy it is."

Though she didn't know the man well, she already knew better than to challenge one of his dares, for it appeared he never spoke idly. He would do as he threatened without qualm. "Fine."

With resentment, and a good amount of something she didn't want to analyze, something that made her insides tingle and her head light, she moved back to let him in.

His big body brushed hers purposely, a body she knew from sneaking glances to be hard and toned and powerfully built. And wet. He dripped on her clean sweater, the one she'd just changed into after scrubbing the inside of the house all day.

Actually, she'd been scrubbing for three days, and was exhausted, though in truth, most of that exhaustion came from worry. What would they do? For in the light of day, Triple M, deserted and financially stuck, was no more a ranch than their apartment had been. She'd been reading ranching books until late at night, but all the knowledge in the world wouldn't help without money.

"Wipe your feet," she said, even as he did it on his own. "And dry off, would ya?"

"Nice to see you, too." As he slipped out of his soaked jacket, his hard mouth softened and he shot her a grin she knew most would consider irresistible.

Zoe didn't consider anything about Ty Jackson irresistible. She would have said...cocky. Trouble-causing. Wild.

Which didn't explain why his crooked smile wormed its way directly to the part of her that was barely controlling her temper, and shattered it. That she was so mad at him had nothing at all to do with how she'd caught him flirting outrageously with one of his ranch hands, who just happened to be a woman. A tall, leggy blond woman named Shirley who looked like a Barbie doll.

"So...did you miss me?" He straightened and sniffed hopefully. "Wait. Is that...God, is that pizza?"

"Yes, and don't even think about it." Slamming the door to shut out the late spring storm, she crossed her arms firmly and once again blocked his way. "We returned the rental car today and brought back supplies. Maddie's whipped up homemade pizza. Her idea of roughing it."

"You should have told me you needed to go into town. I would have taken you on my jet boat down the river. It takes less than half the time."

She gritted her teeth and pretended she had loved that long, bumpy, hot ride because otherwise she might have been tempted to slug him. Triple M had a dock, too, which was an easy walk from the house down a beautiful green hill...but, not surprising, it didn't have a jet boat. "Goodbye, Ty."

His gaze took a leisurely trip down her petite frame, and though those sharp gray eyes heated in a way that made her breath catch in her throat, his smile remained cool and in control. "You think *you* can stop me from coming in? No one gets between me and pizza."

"Watch it, pal. I know how to block."

Darn his all-too-gorgeous hide, he looked amused. "Why don't you play the nice little hostess for once and pretend you're happy to see me?"

Pretend. She didn't have to pretend, if the way her heart raced was any indication. But since that just irked her all the more, she ground her teeth. "You're not staying."

He crossed his wet arms over his chest, the look on his face reminding her he enjoyed a challenge. "Bet I can convince Maddie and Delia different," he said.

No use arguing the truth. The man standing in front of her could convince a nun he was innocent, something he'd certainly *never* been. After a mere three days, he'd have to do nothing more than hug each of her sisters, and then he'd be sitting on the floor, joking and laughing with them as he polished off an entire pizza by himself.

No denying how much Delia and Maddie had both taken to him. Actually they'd done more than be taken. In the past nights that he'd come by, ostensibly to check on them, they'd practically adopted him.

No doubt, Ty Jackson was one of a kind. He marched to his own beat, and never did less than exactly as he wanted. And though it made no sense, Zoe resented his sexy hide for all she was worth. Resented the genuine, affectionate way he had of treating her sisters, resented how his smile could turn her inside out, resented everything.

Especially how he wanted their land. Delia and Maddie might have been able to forget that little detail, but she hadn't.

For the first time in her life, she had a home; shabby, yes, but it was a home. And she'd guard it with everything she had.

Ty hung up his jacket, clearly certain he'd be staying. The sleek muscles of his back stretched under his shirt, and for the first time, Zoe realized he must have come straight from work. His boots were dusty. His long, powerful legs were covered in frayed, worn jeans that had seen better days but fit him like a worn, soft glove. While she watched, he shoved up the sleeves of his shirt, revealing deeply tanned forearms, strong, firm, callused hands.

"See anything interesting?"

Her gaze jerked up to his laughing one, and she was thankful the room was dim enough to hide her blush. "Don't count on it. But you're holding up okay for an old man of…" She considered him with a frown, feigning indifference. "Forty."

"Thirty-four," he corrected her. He leaned forward, smelling of rain, wood and one hundred percent delicious masculinity as he tugged a loose lock of her hair. "But I'll be sure to tell that to the geriatric warden tonight when I check in, thanks.''

Muttering to herself, she whirled away.

One of his hands caught her and held firm as steel. "Wait up.''

His eyes weren't kind and sweet, the way they were when he looked at Delia and Maddie. They were…hot. "I'm busy,'' she managed to say.

"I want to talk to you.''

"About the land?''

He didn't answer.

"Talk to Maddie and Delia, though their answer will be the same as mine. No, this place isn't for sale.'' Even if she had no idea what they were going to do for cash. "No, no, *no*.''

His mouth twitched at her adamant tone. "You keep sweet-talking me like this, and I'm going to get ideas.''

"Go get ideas about *Shirley*.'' She fairly choked on the name of his enthusiastic blond ranch hand and reminded herself she didn't care about him. Not one little bit.

He let out a huge grin. "And jealous, too. That's so sweet.'' His voice lowered, deepened to a rich honey. "Ready to admit it, Zoe? You're hot for me.''

"Ha!'' She lifted her chin. "I'm *too* hot for you. Now, go home. You smell like a cowboy.''

"I *am* a cowboy.'' His eyes glittered knowingly, as if he could see right through her facade to the secret part of her she liked to keep hidden. "And I want to talk to all *three* of you,'' he said.

And what Ty wanted, he got. No use trying to fight it, he'd probably just toss her over his shoulder and cart her into the kitchen, where even now she could hear her sisters' voices.

It was pointless to fight with him. So she shrugged in acquiescence and sashayed away.

Ty watched, a slow, appreciative smile crossing his face now that she had her back to him. God, she was so easy to bait, and he loved to see her flash all that fire she struggled to contain.

She was something; that compact, hot little body of hers spitting all that attitude, her wild hair falling around her shoulders. A strand slipped in her face, which she tugged at with a low sound of annoyance.

Oh yeah, she was riled up good now.

And while there were other things he might love to do to her as well as tease, Zoe Martin was off-limits. They'd both set those limits three days ago. He'd done so because, despite her innocence in the whole thing, he resented like crazy that she was holding Ben's dream. He was far less certain *why* she held back from their obvious, unfortunate attraction, though he got a feeling it was because she'd been hurt and betrayed far too much in her short life. It did disturb him to watch her hide her natural sensuality and passion, especially when he knew that sensuality and passion were directed at him.

She concealed them behind a wall of indifference that exasperated him. Which was why he so enjoyed the bickering; it pulled her out of her shell and revealed the true Zoe.

But she was a weakness, one he didn't have time for.

He'd come to a decision. One that would solve this problem once and for all. He was going to do exactly as Constance had asked. He would manage this place for them. It meant getting the ranch running from nothing. It would take money, hard work and grit, none of which he was even sure they had.

Truth was, he was banking on them not having it. As soon as they saw how much was involved, he figured the city girls would be happy to sell—to him—and head back to Los Angeles.

Nobody would get hurt; they'd go home and he would fulfill his promise to his brother. Perfect. Hoping it worked, Ty followed the tantalizing scent of food, and the equally tantalizing scent of Zoe Martin.

"Go ahead, Ty, you take that last piece." Maddie held out the pan and smiled at him. He smiled back because it had taken her these entire three days just to feel comfortable enough to speak easily to him, and he felt relieved she'd decided to trust him.

Relieved and guilty, because he didn't deserve their trust when he wanted them to leave so badly.

The mouth-watering aroma of melted cheese and sausage continued to call to him. But he'd had four pieces already, and he hadn't come to eat them out of house and home.

"You know you want it," Delia teased him.

They'd had an instant connection, he and Delia. A brother-sister connection that had them immediately bonded. And now he'd bonded with Maddie as well, their relationship was softer, more gentle than the teasing one he and Delia shared.

He wanted to resent these women, and did. But some of that resentment was fading, no matter how he struggled to hold on to it.

God, he missed Ben. He supposed that would never change. But how to keep his dream alive without hurting these women?

Maddie was a haunting beauty, with huge wide eyes that just made a man want to drown in them and offer to slay dragons. Those eyes held secrets, painful ones, and he wondered at them. Delia was tall and slender, a glamour girl. Intelligent, too, with a wicked sense of humor he got a kick out of. And in her eyes was a need to belong. Well, she belonged now, to the ranch he wanted for himself.

Then there was Zoe. She was different from her sisters,

far different. He wasn't satisfied by anything so simple as *friendship,* and he didn't understand it.

"Eat," Maddie said to him again, gesturing with the box. "You've lost weight."

Zoe snorted.

He ignored Zoe and winked at Maddie. She held the pan patiently.

His stomach growled.

Oh, what the hell. He took the piece, studying the third sister, the one who didn't easily fit into any simple category.

Did she feel the same way about him? Hard to tell since she hid everything going on inside that head behind a screen of grumpy indifference.

She wiggled uncomfortably under his scrutiny, then finally swallowed a bit of pizza before demanding, "What are you looking at?"

"You."

She flushed, fidgeted some more, giving herself away. "Why?"

He simply grinned and continued eating, undisturbed, relaxing now that he knew the truth…she was secretly crazy about him.

A comfortable silence filled the room as they ate. They were all sitting on the freshly cleaned living room floor, before a warm, crackling fire, eating picnic-style.

That they didn't have four chairs in the kitchen wasn't the point. The sisters just loved being together, and they were willing to share that with him—and he wanted their one and only possession for himself.

"I didn't come to eat," he said quietly, putting down his pizza.

"Really," Zoe said dryly, brushing off her hands. "I never would have guessed." Her eyes sharpened on him. "You being here wouldn't by any chance have anything to do with you wanting this land, would it?"

Chapter 3

"Zoe, be nice," Maddie said lightly. She swiveled her head, her short, dark hair flying around her face, her dark, deep eyes warm with affection as she spoke to Ty. "She's a bully today because that jerk at the bank in Lewiston didn't hire her." She looked at Zoe again and reached for her sister's hand. "He just didn't recognize a treasure when he found one, that's all."

Zoe swallowed, closed her eyes for a long heartbeat, clearly touched, and just as clearly uncomfortable with Maddie's easy love.

Ty's curiosity upped a notch, so did a strange sense of protectiveness. The drive to Lewiston was long and never easy in the best of times. "Why did you want a job there? It's too far for you to drive it every day."

Zoe recovered from Maddie's affection in the blink of an eye and looked at him as if he were something she'd scraped off the bottom of her shoe. "It's funny how expensive this habit of eating is."

"I wish you wouldn't, Zoe," Delia said quietly. "We'll find a way. We'll sell something, or get a loan."

"Delia's right," Maddie insisted. "We'll make it work together or not at all."

Ty watched the three of them, felt their closeness as a tangible thing.

And it was, he reminded himself. These women were family. They were closer than family, for they'd *chosen* to be related. He'd chosen to be *un*related to the family he had left. It'd been for a good reason, that reason being survival basically, but the fact remained. He had no one.

God, he missed Ben.

Drawing in a deep breath, he realized the truth he'd only guessed at before. These women couldn't afford to get the ranch going, but they were too stubborn to give up. They might never leave and sell him the land. There was only one thing to do.

"I came here tonight to talk to all of you," he said. Zoe frowned, Maddie's brow wrinkled in worry. Delia sat calmly, waiting. Typical, he thought. The pessimist, the worrier, the cool one. Already, they were worming their way into his affections. He couldn't stand the thought of any of them being hurt.

That it was *him* trying to hurt them was unbearable. "I'd like to be your partner," he said.

That was met with stunned silence.

"You're already manager," Zoe said suspiciously.

And how she hated that. "This would be different. I'd be an equal partner. I'd share the losses."

"And the profits," she pointed out.

"Well, yes."

They all stared at him, three pairs of wide eyes, as if he'd lost his marbles.

"Hey, this is a good thing, ladies," he said, smiling into their pensive silence. "You want a ranch. You don't have the needed capital. I do. It would give you money to survive on until you got your stock built up through purchases and breeding."

"Wait a minute. Did you say *breeding?*" Delia carefully set down her drink. "Here?"

She said *breeding* as if it were a four-letter word, and it made Ty laugh. Delia was a city girl, born and bred. Los Angeles was her playground. Hell, she probably *did* think *breeding* was a bad word.

Once upon a time he had felt stifled in a city, claustrophobic. Chicago was a place where one couldn't even turn around without bumping elbows with a neighbor, and he had resented that. Ben had, too, and for as long as he could remember, Ty had wanted out.

He needed open space. Fresh air. His own land, lots of it.

What he needed was *their* land.

"And you have enough money just lying around that you could lend it to us," Zoe said, with serious doubt.

"Yes." He hadn't gotten it by inheritance, that much was certain. His mother had been a whore, his father a career criminal. He didn't have any relatives who would leave him a time bomb, much less something of value. He'd simply been very successful at raising and training horses, investing his profits wisely, making the most of what he'd earned.

"And how much is this going to cost us?" Zoe asked. "In say...*land?*"

Trust her to speak so bluntly. "I'm not going to cheat you out of anything, Zoe. Ever."

Her eyes, the color of drenched moss in the dim light, stared at him warily, unwilling to believe, which hurt in a way he hadn't expected.

"Well, *I* for one know you'd never hurt us," Delia said gently as she scooted around the pizza to put her arm on his shoulders. She squeezed him. "We just don't want to take your money, that's all."

"It wouldn't be right," Maddie said, smiling sweetly and patting his knee. "You keep it for yourself, Ty."

He couldn't believe it, but his throat actually tightened at their easy affection and trust. He hugged Delia back, and touched Maddie's lovely face. Something about the heat warring with fear in Zoe's eyes kept his hands off her, for she wasn't as simple to show easy affection to as her sisters.

But he wanted to touch her; the need shocked him. "I can help," he said instead. "You expected this place to be up and running."

"But, Ty, we hadn't decided that we were definitely going to…breed," Delia pointed out.

Ty had spent every summer since he was ten on a series of ranches in "the country," really just a suburb of Chicago. At first he'd been sent there by the city officials because no one had wanted the trouble-causing boy he'd been. He'd been worked hard, and he had grown to love every minute of it, while still pretending to hate it.

Then later he'd gone willingly, taking Ben, feeling more at home in the great outdoors than anywhere else. He loved horses, loved all animals, and had begged, borrowed and practically stolen to make Ben's fantasy of ranching come true.

It had to be in one's blood to make this hard living work. And if it wasn't in these women's blood, they'd go away and he would buy the land. Then they'd all win.

"Let me get this straight." Zoe studied him carefully. "You want to be involved as a partner, not just to *manage*, but to *own* a part of it."

"Yep."

"You want to control it."

Her mistrust was palpable, and he couldn't help but wonder what had happened to her to make her this way. "I wouldn't even attempt to control you, Zoe," he said softly, everything else fading away but this woman with the beautiful and so-unsure eyes. "If that's what you're thinking."

"You couldn't, anyway," she said, lifting her chin.

"It snows here in the wintertime," Delia said shakily.

"Quite a bit," Ty told her.

"If we had a bunch of animals here, we wouldn't be able to head south for warmer weather."

"You'll love cross-country skiing. I'll teach you," Ty said, shocked to discover he meant it. But they were leaving soon. He was counting on it, he reminded himself.

"Oh Lord," Delia murmured, rubbing her head. "It just hit me. The wilds. We're really living in the wilds."

"Eighty-three thousand square miles of wonder," he confirmed. "That's Idaho. There's no place more wild in the U.S., except for maybe Alaska."

Delia moaned.

"Well, it's not like we're camping," Maddie pointed out in her quiet, infinite wisdom. "You have electricity for your hair dryer, Delia. A tub for your bubble bath."

Zoe let loose enough to laugh, the sound unexpectedly light and happy. Her tense face transposed, softened…and took Ty's breath away. He couldn't take his eyes off her.

"Skiing," Zoe murmured a bit dreamily. "I've always wanted to try it."

The yearning in her voice tugged at him. "You're in, Slim?"

He knew what the stakes were for her; Delia had told him. After years of going to college at night while working full-time during the day, Zoe had finally gotten her business degree. Would she be happy running a ranch when a cool, easy living was all she'd ever wanted?

"And you're going to stick with us?" she wondered. "No matter what?"

They were still watching each other, so that there was

no hiding what flickered between them. Honesty, fear. Need. *Startling* need. "I'm going to stick, no matter what," he said.

He saw the moment his response registered. The promise he was making. Saw, too, her fierce disbelief, and he experienced a strange urge to pound whoever had hurt her so badly in her past, whoever had caused Zoe to accept a promise, any promise, with such mistrust.

"Well, I think you'd make a good partner," Maddie said softly, with a shy smile. "But only if Delia and Zoe agree."

Delia's wide gaze whipped to Maddie. She was so uncustomarily ruffled she forgot to pretend she wasn't.

"I promise to make sure all the amenities run smoothly," Ty said seriously, though he wanted to sigh in relief. They'd never stay long, and while he might actually miss them, he convinced himself he was doing them a favor. "I'll even build a Jacuzzi, Delia. Just for you."

"Oh, really?" She beamed. "You really will?"

"Promise."

"Okay, but I won't raise pigs. Or kill anything that makes red meat," Delia said firmly.

"No problem. We can start with horses if you'd like."

Delia flipped back her hair and took a deep, calming breath. "Oh God. Okay. I'm in, too. Maddie's right. You'd be a great partner. Zoe?"

All eyes flew to Zoe, including Ty's. She looked at him, unusually intense.

And again that strange, inexplicable communication happened between them. She was looking for honesty and he'd claimed to have given it, but he hadn't, not fully.

He was counting on them leaving and guilt hit hard.

She deserved more, but unfortunately he couldn't give it.

The room was thick with unspoken hopes and dreams.

Ty watched Zoe, waited while that current tugged between them.

Stubbornness set her jaw, and he knew from the sudden disappointment filling him what her answer would be before she even spoke.

"You know what?" she said softly. "We'll do this, we'll manage to get this ranch running, but we can do it on our own. We won't be a burden to anyone."

"I never said you'd be a burden," he said carefully. What had given him away? Had she read his guilt for what it was? "I *offered*."

"Zoe, I—" Delia pinched her mouth closed at the look of determination on Zoe's face. "Never mind. You're right."

Maddie sighed, then smiled and took Zoe's hand, effectively disarming the tension. "Thanks, Ty, for offering." She spoke softly but firmly, sparing one last glance for her still-silent and brooding sister. "But we'll be fine."

They were united, together. Reluctant admiration shot through Ty. Seems they had grit after all.

Then he looked at Zoe, who was looking at him with a definite challenging light. He felt his blood stir to meet that challenge. They would still work together. After all, he was manager of their property for the next year whether they liked it or not. It would be interesting, to say the least, considering she was stubborn to the last drop.

So was he.

"But Ty, honey?" Delia smiled beguilingly. "Think I could still have that Jacuzzi?"

Zoe took a walk after dinner in the cold night, desperately in need of some perspective, which she couldn't get being in the same room with the enigmatic, sexy Ty Jackson.

Leaving Ty happily and easily charming Maddie and Delia, she stomped along. Why did he do that? she wondered. He certainly didn't bother with any charm when it came to *her*, yet with her sisters, he poured it on. It wasn't fake, either, which also confused her. No, when he spoke to Maddie or Delia his eyes were warm and relaxed, his manner genuine and easygoing yet somehow protective.

But she wasn't fooled.

Letting her pent-up energy take her where it would, she roamed. In daylight, Triple M was too gorgeous to believe. Behind the house, there were the three peaks, behind them more mountains for as far as the eye could see. The fertile black soil was covered with lush growth. Tall green grass, myriad colors of wildflowers, the azure-blue sky, the deeper blue of the raging river, and interspersed among it all were the two rustic red barns, the ranch house and a series of run-down cottages.

A picture-perfect scene.

Except that the barns were empty and in desperate need of repair. So was the house. Brightly colored wildflowers grew like weeds in the empty pastures.

At night, though, like now, Zoe could walk through and imagine it how it *should* be.

She gave in to the panic gnawing at her belly. They had savings, but they were small. Too small. God, she thought, leaning against a wooden railing. What would they do? They couldn't go back, there was nothing for them in L.A.

This was where they belonged, she could feel it, but she was deeply afraid about their future.

For whatever reason, Ty wanted this place, too. But she was every bit as rough and tough as he, and utterly indestructible, despite the broken promises in her past.

She told herself she hardly ever thought about that anymore, her mother's hastily whispered vow to return as she dumped a terrified three-year-old Zoe in the group foster home.

Good thing for Zoe that home had been so strong, so supportive. There had been some rough kids she'd had to fend off occasionally, but the owners of the house, the Fontaines, had been kind, loving and very warm. Without that base in her life, who knows how or where she would have ended up.

Yet she wasn't stupid enough to ignore the fact that she had indeed been perversely affected by her beginnings, no matter how much she shoved those beginnings away. She knew she didn't trust well. She knew she used gruffness and irritability as a shield to keep others at bay. And she protected her wary heart with a grid of iron, never allowing anyone but her sisters too close. Even then, she'd held back a good part of herself, though it shamed her to admit it, for in return they had given her everything.

Fact was, Zoe liked control. A lot. And she went out of her way to ensure she always had it, which included holding tight reins on her feelings. But she didn't have it here and she didn't have it with Ty. One look into those sharp, knowing eyes and she knew the truth. Ty Jackson wasn't the type to be controlled, which was reason enough to steer clear of the man. Not a problem, even if he had the best butt in Idaho and a smile that made her heart stutter. She'd steer clear.

She didn't need the heartache.

What she *did* need was to survive, and she was a master at that. All she had to do was turn this ranch around, and fast. As in yesterday.

She could do it. *They* could do it.

But the little flutter of nerves had her pushing on. She drew in a deep breath of night. Dark in Idaho was unlike anything she'd ever seen in Los Angeles. It was…black. And complete. The sky was littered with stars, the air cold and crisp. It smelled like…camping.

And now it was home. *Home.*

God, what was she thinking? They were out of her element, there wasn't a Taco Bell within a hundred miles! There wasn't even a major city within a hundred miles.

But deep down she knew she wasn't worried about Boise. Shooting the house a disgusted look over her shoulder, she kicked at some dirt and walked into the night, her inefficient tennis shoes sticking in the mud.

She was worried about her sisters.

And, if she were being honest, she was worried about Ty.

One of them was bound to fall for him. Delia loved a man with a sense of humor hidden behind the body of a Greek god, and Ty definitely fit the bill. And Maddie, she seemed to be such an easy mark for any man, with her low self-esteem and constant need to be…well, needed. Someone like Ty could take advantage of a woman like her in less than two minutes.

Only one problem with the theory of Ty hurting one of her sisters—he wasn't looking at either Maddie or Delia with that fiery passion hidden behind sleepy bedroom eyes. He was looking at *her*.

What had that been over dinner, that strange connection between them? For a long, uncomfortable amount of time, she hadn't been able to tear her gaze from his. Not that the big, lean, muscular man was a hardship to look at, but it unnerved her, this attraction she didn't want.

Just the thought had her walking faster into the night. Behind the shack of a barn, and nearly a hundred yards away, was another building, a second barn. With all her energy, it was no problem to cover this distance quickly. She was oddly unafraid of the dark, even with all the night sounds echoing around her. In fact, she felt more at home here in the wilderness than she ever had on the crazy streets of Los Angeles.

This barn was much nicer than the one closer to the

house, and she knew why. It wasn't used by Constance's ranch, it was part of the land leased by Ty. This part of Constance's land was closest to his, and at certain times of the year, such as now, when it was still cold at night, he kept horses stabled here.

Through a thicket of trees and up a gentle slope she thought she could see the lights of his own ranch house. But because she didn't want to imagine his life there, she turned away and opened one of the heavy double barn doors.

"Well, hello there."

Zoe nearly jumped out of her skin at the unexpected voice, which was mixed with the sounds of the horses within the barn, stomping impatiently at the late intrusion.

"It's just me. Cliff." The man turned his flashlight on himself as he dismounted from his horse. "How'ya doing tonight, ma'am?"

Zoe recognized him as one of Ty's men. He was young, late twenties at the most. He smiled easily, laughed just as easily, was sweet and kind to a fault; altogether the opposite of his boss.

"I'm just checking the horses," he said, as if he needed to put her mind to rest. "We've got one close to foal."

Zoe's troubles fell away at the thought. "Really?" She pictured a brand new baby horse, all awkward and adorable, struggling to stand next to its mother, and went warm and fuzzy inside. "I've never seen a pregnant horse before."

"Can't have that," Cliff drawled, smiling at her. He walked past her into the barn and hit one of the switches on the wall. Soft light filled a small portion of the barn. So did an intriguing mix of scents that Zoe hadn't gotten used to yet, but liked. Sweet hay, horse…man.

Even here, she thought with wonder, she could smell Ty.

She told herself that was dumb and concentrated on looking around. There was a double row of stables here, and a couple of curious horses peeked out over the doors. A sable-colored mare stood closest in her stall, staring over the wood with large, melting eyes.

Zoe moved closer, mesmerized. In the past few days she hadn't had time for this, with getting the house cleaned and everything situated. She reached out with a slightly nervous hand, charmed when the horse pushed her big head closer, stretching her long neck.

Then Cliff was there, right next to Zoe, holding an apple. He pulled out a pocketknife and sliced off a piece. Gently, he took Zoe's hand in his warm, callused one, put the wedge of apple on it and held it out. Zoe went still at Cliff's touch and waited for that burst of awareness, the same one she got whenever Ty inadvertently touched her.

Nothing.

Disappointed, she looked up into Cliff's handsome face, wondering why. It didn't seem fair in the least that this man did nothing for her. It wasn't unusual, she'd gone most of her life without being tempted in the slightest by the more rugged male species. She'd managed to lose her virginity early due to pure curiosity, but a shrugging disinterest in the activities had assured her she wasn't missing anything.

Here she was at twenty-six, a woman who didn't seem to lust as most normal women did. So why was she suddenly doing just that with Ty of all men?

Well, if she had to be experimenting, then it should be with someone kind and gentle like Cliff. Maybe if she tried just a tad bit harder...

Oblivious to her thoughts, Cliff held the apple up to the eager horse. "Watch," he whispered conspiratorially, winking when Zoe beamed up at him, giving it her best shot.

The beautiful animal, whose sides were bursting, obviously filled with pregnancy, reached its sniffing, hopeful face toward them and…bright light flooded the place.

The horse snickered, annoyed. Zoe blocked her eyes from the bright glare.

"This is certainly cozy."

Zoe blinked until she could see. Ty leaned negligently back against the wall, arms loose, fingers hooked into his belt loops, legs crossed in a deceptively casual pose. Every switch on the wall had been flipped on. "Sorry if I interrupted anything," he said, looking anything but.

Cliff smiled at him and shook his head. "Just giving Abby a bedtime snack." But he dropped his hand from Zoe's.

Ty nodded, his expression inscrutable. "You're all done for the night?"

Cliff's smile faded some and he shuffled his feet slightly. "Well…"

Ty lifted a brow, all stern and unrelenting, none of the sharp wit that Zoe had come to think of as innately part of the man in evidence now. "Well, what?" he snapped.

Zoe opened her mouth, but not sure what to say, she shut it again.

Cliff shifted his weight. "I didn't have time to—"

"You had time to come on to Ms. Martin."

Now Zoe opened her mouth again, suddenly positive she did indeed have plenty to say.

Before she could, Ty pushed away from the wall, and when he did, Cliff shot Zoe a half-sheepish, half-apologetic glance, moving clear from her.

"Ah…gotta go," he mumbled.

With enough bright lights shining that she could see every line on his tanned face, Zoe had no trouble detecting Cliff's blush, or his embarrassment. She glared at Ty, who didn't appear to notice. When Cliff had fumbled his way out of the barn, leaving the door open in his haste to escape,

Zoe ground her teeth and turned to Ty. "Well, that was...*nice.*"

His eyes flashed. "Don't flirt with my help."

"Flirt?" A shocked laugh left her. This had to be a joke. But it wasn't, she realized, looking at his furious face.

"If you want to flirt," he growled, "you do it with me."

Carefully she closed her dropped jaw. "You're the last man in Idaho— No, the last man on *earth* that I'd flirt with." Tossing her hair back, she stormed over to him. That her chin didn't even come to his tense shoulder didn't stop her; she wasn't afraid of him. "And don't you ever tell me what to do."

"I'll tell you whatever I please when it's my business."

"This is just because I refused to take you on as our partner."

"Believe me, it has nothing to do with that—"

"You flirt with Shirley."

He laughed then, some of the tension leaving him as she stood him down. "I do not."

"I saw you."

"What you saw, Zoe, was me turning her down. I don't mix business and pleasure. *Usually,*" he added, taking the last step between them.

The breath backed up in her throat at the look on his face. The shadows covered some of his expression, making it difficult to tell if all that heat was anger or arousal. She preferred the former.

"Did you hear me, Zoe? Stay away from my ranch hands."

"You're a...a bully!"

He laughed again. "Is that the best you can do?" Before she could come up with better, he'd taken her shoulders and pressed her back against the stall. Zoe was sandwiched between the hard, cold wood and Ty's equally hard but warm body, and her mind went blank. He surrounded her, and it wasn't a threatening sort of feeling at all, though it should have been. His broad shoulders blocked the light, blocked out everything but him.

"You were..." She struggled to keep her train of thought, difficult when all the blood rushed out of her head at the rough, unexpected embrace. "Rude to Cliff."

"I know." His forehead lowered to hers at the startling admission. "What is it about you that drives me so crazy?"

It was a rhetorical question, but with his lips hovering only a scant inch from hers, Zoe felt the compulsive need to keep talking because if she stopped, he might kiss her and then she would be lost.

"Don't worry," she said quickly. "I drive everyone crazy, it's not just you. Ask Delia—"

"Delia's not here." His large hands captured her head with surprising gentleness. Slowly he tilted it up, better aligning their mouths so that if he so much as breathed, they'd be connected.

It couldn't happen, she thought, unreasonable panic welling. This was crazy, they had no business doing this, none at all. Forget her wild fantasy involving his wicked mouth covering hers, of his tough, powerful body doing things to her own, of his deep, husky voice detailing each one of those things... Goodness. Forget it, this was *not* what she wanted.

But he was going to kiss her if she didn't do something, anything. "Ty...I don't think—"

"That's right," he murmured, his eyes heavy-lidded. "Don't think. *Feel.*"

"But—" He was watching her mouth with a hot, intent purpose that had her knees knocking together. "Ty..."

"Hmm-mmm..."

He wasn't going to listen to her. Well, she knew what to do, she was from Los Angeles, and well prepared. "Ty..."

"Shh." His hips slid over hers, the hard ridge between his thighs unmistakable. He did it again, finding the soft notch between hers, and she was putty in his hands. "Ty...I don't—"

"Zoe." Just that, just her name on a groaning sigh.

Nope, listening was beyond him, it was nearly beyond her. So she did the only thing she could think of to stop him.

She punched him.

Chapter 4

One week later, as spring gave way to summer, Zoe began to regret her rash decision in turning down Ty for a partnership.

And also for punching him in the belly.

Ty had pretty much ignored her, brooding and silent whenever they were together. However, with her sisters he'd been Mr. Charm.

Zoe told herself she could live with that.

What she couldn't live with was the ranch in its current condition. The only income they generated was the land Ty currently leased for his own operation. Which meant one fourth of the land looked good and cared for. He had fenced in pastures for his horses, and not only were they beautiful and impressive, it was an unbelievable thrill to stand outdoors, on land that belonged to her and her sisters, and watch nature take its course.

With the warm season came a patchwork of colors so brilliant it hurt the eye. Wheat, peas, alfalfa and wildflowers all grew naturally, blowing gently in the breeze, framed in by the river and the mountains. It was gorgeous beyond anything she'd ever known, and her love for the place grew.

She didn't want to give up on it, but they had to be able to survive.

Enchanted by the magnificent land, despite the isolation and clear-cut problems, Zoe and her sisters had agreed— they'd stick it out until the end. For better or worse.

Only for Zoe, it'd gotten worse. She'd had no clue how hard it would be to see Ty Jackson on a daily basis. Hell, on an *hourly* basis.

He was everywhere.

Long, powerful legs strained his snug, faded jeans. Tough, rugged shoulders managed to take on amazing amounts of work and responsibility. And his silent, crooked, knowing smile that taunted her.

"What's the matter, Slim?" he called out from his spot twenty-five yards away.

"Did I complain?" she snapped, turning her back to him.

Being manager could have meant any of a thousand things, but thankfully he seemed to respect them enough to let them make their own decisions for the ranch. Unfortunately they had no idea what those decisions should be.

Ty had a full staff of trainers and ranch hands at his own place, and since Triple M didn't, and couldn't afford one, he'd committed to riding fences on their land today, a chore desperately needed. To Maddie and Delia's combined delight, and Zoe's suspicion, Ty had taken Zoe as his helper.

This amused her sisters because they both sensed exactly how explosive she and Ty were together, and since the closest video store was an hour's drive away, it served as their entertainment.

Maddie had days ago suggested, in her sweet, calm way, that Zoe try harder to get along with Ty, that maybe Zoe was mad because Ty did what no one else did—made Zoe *feel*.

Maddie didn't know what she was talking about, grumbled Zoe as the sun beat down on her. She saw no reason to try to get along with the man who was only being nice to her to get her land, no matter how good his arms had felt around her.

He drove her crazy on purpose, she thought darkly, wiping her damp forehead with her arm. He thrived on it, as if he was as strangely frustrated as she at their strange, unaccountable attraction.

Ever since that night she'd slugged him, he'd stopped teasing her at every turn, but he still, when she least expected it, shot her one of his...*looks*.

The scorching, hungry, "maybe I'm going to kiss you in spite of you hitting me" look that made her bones melt. Made her yearn and ache and...yes, dammit, *feel*, in a world where she'd learned that feeling only hurt. She'd been with Delia and Maddie for years, and still she'd managed to keep a good part of Zoe to herself.

So what made it so hard with Ty?

He hadn't attempted to kiss her again, yet he'd kissed her sisters regularly. Sweet little pecks with closed lips. He kissed other women like *Shirley*—which for reasons Zoe didn't want to think about, made her want to strangle him, especially since those kisses were not so sweet and not so little at all.

Zoe knew this because she'd had the misfortune to catch him kissing the woman in the barn. Well, to be honest, as Ty had told her, Shirley had kissed *him*. But it'd been a long, deep, messy-looking kiss.

She groaned and squeezed her eyes shut against the strange pooling of heat between her thighs.

What made that memory even worse was the way Ty

had looked when he'd finally managed to pull back. Dark, intense...aroused in spite of himself.

And some pathetic little part of Zoe wanted to feel that way, too. Wanted Ty to make her feel that way.

Was she that awful? She hadn't hit him that hard, had she? And it was only because she'd been frightened, not of him, but of what he made her feel.

God. What was she thinking? Zoe didn't care why he didn't kiss her! She was thankful, yes, she was.

She didn't want to be that desperate for anyone. If she just stuck mostly to herself, she'd be just fine. Yes, she had Delia and Maddie, but she knew deep down, one day they'd get married and have children and drift away from her. They'd find others in their lives to love and she would be fine with that.

She'd be alone again, and she'd be fine. Just fine.

Ty patiently held the wire. The sun gleamed off his reflective sunglasses so that she couldn't see his eyes, but she imagined they were lit with amusement—at her expense. "Don't tell me you broke a nail," he called out.

"Shut up," she called back in what she meant to be an amiable tone, but she sounded weary even to her own ears. Straightening, she stretched her aching body, knowing she'd lie down and die before she admitted she was tired. Die, too, before admitting she'd been thinking of him.

Shoving her long, out-of-control hair back, she wished for a hair band with all her might. She lifted her hands to raise it off her hot neck, but her hands were disgustingly dirty. Shrugging her shoulders at this minor inconvenience, just one more in a long line of many, she snipped off an extra piece of wire and twisted it in her hair, far more concerned with comfort than looks.

It'd be hell later, untangling the wire from the snarls in her curls, but that was a worry to be saved for nightfall.

"Hey there."

He'd come right up behind her. She jumped a little because his voice was so rough yet silky, and it did something funny to her nerves. "Stop sneaking up on me."

Solemnly, he held out a pair of gloves. "Keep these on," he demanded. "You'll ruin your skin."

"You must be confusing me with Delia." It was only fair to share her rotten mood with him since he'd caused it. "I could care less about my nails."

"Hmm." His work-roughened hands brushed hers, and at the contact, her stomach tightened all funny. She jerked her hands away, annoyed at both of them.

"Touchy," he noted.

"Just keep your paws to yourself." No one's touch had ever made her feel all tingly inside. Why his? Why now? And if she smacked him again, would he understand that it was just her irrational fear and nothing personal?

"Touchy *and* full of insults." He grinned. "You're a real joy to work with."

"So are you," she said evenly. "Just ask Cliff."

He didn't even look ashamed. "I apologized to him."

"Not to me."

"You slugged me!" He slid a hand over his perfectly flat stomach as if remembering the punch vividly.

Why, she wondered for the hundredth time, was he so gentle with the quiet, withdrawn Maddie, so funny with intense Delia and so absolutely ungentle and unfunny with her?

Instead he was bold and wicked and fierce, and she refused to feel bad, or at least admit that she did. "You could have chosen Maddie or Delia to help you today, so don't complain that you're stuck with me."

"Who's complaining?"

Well, he had her there. Feeling awkward with him so close and so big, she looked around desperately for a distraction. She didn't have to look too far. The dry, parching heat was getting to her. "I wish I had a rubber band!"

"Here." He reached into the truck and opened the glove box. His wallet fell out, opened, to the floorboard. Ignoring that, Ty found a rubber band and handed it to her.

"Thank you." But the words were hard to say because she was looking into the truck, down at his open wallet. And at the two—*two!*—condoms in it. A little squeak of shocked embarrassment escaped her.

Without any sign of self-consciousness, he replaced the wallet and straightened.

"Better?" he asked, gesturing to her now-contained hair.

She could only stare at him. He carried two condoms on him, was all she could think. "Two?"

He let out a slow, sexy grin at that and she nearly swallowed her tongue, realizing she'd spoken out loud. "I mean—"

"I know what you mean," he said. A long finger stroked her cheek, while his eyes flared with a surprising amount of heat. "I'm not promiscuous, I just like to be prepared. And sometimes one just isn't enough." His smile spread. "It wouldn't be with you, Slim."

"I— You— Oh." Hopelessly flustered, she studied their feet, blushing all the more when he laughed softly. And she decided if he was enjoying this, she might as well ask "Just how *not* promiscuous are you?"

"Well...those two would probably fall apart if I needed them, they're so old," he admitted ruefully.

That cheered her up considerably. Until he tipped up her chin and said, "I'm thinking of replacing them." His thumb glided along her lip, making it tingle, and the look in his eyes made her heart take off like a shot.

He did it on purpose, she decided, just to see her all ruffled, and she renewed her efforts at resenting him with all her locked-up heart.

Before she could stalk off, he easily captured her hands again, studying them carefully. "I want you to wear the gloves so you don't get cut and scratched." His thumb slid lightly over a reddened knuckle.

Just a simple touch. One little touch. And because of it, she had to open her mouth to breathe. Then he bent and blew lightly on her wound, just a slight puff of air, and she nearly moaned out loud.

She snatched back her hand. "Knock it off." She was proud of her even, haughty voice. He didn't have to know that her bones had just melted away, leaving her drowning in a pool of longing.

He just looked at her, all one hundred eighty pounds of uninhibited, rowdy, knowing male. "What's the matter?"

She lifted her chin and glared back. "You're wasting precious daylight hours. I'm going to have to dock your pay."

"I'm not getting paid."

Which was another puzzle she'd been meaning to solve. "You cared for Constance that much that you'd do this for one year without compensation?"

He met her gaze evenly. "Yes."

That sort of generosity was unheard of where she'd come from. There was a reason for it, she reminded herself. Just as there was a reason he was trying to butter them up.

"We *are* going to pay you, you know," she grumbled, looking away. "Soon as we can."

He smiled then and leaned against a post, all sinewy grace. "The gig is up."

"What gig?"

"Why don't you save us both a bunch of trouble and admit how you feel about me?"

She managed a laugh. "It's not flattering."

That infuriatingly sexy smile stayed put. "You're crazy about me."

"Crazy, definitely." She flipped her precarious ponytail back, using annoyance to cover her fear. Had she given herself away? He couldn't have guessed her deepest, darkest, most secret fantasy, could he?

Her secret little hope that someday *he* would be the crazy one. *Crazy for her.* Not for the land, but *her.*

Just thinking it in the light of day had color rushing to her cheeks. She put her hands on them, feeling the dirt streak on her skin.

She could only imagine how she looked. And how was it that she felt as though grime clung to her every pore, while he looked cool and clean? He even smelled good, she thought resentfully. Lingering soap and one hundred percent male. No man should be allowed to smell that good. Standing there thinking about it, she wavered in the heat.

No wonder women fell over him. It was disgusting, yet she leaned just a tad closer to catch another whiff.

She must be more tired than she thought.

His eyes narrowed on her, reminding her she didn't like that he noticed every little thing about her, especially the things she didn't want him to notice. "You're slacking off, Jackson," she muttered, turning away. "Get back to work."

"Let's take a break."

"I don't need one."

He hauled her back around, his hands firm on her hips. "*I* need one," he insisted, searching her face for who knew what. "I'm tired, Zoe. Very tired."

"Oh. Well then, I don't want to show you up or anything and make you feel bad." She sank gratefully to the tailpipe of the truck—actually, *rambling heap* better described the ancient, beat-up thing that had been left on the deserted ranch.

When Ty offered her iced tea from a cooler he kept in the back, she nearly whimpered in pathetic thanks.

On the gentle slope below them she could hear the rush of the river, and it sounded cool and inviting. A single falcon flew overhead, its wingspan wide and sure. Zoe watched, fascinated, reminded that she was indeed in another world from her accustomed city. "It's so…hushed," she whispered.

"Peace and quiet are the catch of the day," he agreed, tossing his hat into the truck.

"I know. The view is so close I feel it reaching out to touch me." She flushed, feeling stupid for voicing her thoughts.

Ty was staring at her, appreciation and frank approval in his gaze. "You *do* feel it, the magic in the air here. I wasn't sure."

"Yes," she admitted. "I feel it."

The awareness between them was thick as ever. He didn't seem any more inclined than she to deal with it. Ty tipped back his head and drank. A drop of the clear, cool drink ran slowly down his neck, leaving Zoe with the most shocking urge to lean close and lick it off.

"Oh Lord, I've lost it," she muttered weakly, closing her eyes to both the man and the sun. "Completely lost it. It's too hot or something."

Odd as it was, Ty let the opportunity to rile her pass, remaining unnaturally silent.

Startled by that, Zoe opened her eyes and stared at him.

He leaned against the side of the truck bed, one foot bent and braced against a tire, his elbows supporting his weight as they rested on the top of the truck. His shirt stretched intriguingly over his wide chest. His jeans, streaked with dust, emphasized his long, powerful legs. Tipping up his face, he caught the warmth beaming down.

A man seemingly at rest.

And yet his every muscle vibrated with tension.

"What is it?" she asked softly.

Another man might have leaped in with denials, or at least shrugged her off.

Ty did neither, didn't budge. That terrible stillness held him, further alarming her. What if he were having a heart attack? Sunstroke? She was helplessly ignorant about such things. "Are you…sick?"

His lips quirked then, though he still didn't move. "Don't worry, Slim. First aid isn't required."

The urge to tease him out of this unnerving mood was strong, but something stopped her. Whether it was the utter flatness to his expression, or the alarming stillness in a man who never stopping moving, she didn't know.

She hopped off the tailgate and moved in front of him. "Ty?"

When he still didn't bother with a response, she reached up and flicked off his sunglasses.

Now he looked down at her with those fathomless steel eyes. "Break's over."

She didn't pretend to know him well, but something was wrong. He seemed so…well, regretful, and he wasn't a man to waste time on regrets. "Ty, come on. Truth."

"Truth." He nodded, turned and kicked the tire of the decrepit old truck with angry vehemence. "Truth is, this life is too hard for you."

That was a good one. Compared to the life she'd already led, this was a cakewalk. "You're wrong about that," she said evenly.

"It is," he insisted.

"So I suppose you want me to sell to you and hightail it on outta here."

"This isn't what you expected, Zoe. You know it's not. It isn't good for Maddie and Delia."

Maddie and Delia. Of course, it all came down to them, because who really cared what the tough, cold Zoe thought? "They're fine," she said, more harshly than she meant.

"But for how long?"

She kept her voice even. "Sorry you agreed to stay on for the year?"

He looked disgusted at that thought. "No."

"So it's true, then," she said slowly. "You want us to run off with our tails between our legs and leave you the land."

"No." But he turned from her.

"Ty."

"No!" He nearly shouted this, then dropped his head back on his shoulders and stared at the lazy white clouds floating across the sky. "Hell. I'm not regretting helping. That's the last thing I'd regret. I'm talking about money, Slim."

"What about it?"

"You don't have any, for one. Constance didn't have any to leave you. This place is dead without it, and you won't let me help financially."

"We'll manage."

"How?" He shook his head, frustration spilling out of his every pore. "Why won't you let me in as partner?"

"So we could spend your money?"

"Well…yes. Dammit, yes."

"Is that what this is about? Your pride?"

He let out a rough laugh. "You have a way, Zoe, of putting things. Makes me feel about two feet tall."

"We could care less about money." She thought about it, then amended that statement with a fond smile. "Well, Maddie and I, anyway. Delia, she's another story."

"You all deserve more." He shoved his fingers through his hair and walked around in a slow circle. He'd not slept agonizing over this. It was hard to relinquish Ben's dream, and this land had truly been his brother's dream, but he couldn't, wouldn't cheat these women of theirs, either.

He just couldn't do it. Couldn't live with himself if he pushed them until they gave up.

"So you're upset that this life is too tough for us?" She laughed at him. *Laughed.* "And who appointed you our keeper?" She put her hands on her hips and faced him, eyes flashing, hair wild, looking stunningly primal. "I'm a big girl, Ty Jackson, and I've been through lots of crap. This is nothing."

He wondered just how bad that "crap" had been. No use mentioning he agonized over that, too, because she wouldn't believe him. "I know—"

"No," she interrupted flatly. "You don't. I'm stronger than most, though, so if you really think you're responsible for me and that you have to take care of me, think again, buster. No one but *me* takes care of me."

How to explain that what he felt for her wasn't "responsibility." Hell, it wasn't even close to brotherly, hadn't been since the beginning and had only escalated since their brief embrace in the barn, just before she'd clobbered him with a surprisingly effective right hook. But he couldn't put those feelings to words because he didn't have the words for something he didn't want to face. "I just—"

Her finger poked into his chest, her head barely meeting his shoulder as she continued to rant with the sun beating down on them. "I make my own decisions, one of which was to come here. It's a mess, I agree on that. But a mess my sisters and I will deal with together. And together, *alone,* we'll fix it."

"How can you fix it without money?"

"I can hammer just as well as you, that doesn't take cash. And—"

"And you have no idea what you need here. This was a horse ranch, but you have no horses. No money to buy them. And no idea how to work the land to raise crops instead, not to mention no money for that, either."

"I have a little money." *Very* little. "Delia does, too, though not much because she can't keep cash to save her life. Maddie doesn't have anything, but—"

"It's not enough," he said firmly.

She put her hands on her hips and faced him. "So I ought to just sell it to you, I suppose."

"Sounds good to me."

They were standing toe to toe, nose to nose in the dirt by the truck. "No go. Never. No way," she clarified.

He growled in pure frustration. "You're just being stubborn."

"We'll be fine."

"A loan won't give you the know-how."

She swiped at her forehead, streaking more dirt. She looked stubborn, full of determination and beautiful. "I know. But I have a manager. Unless...you're done here."

"Do you want me to be done?"

"No. We...need you."

He gaped at her surprising admission, while she sighed, clearly not happy about having to admit it.

"Do you?" he asked quietly.

"Yes." She drew a deep breath. "So...will you help?"

"Good question." He could smell the light, tantalizing scent of her. He could feel the heat from her body seeping into his. Their thighs almost brushed, and at his sides his hands curled into fists to keep from grasping her hips and bringing them to his.

"Know what I think?" she whispered.

"What?" His voice wasn't quite steady, and he cleared his throat at the awareness shooting like electricity between them.

"I think you need us, too. You just don't even know it."

God, he wanted to put his hands on her again, his mouth on hers. And he didn't want to see that flash of fear in her eyes when it happened. He didn't *want* to feel this way about her, but he did.

"Isn't that true?" she pressed.

Why couldn't she back off? She didn't want to show him the real Zoe hidden beneath her tough facade; she should just leave him and his feelings the hell alone. He took back his sunglasses and placed them on his nose.

"Chicken," she taunted. "Too chicken to talk to me."

"I want to do a whole hell of a lot more than talk," he assured her, watching her flush with little satisfaction.

"There you go, being a bully again."

That did it. Really did it. She gasped when he stalked toward her, backing her to the side of the truck.

"Ty. What—"

He did what his body demanded. And maybe he was being a bully, but he didn't care.

He swallowed her startled breath with his mouth.

Chapter 5

Zoe's body reacted first, with a delicious shudder as Ty's mouth ravaged hers. Her bones dissolved, but instead of falling she found herself plastered against him. She let the kiss take her, and oh, what a kiss.

The small part of her mind still functioning reminded her that she didn't do such things no matter how wonderful this mindless, floating feeling was. Reminded her she wanted a new life for herself and her sisters, and that didn't include sleeping with anyone, much less a man who wanted her land for his own.

But the sun felt good on her face, and Ty's mouth felt even better against her, so it was a long, hot moment before she found the strength to resist.

Ty tensed when she pushed at his chest. He lifted his head and stared at her warily. "You going to hit me again?"

She sighed and pushed harder. "No. Go away."

"What's the matter?"

He was too tempting, that was the matter. "I don't feel like it, that's all."

His mouth, still wet from hers, curved, but he dropped his hands from her. "You felt like it a moment ago."

"Changed my mind."

He looked as though he might have argued, but the sound of a motor revving on the dirt road stopped him. He cocked his head. "That's one of your sisters."

"How can you tell?"

"Listen to it. The engine sounds like it's on its last legs."

She listened, and he was right. The engine coughed and stuttered. Then it came into sight, and it was indeed the second of Constance's two trucks.

Zoe hadn't been able to believe the run-down condition of the vehicles. It was a silent and gut-wrenching testament to how desperate Constance must have been in the past years of her life. Too old to make a success out of the ranch without a family, and with not enough money to pay someone else, Constance had been stuck.

It was enough to break even Zoe's stoic heart, and while she waited for the truck to come closer, she stole a glance at Ty.

He remained a mystery. Tough, independent. He dodged all personal questions about himself, not to mention how his staff seemed to go out of their way to avoid him. He most definitely was a loner.

Yet he hadn't let Constance down. He might have been unable to get her trucks fixed for her, but he hadn't left her alone. He'd been there for her, until the very end.

Which gave her a funny warm feeling to think about. The ancient, beat-up old truck stopped, and Delia, Maddie and Cade McKnight stepped out into the bright sunshine.

Cade saw Zoe and waved. Even now, after Constance's death, Cade was determined to figure exactly which of them was the true heir—not because he wanted to kick two of them off the land, but because he loved a good mystery.

He was sharp, tenacious and very good at what he did. He was also tall, dark and handsome enough that Maddie's cheeks were red.

So was Delia's whole face, which made Zoe want to laugh, because for some reason Zoe didn't quite understand, Cade seemed to get under Delia's skin.

Oblivious, Cade shook hands with Ty, then smiled at Zoe. "I see you met your neighbor."

Zoe bit back her grimace. *Met him and was just kissing him senseless, thank you.* "Ah...yes."

Ty lifted a brow, daring her to speak her mind.

Zoe looked away. "We were just...um...fixing fences," she said lamely. "Working really hard, too." Sweat trickled between her breasts. "Hot today, don't you think?"

No one but Ty seemed to notice her discomfort. His smile spread, and with no one watching him, he winked at her conspiratorially.

If they'd been alone, she thought she might have slugged him again.

"Cade wanted to see how we were doing," Maddie said.

"Yeah, well, he could have called for that." Delia ran a finger over her latest self-applied manicure. Her nails were electric blue with bolts of lightning on the thumbs. "What he really wanted, Maddie, was another home-cooked meal."

Cade grinned.

"Well, he's in luck, then." Maddie smiled. "We're having a pot roast tonight. With homemade bread."

Cade's eyes lit with hope. "You're too good to be true, Maddie."

Maddie flushed under the praise, looking pretty and cool in her fresh white jeans and a blue denim top, despite the fact she'd been working hard inside all day. Delia looked smooth and very sophisticated as well, with her black silk shell and jeans, leaving Zoe to swipe the grime on her hands down the front of her own already-dirty jeans, wishing for a hot shower.

Cade looked around the empty land with a sad frown. "I guess I also wanted to see if you'd made any plans. I know this place wasn't quite what you'd expected. I didn't know if you'd definitely stay...?"

Zoe looked at her sisters and was relieved to see the same determination on their faces as she knew was on hers. "We're staying," she told him firmly. "No question. But you could have told us, Cade."

He looked ashamed but not apologetic. "Would you have come?"

Zoe fell silent, unsure. Would they have? She didn't know and that made her sad. She would have missed out on the pull of the land, the freedom...the tall, handsome face of Ty as he watched her quietly with an intense expression.

"This land meant everything to Constance," Cade told them. "And to think of it being unoccupied and neglected, as it was before you got here, destroyed her. You three weren't the only ones who got something out of the inheritance, she did, too—the knowing that Triple M would live on." Cade paused. "So what will you do?"

"We'd like to ranch," Zoe answered. They'd stayed up late every night talking about it. "But we can't be sure until we make plans and pin down the financial side of it."

"There aren't many options on land such as this."

"No." Zoe had been worried about this as well. If they didn't raise horses or cattle or crops, which she knew nothing about, what would they do? They had expected the ranch to be running, with a full, knowledgeable crew, and that she hadn't checked it out thoroughly was a guilt she would have to live with. They couldn't live here like this for long, they had to make money. A ranch seemed the logical choice, but they knew so little. She hated to be dependent on anyone, but how else could she do this other than to get help from someone who knew what to do? She glanced at Ty and her nerves tightened. "We're not leaving, though, whatever we decide."

"Good." Cade looked at everyone. "I guess Ty has filled you in on the gaps in the story."

Zoe's stomach took a little dive. "Gaps?" She stole another glance at Ty, but suddenly his eyes, open and friendly only a second before, had completely shuttered, giving none of his thoughts away.

"This can wait" was all he said.

"No need, we're all here." Cade leaned into the truck, grabbed a container of water and took a long drink. "The sky's as blue as a crayon today, but it's sure dry out here, isn't it? Not nearly so warm in the city, let me tell you."

"Well, city boy, feel free to pack it on home, then," Delia said blandly. "You could just call when you don't have any news, you know. You certainly don't have to come out here to say nothing and complain about the weather." Daintily, she picked her way through the dirt to the truck, ignoring Cade's unperturbed grin.

"I bet the change of scenery is nice for you," Maddie said quickly, always the peacemaker. "You know you're always welcome, Cade."

"Thanks, Maddie." Cade swiped at his forehead, but in truth, he looked just as at home as they did, wearing faded jeans and a snug T-shirt revealing the city boy was well nourished and perfectly fit. "But it's kind of you, Delia," he called out. "To worry about me traveling so far to help you."

Delia rolled her eyes, and Zoe, wondering why no one else was going mad, lost her patience. "What gaps!"

Cade sighed, and his smile faded. "None of your parents

have yet been successfully found, much less traced back to Constance. It doesn't matter for the inheritance.''

Zoe swore softly, bitterly disappointed. Cade touched her shoulder. ''Constance didn't need more proof than what she had—three women born approximately when she thought her granddaughter might have been born, and who were in the right place. She felt certain it was one of you. She knew how close you were, how much you loved one another, and that was enough for her.''

Zoe nodded and fought her crushed hopes. Whether she liked to admit it or not, she would have given her right hand to know what had happened to her mother that day she'd been dropped off so many years ago.

And she would have died before admitting to a soul that she was twenty-six years old and still haunted by what her mother had done, that she needed to know *why* she'd been deserted, and that need grew daily.

''Other than the fact that none of you have a father on your birth certificate, and that you'd all been left by a mother who disappeared out of your lives, we have little to go on,'' Cade admitted.

Zoe spoke kindly because he was doing everything he could, but it was hard to be patient when she was dying for more. ''So what 'gaps'?''

''We're busy now,'' Ty interrupted. ''We've got fencing—''

''Ty, I've got to know.''

''Fine.'' Abruptly he turned away, back to the fence. Hunkering down, he set to work, ignoring her.

''Cade?'' More urgently now, Zoe turned to him. ''Tell us.''

''Should we go back to the house first?'' he wondered.

Behind them, Ty's hammer hit a post hard. Zoe glanced at him, at the tense set to his body, but she didn't have time to worry about the moody, brooding cowboy when her own life was on hold. "No, please tell us now."

Delia came closer again and lost most of her defiance as she stood united with her sisters. Cade flashed a look that begged them for understanding, but Zoe wasn't prepared to blindly give anything.

"Constance was only a prayer away from bankruptcy," he said quietly, easily, but it was clear how badly he felt in every line of his tall, rangy body. "And if she'd gone bankrupt before her death, there'd have been no land to inherit."

"That's no secret, is it?" Delia asked. "It was pretty clear to us from the beginning how much money trouble she'd had."

"That poor woman, all alone, facing that," Maddie said with pain in her voice. "I wish we could have found her sooner."

"Losing this land would have killed her," Cade admitted. "Triple M Ranch was everything to her. The only thing that meant more was finding her granddaughter."

"If she was so poor, then how did *you* get paid?" Delia asked. "I'm sure you're not cheap. And now that I think about it, why do you keep on this case even now, when there's clearly no money in the estate for you?"

"I'm getting to that." Obviously a man used to hostility, Cade calmly took another long drink of his water. "Aah, that's good." He looked at Delia evenly. "Constance had a benefactor."

"You mean like maybe an older man who loved her and couldn't stand to see her hurt?" Maddie's face softened. "Oh, how romantic."

"Not an older man, no," Cade said. "But it was someone who cared about her a great deal, and yes, someone who didn't want to see her hurt."

"Dammit!" roared Ty.

Everyone looked at him. He ripped off his gloves and sucked on an injured finger. He'd shucked his hat a while back so that the sun shone off the dark hair that fell nearly to his shoulders. He was taut as a bow, an explosion just waiting to happen.

Zoe's bad feeling got worse, and she turned back to Cade. "You're telling me that this someone paid off both her debts *and* your fee? Just because they cared? That's a whole lot of caring." In her opinion, no one did something like that without a really good reason.

A motive.

And motives were usually selfish.

"It is a lot of caring," Cade agreed. "And because of it, you're here."

With a quiet oath, Ty dropped the hammer and turned to face them, hands low on his hips in a stance of great irritation. "If you're all done having a nice little break, then scatter, would ya? I've got work to do and you're distracting me." He stalked to the truck, but before he could hop into the driver's seat, Cade spoke to him.

"I think they should know who that benefactor was, Ty."

"Well, I don't. There's no reason to tell them."

"You're wrong." Zoe stepped closer, quivering with the need for answers. "We have every right to know, and I want someone to tell us right now what's going on."

Cade shot Ty a sympathetic glance, but he spoke regardless. "It was Ty."

Stunned silence met this remark. Zoe felt the shock bounce through her, which only deepened when Ty looked at her, his eyes bleak and miserable.

"You," she whispered softly.

"Me," he agreed, just as softly.

"Delia said you were considering making him a partner

in the ranch,'' Cade said. ''So I thought you should know how responsible and trustworthy he is.''

''We're not considering a partnership,'' Zoe said, turning away, her shoes crunching in the dirt. She stared blindly at the gentle green slope that led down to the raging river.

''Well, I think you *should* consider one,'' Cade told her back. ''Because, frankly, I don't see how you'll do it without him. Ty is the best at this, you couldn't get anyone better.''

''Oh, Ty,'' Maddie murmured. ''How incredibly wonderful of you to take care of Constance that way.''

''And expensive,'' said the pragmatic Delia, but even as cynical as she was, she looked very touched. ''I'm not sure I know how to thank you.''

''I don't want thanks.'' His jaw was set, and hostility rolled off him in waves.

''What you did meant the world to Constance,'' Cade said to Ty quietly. ''And you deserve the proper recognition for that.''

Ty clamped his mouth shut as if too much of a gentleman to say what he thought about that. ''I didn't do it for any of you,'' he said finally.

Okay, Zoe thought, maybe he wasn't too much of a gentlemen to express his thoughts after all. ''Why did you do it, then?''

Ty slid into the driver's seat and snapped on his seat belt. ''Your ride is leaving. You walking back?''

Being ignored made her testy, and just a tad bit pushy, though even a small child would have had the sense to leave this man alone right now. ''Maybe it was more simple than that,'' she suggested. ''You wanted to buy this place.''

''I already told you that,'' Ty said through clenched teeth.

Cade looked confused at Zoe's hostility. ''I don't think you understand. If Ty hadn't paid for me to continue the search for Constance's granddaughter, and if Constance hadn't been satisfied with what I'd found, Ty wouldn't have had to *buy* this place.''

Ty started the truck and rudely revved the engine.

''But of course he would have bought this place,'' Zoe said loudly, glaring at Ty. ''He already told us he wanted it.''

Cade shook his head. ''Over the years Constance got very close to Ty.'' He had to yell over the noise of the truck. ''She felt as though he were her family, and indeed for a long time, he was all she had. She thought the world of him.''

The engine revved again. Music filled the air now, loud pumping, ridiculously upbeat music that was at a direct conflict with the tense atmosphere.

It was hard to reconcile the brooding, terse male sitting in the driver's seat with the kind, caring warm man Cade was describing.

Harder still to let go of her years of innate suspicion and wariness to admit that maybe, just maybe, she was looking at a man who was not as she wanted to make him out to be.

He wasn't selfish.

He wasn't sneaky.

He wasn't out to hurt anyone.

And maybe, just maybe, he could indeed be trusted.

Even if he was ornery as a prickly bear at times. ''What does this have to do with the land?'' she yelled to Cade, at the precise moment Ty reached over and flicked off the earsplitting, pulsing music.

Her voice echoed unnaturally, and she glowered at the back of Ty's still head as everyone looked at her.

''It has everything to do with the land,'' Cade told her. ''If I hadn't found you three lovely ladies, Ty himself would have inherited the ranch.''

Chapter 6

"You could have told me."

This from Zoe, and as they were the first words she'd spoken since Cade's untimely announcement, Ty considered himself lucky.

"I can't believe you didn't."

He tightened his hands on the steering wheel as they bumped and rocked in the truck over the rough road on their way back to the house. "It never came up."

She gaped at him, shook her head and turned away, staring out the window. "You're something, you know that?"

"Oh, really? Well, you're not much different." Anger felt good since it erased any lingering guilt he might have been wrestling with. "Ever since you came to Triple M you've been staring at me as if I were some sort of bug. A total creep. As if you expect me to hurt you—"

"I'm not afraid of you."

"I didn't mean a physical hurt." Arguing with her was like arguing with Ben, who'd been nearly as stubborn as she. Ty had never been able to win a verbal war with him, either, and suddenly he ached so much he was exhausted with it, which made him all the more furious.

He pulled up the long gravel drive to the house and braked. In the confines of the truck, the air sizzled, and he assured himself it was all temper and nothing more. Zoe had been shooting him with mental daggers the entire drive and he'd had enough. "Look at you," he said. "You're braced for battle like I'm the bad guy."

"If the shoe fits…"

"Tell me, Zoe, what's so bad about me helping Constance?"

She stiffened and he was tired of her silent hostility. "A woman that could have been your own grandmother? Does helping her make me a criminal?"

She remained tense against the door, as far from him as she could possibly get, but then suddenly it was as if his words deflated her. Her shoulders drooped. She rubbed her temples, her hair falling forward out of her makeshift ponytail. "God, I always do that. I don't know why," she admitted quietly.

"Always are a pain, you mean?"

A smile tugged at her mouth, and she dropped her hands from her face to her lap as if she were too tired to hold them up any longer. "That, too. I meant, I'm always looking for trouble. Delia says it's my middle name."

"Gee, I don't know what she's talking about."

"I'm sorry for that."

"But not for thinking the worst of me at all times, I guess," he said wearily. She was one of the most irritating women he'd ever met. And the most fascinating. "Do you have any idea how much you tie me up in knots?"

"Me?" Now she looked up, clearly startled at his unexpected bluntness. "What do you mean?"

He threw up his hands. "I don't know what the hell I

mean. You have all these thoughts running through your head that I can only imagine, but I'm pretty sure, given your expression, they're not exactly flattering."

She opened her mouth, but nothing came out. A tactful silent agreement.

Because he couldn't help himself, he shifted closer, lifting a hand to the back of her seat, fighting his sudden urge to touch her glorious hair. "Yet only a little while ago," he continued in a low, unintentionally husky voice, "you were kissing me as if your life depended on it."

She let out a little puff of breath, a sound that became erotic in the close confines of the car. Of their own accord, his fingers touched her then, just lightly on her cheek, trailing to her ear and sinking into that hair he'd been dying to touch again. "How do you think that makes me feel, Zoe?"

She swallowed hard, closed her eyes at his touch. "As confused as I am, I imagine."

Tempting as it was to just drop her off and keep going, he turned off the engine. They had to work this out, although he would have rather gone back to his own place and buried himself in his own work. Hell, he would have rather gone *anywhere* than face this green-eyed, auburn-haired beauty he couldn't seem to stop thinking of. "I want you to understand something," he said slowly.

"About the will?"

"Yes."

"About the little fact you didn't tell us you were in line to get this land?"

"Yes, about all that. And more." He hesitated, willing her to believe. "It's true, I would have inherited this land from Constance if you hadn't been found. And yes, I would have combined this ranch with my own land."

"Why the big secret, Ty? Why didn't you just tell us right away?"

In truth, he didn't know. Other than he had never helped

Constance for the possible glory. He hadn't even helped her because he wanted her land so badly. He'd helped because he knew what it was like to be frightened and desperate. He'd hated the helplessness of it all, and hated watching Constance fight it.

And why should she have had to, when he had the means in which to step in and prevent it? Bottom line, he had helped because he had wanted to, because it meant something to him to be able to do it, and because it had been the right thing to do.

But he didn't feel like spelling any of that out to Zoe, not when she was so sure he'd done it to get the land.

"Why did you help her find us?" Zoe asked him. "Why would you do that if you didn't have to? You could have had everything you wanted, and for free. Instead you bought yourself right out of an inheritance."

She thought he'd had an ulterior motive, which infuriated him. He was angry at himself for letting what she thought bother him, and angry at her for thinking so little of him in the first place. "How could you understand so little about loyalty and caring when you have two sisters?" he wondered. "I've seen how close you are."

She dropped her gaze and turned her head away, but he'd had enough of her escapes and wasn't going to let her get away with it again, not when he needed answers. With a finger beneath her chin, he lifted her face. The signs of her discomfort were there in her flaming cheeks, her flashing eyes, but he didn't let up. "Tell me."

Annoyed, she slapped his hand away and made a scoffing noise. "This isn't about me. I want to know why the big secret. You let us think you were nothing but a fellow rancher, but you were much more to her than that. You were more to her than…" She broke off abruptly, swallowing hard.

"Than what?" He gentled his voice, his temper gone as he realized the truth.

"I don't want to talk about it—"

Too damn bad. "I was more to her than you?" he pressed. "Is that it? You're upset because a virtual stranger was in her life when her own granddaughter, possibly you, couldn't be?" He knew he'd hit the jackpot when she flinched as if he'd hit her. Some part of him, a part he'd been holding back from her, cracked open, allowing a rush of feelings to surge through, the first and foremost being a compassion he hadn't expected. "It's not your fault, Zoe."

She tried to look away, but he wouldn't let her. "It's *not*," he repeated gently. "You didn't know where she was, or even that you might have been related to her. You can't blame yourself."

But she did, he could see it in her eyes, and he realized she wasn't nearly as tough as she thought she was.

"She was destitute," Zoe whispered, showing more emotion than he'd seen. "Alone."

"And you know what that's like, don't you?"

"I had my sisters."

And he'd had Ben, thank God. "You know, maybe we're not quite as different as you think."

That brought a smile. "I'm a city girl. You're a cowboy. How much more different can we get?"

"Labels, Zoe?" he chided with a laugh. "I expected better from you."

She looked pointedly at his boots. At his hat lying on the back seat.

"The clothes don't make the man," he told her. "And I'm a horse trainer, not a cowboy. I'm more city than you think. I came from Chicago." He had no idea why he said it, he never said it.

She was just as surprised as he. "How long have you been here?"

"Forever," he said flatly.

She nodded, understanding better than most he didn't like talking about his past. "You were so good to her. I don't know why I snapped before, I'm sorry. I think…" Her voice lowered as if she were ashamed. "I think about how often I've wondered about my family. About where and who they were—" She rubbed her face again, looking weary. "Never mind. It doesn't matter." She reached for the door handle.

"Wait." He put his hand over hers, not wanting her to go, not when he was getting a prolonged glimpse of the Zoe she usually kept hidden from him. "It matters."

"I don't know why I'm telling you these things, I hate to talk about myself."

"You haven't told me much, except for what you think of me." He smiled. "You've been pretty clear on that score."

She grimaced. "Yeah." She bit her lower lip. "Look, I often shoot off at the mouth, letting out the first thing that comes to me."

"No. Really?"

She smiled at his dry tone. "I should work on that, but…" She lifted her shoulder. "Truthfully, I haven't the foggiest idea how I feel about you."

On that shocking statement, she got out, then bent slightly at the waist and looked at him.

He looked back.

"Did you know you were going to inherit when you went about helping Constance to find her granddaughter?" she asked.

"No."

The green in her eyes deepened. "Without us here, you'd be one happy camper."

"But you *are* here."

"Yes, we are. You never told me why this land is so

important to you." She leaned on the door, and her light scent came to him on the breeze, wafting through the window. It was soft and sexy. Exciting.

But she was asking him a very personal question. He breathed through his mouth instead of his nose and concentrated. "My land is too small. I want to expand."

"Uh-huh. And…?"

"That's a pretty good reason all by itself."

"But it's not the only reason."

"Maybe not," he allowed.

"We're not going to give up."

"I realize that."

"And you're not going to…get mad?"

"Mad?" He shook his head. "You're going to make me mad just asking that ridiculous question. It's *your* land, Zoe. And Delia's and Maddie's. Yes, I want it. Yes, I'll buy it when and if you want to sell, but that's it. There's no trick, no ulterior motive, no nothing."

And that genuinely confused her, he could tell, which went a long way toward tempering his anger. She couldn't possibly comprehend what his attachment was. And if she knew about Ben, she'd understand even less.

"There's more you're not telling me," she insisted.

"Okay, let's make a deal," he suggested. "I'll tell you my deepest, darkest secret and you tell me yours."

"Fine." She crossed her arms tightly over her front, a defensive pose if he ever saw one. "My secret is I don't think I like you very much."

This made him laugh. "Well, we share that." He was strangely relieved that she wasn't going to push, because it was too personal, too deep, watching Ben's dream die.

And like Zoe, he trusted no one, not even this woman and her sisters, who were already worming their way into his weary heart.

He was certainly not prepared to open that heart up for

inspection. Not with Zoe, a woman he'd just discovered had the unsettling ability to hurt him.

Zoe sighed, then turned on her heel and walked toward the house.

Ty watched her go, wondering why he felt so off the hook and yet discontented at the same time.

Cade shoved in the last bite on his plate and moaned with pleasure. "God. Maddie, you're a genius. It's wonderful."

Delia eyed his scraped clean plate with a lifted brow. "Well, thanks for coming, and now that your plate is empty…" She glanced meaningfully toward the front door. "Don't let us keep you."

Cade grinned instead of leaving and lifted his plate toward her. "Why, yes, thank you, Delia. I'd love seconds. Kind of you to notice."

Delia inhaled deeply, as if searching for her calm.

Maddie laughed and got up from the table, taking Cade's plate to refill it with another steaming helping of pot roast. "Cade, Cade," she said with a smile. "You're learning the hard way."

"Most definitely," Zoe agreed. "The last man who teased Delia disappeared."

Maddie handed Cade his plate, shaking her head when he laughed. "It's true."

"And he was never seen again," Zoe added helpfully.

Cade dug into his second helping with as much gusto as he had the first. Undaunted, he winked at Delia as he spoke to Zoe. "So she's a real witch, huh?"

"You should see her when there's a full moon." Zoe grinned when Delia lost all semblance of cool and sputtered.

"Zoe, I liked it better when you were all sullen and pissy

over Ty," Delia decided. "Being grumpy makes you silent, my all-time personal favorite mood of yours."

Cade laughed. "Ah, the love in this room is heartwarming."

"Don't say we didn't warn you," Zoe murmured to him as Delia shoved back her plate and stood.

"There *must* be a reason you're still here," Delia said coolly.

"Yes," he agreed smoothly, meeting her annoyed gaze. "Because you're so sweet and kind. It warms my heart." He lifted an innocent brow.

Delia rolled her eyes, and for the first time all day, Zoe found herself starting to relax. Being with her sisters did that for her, she thought with an unusual burst of affection, even when they were happily bickering and snarling.

Family togetherness at its peak.

But more than ever she was thinking about her other family. Her mother, wishing for answers, yearning for the truth, knowing she was looking at that truth and just not wanting to face it.

She had been purposely and cruelly deserted. Not orphaned. Not stolen.

Deserted.

But lately she'd had other things that occupied her mind every bit as fully as that. Ty Jackson, for one.

She hadn't been able to put him out of her mind.

The way he'd taken care of Constance. The way he'd helped them from the very beginning here at the ranch, even when their being here had destroyed his inheritance. The way he continued to remain civil when she'd continued to turn him down on his offer for a partnership.

But it was far more personal, like the way he'd looked that night in the barn, all fierce and hot as he'd stared down at her mouth in a way that told her exactly what was on his mind. And then there was the way he'd kissed her today in broad daylight out in the middle of the field, how his hands had felt on her body, snugging her close to his hard, warm one.

Heat seeped into her at just the memory, warming her from the inside out, and she didn't think the feeling was entirely uncomfortable.

In fact, she sort of liked it.

"Zoe?"

It was a bit mortifying to realize everyone was staring at her, clearly waiting for some sort of a response, and she had not a clue as to who had even spoken. "Um...what?"

"I was saying," Cade repeated with amusement, "that there is something else I wanted to go over with all of you."

"Oh. Okay."

He looked at each woman in turn, his expression kind but suddenly serious in a way that had them each leaning forward. "I have a small lead on Constance's son," he said. "Ethan Freeman."

"Yes!" Zoe whispered in triumph.

"*Small* lead," Cade qualified with real regret. "So don't get too excited yet. All I have is the fact he apparently stayed in a motel not far from your foster home on and off during the period in which the three of you arrived."

"So he knew where his daughter was!" Zoe interrupted, unable to help herself. This was news indeed, for not one of them had memories of their father, not even a name. Each of them—Maddie, Delia and herself—felt they'd been in the sole custody of their mother before they'd been left at the home.

Now this, the news that one of them had had a father who *did* know where they'd been taken.

"Did Ethan visit the foster home?" Delia asked.

Cade sighed and sifted his fingers through his dark hair

in frustration. "Still working on that. Those records aren't easily accessed."

"Surely the Fontaines would tell you." Zoe couldn't imagine them holding back. The couple that had run the group home had raised countless kids with as much love and affection as they had available. Not easy when facing both financial and legal barriers on a daily basis, not to mention kids who didn't always respond well to their environment, having been shifted around too many times to count.

They'd been lucky on that score, Zoe reminded herself, looking at her sisters. They'd been happy and well-cared for, and had gotten to stay in one home for their entire childhood.

The Fontaines had been responsible for that, for fighting for long-term care. This is why Zoe knew they'd do everything in their power to help them now. No way would they purposely hold back information. Not when one of their kids could learn about their past.

"Unfortunately, it's not so simple," Cade said. "The records aren't kept on the premises at the house. It's all in the system. It's got to go through the courts. And we all know what that's going to be like."

"Like pulling teeth." With a soft, heartfelt oath, Zoe surged to her feet, unable to remain still. Delia joined her in the pacing, holding her hand, silently uniting them.

Maddie remained frozen in her chair, quiet, and Zoe realized it had been some time since her sister had spoken. Concerned, Zoe stopped behind her, put a hand to her tense shoulder. "Maddie? You okay?"

She nearly leaped out of her skin. "Fine." But she spoke quickly, and out of breath. Her skin had lost all color.

Delia frowned at Zoe, lifting a questioning shoulder. "Are you sure, baby?" she asked Maddie, smoothing a strand of Maddie's hair off her forehead.

She nodded, but remained quiet.

It had always been this way, for as long as Zoe could remember. She and Delia curious for any dollop of information about their past that they could soak up.

And Maddie, always stubbornly mute and miserable in the face of the memories; unable, or unwilling, to talk about them.

Zoe had long ago figured out that Maddie didn't want her past dredged up. Zoe herself didn't remember much from her first years with the Fontaines, remembered even less of her life before them. But she did remember Delia and Maddie from the beginning.

Remembered also that Maddie hadn't spoken, much less laughed or smiled, until she'd turned five, though to this day Delia and Zoe didn't know why or what Maddie had suffered to cause such a trauma.

Growing up in a group home with lots of people had been rough for Maddie, but with Delia and Zoe sticking by her, eventually she had come out of her shell. If Maddie was Constance's granddaughter, that also meant Constance's son could have caused Maddie's early emotional problems.

Zoe drew a deep breath and straightened. No reason to feel this murderous toward a man who might be innocent. A man who might be *her* father, not Maddie's at all.

Cade sighed. "I'm sorry I can't tell you any more, that's all I have. But I'm going to get those records and I'll do what I can to figure out if and when Constance's son visited the home. And which of you he visited. At the moment, it's our only lead."

"Why are you doing this?" Delia still held on to both of her sisters in an unconscious gesture of unity.

Zoe felt that unity and was thankful for it, but knew Delia needed this togetherness even more than she did. She thrived on bossing them all around. And on loving them.

"I would think the why of it is obvious," Cade said quietly. "I'm trying to solve the mystery of the inheritance."

That silenced Delia for a moment, but not Zoe.

"You said Constance was happy with knowing it was one of us." What if there was a catch? What if all this could all be taken away from them?

"She was," Cade said firmly. "I told you. When she learned about the three of you, about your past and how close you were, how you considered yourselves true family, it didn't matter to her which of you it was. She wanted this land to go to the three of you."

"Then why does it matter to *you* which of us it is?" Delia asked, eyes narrowed, voice cool as a cucumber.

"Because it *should* matter to you," he replied calmly.

"It doesn't." Maddie's voice was surprisingly strong as she lifted her head and spoke for the first time. "I think maybe it's best if you just leave it alone, Cade."

Leave it alone. The words echoed in Zoe's head. She couldn't, God, she couldn't. She had to know where she came from.

Cade looked at Zoe, as if he instinctively knew the inner battle she waged.

Was she willing to let it go to ease her sisters' minds? he asked silently.

No. No, with every fiber of her being, she had to know. Not because she wanted to be owner instead of her sisters, but because for the first time in her life she wanted to truly *belong*. She wanted a past.

She felt the weight of her sisters' thoughts, felt, too, the weight of the guilt of her own selfishness.

Could she let it go? For them?

Truth was, she could and would do *anything* for her sisters, though her heart ached at the prospect of dropping it.

Of never knowing the truth. A truth she'd been wondering at her entire life.

What had happened to her mother? If she let it go, she would never know.

And then there was another matter entirely, one that couldn't be ignored. "We can't pay you," Zoe said finally, with immeasurable sadness. "It's kind of you to want to solve the mystery, but we don't have the means to pay you. We're hardly above water here as it is."

"I know." Cade looked at her with understanding. "But the fee is taken care of, Zoe. That's one thing you don't have to worry about."

Ty.

He showed up everywhere, even here, in the most private part of her life.

She drew a deep breath and faced yet another problem. The fact that she was far more indebted to that man than she ever wanted to be. She owed him, a perfect stranger, and she hated that.

"My job is to find out the truth," Cade said quietly, watching her.

Delia and Maddie could turn their backs on this and be happy, and she wanted their happiness more than anything, but she just couldn't let it go.

Zoe was tempted to keep her eyes on Cade's so she wouldn't have to see her sisters' response, but that was the chicken way out. She turned to them. "I'm so sorry," she whispered. "God, I'm sorry. But I have to know."

Maddie's eyes filled with love. "Oh, sweetie, of course you do. Don't be sorry for that."

"No, don't be," Delia agreed, reaching over and wrapping her arms around Zoe, too. "It's okay with me if it's okay with Maddie."

"It is," Maddie insisted. "I promise."

Zoe's throat was thick with emotion when she looked over Delia's head at Cade. "Do it," she said softly, hope and fear and a thousand other emotions drilling her. "Find out the truth and tell us. We'll be here."

Chapter 7

"Find out what?"

Zoe whipped around to face the doorway of the dining room, but she would have known that rough, velvety voice anywhere now. It invaded her thoughts, her dreams.

Ty stood propped against the jamb, his lean face unreadable at first glance. His day-old growth of beard only added to the mystery, hiding his face in a dark shadow, but the lines around his eyes spoke of exhaustion, reminding her that he'd put in a long day here, and then more hours at his own ranch.

He lifted a shoulder in lieu of an apology. "I knocked, no one answered."

"I suppose you followed your nose, then," Zoe said, gesturing with her head toward the table laden with food.

"I suppose I did," he said with a cocky grin meant to disarm, and it did.

Maddie, ever the hostess, rose and went for another plate. "Come sit," she said in a subdued voice to Ty. "We have plenty."

He hesitated, his hand on the plate as he dipped his head down and studied Maddie's drawn, tight face. "No smile?" His voice was gentle in a way that Zoe never heard directed toward her. "You don't laugh enough, Maddie, you know that? And you look so pretty when you do."

"Oh, you..." Maddie waved him off and blushed.

Ty lifted his nose and sniffed theatrically. "Smells terrific. I'm starved."

"Well, that's new," Zoe said sarcastically.

"Please sit, Ty. We have plenty," Maddie said again, as Zoe knew she would. The more people Maddie got to feed, the happier she was.

Ty filled his plate with obvious pleasure. He took a big bite of pot roast and sighed deeply, rubbing his stomach as though he were in heaven. "Oh man, this is amazing. I'm not kidding, Maddie. Your cooking is unbeatable."

Maddie relaxed under the attention and actually opened up enough to smile shyly.

"Well, that's better," Ty said, smiling, too, and reaching over to give her a quick squeeze around the shoulders. His eyes found Delia next, narrowing in on her in mock seriousness and said, "Don't tell me. Man trouble. No guy within five hundred miles good enough to take on, is that right?"

Delia laughed. *Laughed.* "You got that right."

Ty shoved an unbelievable amount of food down his throat as he considered. "How about Cade here?" he asked Delia, gesturing with his fork, grinning when Cade pretended to choke on his water. "He's not a bad-looking guy. And as a private investigator, he probably makes okay money, too. A bonus for a woman who appreciates the finer points of shopping."

"Oh, please," Delia said, sniffing disdainfully. "A private investigator? I can do better than that with my eyes closed."

"Yeah," Ty said, grinning widely now because Cade looked so absolutely insulted. "Probably can."

"Hey!" Cade protested, waving his fork. "I'm a major catch, you know."

Everyone laughed.

And that was it. Zoe shook her head in amazement as everyone continued to talk easily. That simply, the tension-filled mood was broken, and Ty had done it single-handedly, where she couldn't possibly have managed it.

In fact, she'd *caused* it.

It was hard to resent a man who could do that. How could the dark, explosive rancher be such a softy, so intuitive as to know how to draw out her sisters? He was so gentle with the quiet, withdrawn Maddie, so funny with the intense Delia.

But with her he was fierce and passionate. He was bold and wicked and uninhibited and rowdy.

And suddenly, just thinking about it, her insides started to tingle.

What was *that* about?

Women wanted him, there was no mistake about it. She'd seen Shirley watch him. She'd been into town with him to pick up supplies and she'd seen strangers on the street, normal women, just melt away at the sight of him.

It made her feel startlingly…jealous. *Jealous!* God, she hated that. She had no hold on the man, no future with him.

She had no future with *any* man.

Zoe was so lost in her own thoughts on this matter, it took her a moment to realize Ty's attention had centered on a new subject. *Her.*

"What!" she snapped.

The corners of his mouth twitched, but his eyes remained serious. "So defensive." Then, right in front of her sisters and Cade, he reached out and tugged on a lock of her hair, completely unaware of how it turned her heart to fluttering wildly in her chest. "Why is that, Zoe?"

She slapped his hand away, scowling to cover her confusion about her reaction to him. "I don't know what you're talking about."

He let his grin show now. "Sure you do. That's why you're so mad." He took a bite of his food and studied her. "Takes a lot of energy to remain as defensive as you always are."

"She's always been that way," Delia said lightly, only her eyes showing her concern as she looked at Zoe.

Zoe had always been a little guarded, and since she couldn't deny it, she tightened her jaw. Anyone who'd been dumped in a home with a heart full of broken promises would be an expert in self-preservation, she told herself.

Besides he was only being so nice and funny and cute because he was banking on them leaving.

He watched her while he continued to eat. Stifling the urge to squirm, she pretended a great interest in her glass of water. She listened to the conversation between Maddie and Cade about the type of spices Maddie liked to use in cooking.

Zoe studied the ceiling pattern, but it was no use. She could still feel the weight of Ty's gaze on her, waiting.

Finally she couldn't stand it any longer and sighed, facing the man whose singular ability to render her a nervous wreck was really getting on her nerves. "What now? Is there food between my teeth?"

"Nope. Just looking at you." He shoveled another bite into his mouth and chewed slowly, his eyes never leaving hers.

His eyes weren't solid gray as she'd thought, they had little specks of blue in them, and long, thick black lashes that any woman would give her right hand for. They were far too pretty to be wasted on a man. "It's rude to stare," she pointed out.

"It's also rude to glower at your guest," he pointed out right back. He smiled. "I understand glowering is your favorite expression, but did you know if you keep doing it, your face will freeze like that?"

Everyone laughed, even Maddie, who was grinning. *Grinning*.

Even Zoe found herself having a hard time continuing to frown under the circumstances, with Ty looking at her so innocently.

He'd drawn them all out, she realized. Effortlessly.

It should bug her, she *wanted* it to bug her, but even she wasn't that selfish.

What really got to her was that she was feeling, feeling for him, in a world where she didn't want to feel at all.

Days later, under an early morning gray sky, surrounded by Idaho wilderness, Zoe was dangerously silent. This was unusual because Ty could see the steam coming out of her ears, and a mad Zoe wasn't usually a quiet one.

He had no idea what had set her off this time; it could have been any of a thousand things. Worry about getting the ranch running again must be foremost. Frustration at the condition of the place might be another. Money, or lack of, yet even another.

He only knew that her eyes were hot and her face miserable, a combination that did something to him he didn't like.

It softened him.

The day darkened as heavy clouds moved across the sky. A storm was coming in fast. They stood outside the old barn, a clipboard in Zoe's hands as they made a list of repairs. The *necessary* repairs only, because stubborn as

Zoe was, she wanted to do this alone with her sisters, without his financial help.

Which meant money was scarce, very scarce.

Ty had been rattling off items an operating ranch couldn't do without, and Zoe had been silently writing everything down, until now. She stood there, braced against the wind as if preparing to ward off her archenemy. They could hear the river waging its timeless battle. Around them the green lushness of the land seemed to darken with the oncoming summer storm. Far in the distance came the roll of thunder. A large drop of rain hit Ty on the arm, but he ignored the beauty around him to stare at the pensive woman standing before him.

What gave her that look? he wondered. The one that made his arms itch to hold her?

"The door has got to be replaced," he repeated for the third time, and once again, her pen didn't move, she just stared—or glared—off into the impending storm, lost in her own world. Her hair, loosened by the wind, whipped around her face. A booming crack of thunder didn't even faze her.

"And the pigs that you'll purchase can fly," he said softly.

Under other circumstances he might have laughed when she didn't react, but there was something haunting about her expression, as if all that pent-up anger was really just a front and beneath it was a lonely, frightened woman. "Zoe?"

She jumped a little and narrowed her eyes, glaring at him as if he'd just let off a firecracker in her ear. *"What?"*

"Are you okay?"

"Of course."

"Of course," he repeated with a little laugh. "If you weren't, would you tell me?"

She was silent. Lightning flashed sharply.

Zoe's lips tightened as she shifted the pen in her fingers. The wind had layered her shirt against her body like a second skin, revealing tight, toned curves.

She was cold and he couldn't tear his eyes away.

Another drop fell, and another.

"Look, we're here to get this list made," she said with a shiver, and looked uneasily into the sky as yet another bolt of lightning streaked across it. More thunder and the air echoed like a drum, so loud that they could no longer hear the river. "So stop dawdling," she complained.

"I can't say Delia didn't warn me," Ty said dryly. "But man, was she right."

"Delia's never right, she just thinks she is."

"She was right about this, believe me. You're grumpy as hell in the mornings, aren't you?"

Her hand, the one that held the pen, fell to her side. The furrow between her brows deepened as she frowned. "I'm grumpy as hell *all* the time, you already knew that. And why were you talking about me to Delia?"

"Because Delia likes to talk. And you know what? I don't think you're always grumpy at all. I think you just like to hide behind it." He stepped closer, his boots crunching in the dirt that was pitted with the sparse but huge drops coming down.

Zoe lifted her chin, too stubborn to suggest they move into the barn, even as the sky let loose, dropping what seemed like gallons of water right out of the sky.

They were drenched within seconds.

Grabbing her hand, Ty yanked her inside the dark, musty barn just as thunder roared again, so loud his ears rung. Rain pounded the roof like a drumbeat.

She ignored the fact that water ran down her face in rivulets, disappearing into the neck of her shirt, which was equally wet. She ignored the fact that he was wet, too. And that they were nose to nose, breathing hard as if they'd run a mile.

"Why do you do that?" he demanded.

"Do what?"

His body was nearly flush with hers, so close he could see the pulse at the base of her neck as it went wild. Yet her face remained cool, and between them she crossed her arms, putting that barrier between their drenched bodies.

It was frustrating as hell. *"That,"* he accused, slipping his hand up, spreading it lightly on her throat and neck. Her skin was wet and unbelievably soft. Her hair had rioted, the dripping curls everywhere. "You pretend you don't feel anything, when I know you do. It drives me crazy."

His touch drove *her* crazy, but he didn't have to know that. Talking was difficult with his hand on her, with his fingers flirting softly with her skin. Skin that had gone hot and itchy for more.

Her heart thundered in tune to the driving rain. She dropped her arms to her sides and shivered as he brought his deliciously warm body closer. "I'm n-not cold," she said, stuttering as her teeth chattered. "You don't have to keep me warm."

"If you're not cold, why are you shivering?" he asked. "For me?"

"No."

A lie and they both knew it. "If I kiss you," he murmured huskily, leaning close, his eyes sleepy and sexy, "are you going to hit me again?"

"I didn't hit you last time, did I?" His fingers were moving on her now, flirting with the neck of her shirt, doing a little circle near her collarbone that had her legs feeling rubbery and weak.

God. Why couldn't he just accept the unfeeling facade she was trying to give him? Why couldn't he just leave her alone? But no, he wanted her. He wanted Zoe, the *real* Zoe, the one she couldn't give him because she had buried that woman too deep.

Outside the barn, the storm raged. Rain hit the roof like a herd of wild horses, pounding, drumming. It matched her pulse as she stared wide-eyed at the man holding her a willing captive.

She thought she just might forever associate the sound of the rain with how she felt right now, as if she were on the edge of a huge abyss, waiting to fall, fall, fall…for a man.

Not just any man, but this one. Ty Jackson. ''I don't think kissing is a great idea,'' she said.

He was as wet as she was. His clothes clung to every tough inch of his big body as he continued to invade her space with more than six feet of aroused male. ''I do,'' he said.

''Back up.'' She straightened her knocking knees ruthlessly. ''You're crowding me.'' Because her voice sounded whispery and weak, she licked her lips and cleared her throat. ''We have a list to make, and if you're not up for it, just say so.''

''Oh, I'm up for it.''

Her gaze jerked to his, but she hadn't been mistaken on the content of that comment, not with his eyes so hot. His hand stroked upward, cupping her jaw; his thumb rasped over her lower lip, which opened slightly as she fought the urge to suck it into her mouth. It was such a shocking yearning, she couldn't believe it. So she bit him instead.

''Ouch!'' He stared at her in injured shock.

''The list,'' she reminded him breathlessly, when he'd yanked his hand back.

''You bit me!'' He sucked the finger into his own mouth and the strangest thing happened to her tummy. It got all tight and bouncy as if full of butterflies. Her thighs quivered. "I'm sorry." She laughed a little shakily. "I'm not sure what happened to me."

His stare turned from hot to thoughtful, then speculative. "You're nervous," he decided.

"No."

"Yes, you are." His voice softened so that she had to strain to hear him over the noise of the thunder and driving rain. "I would never hurt you, Zoe."

Feeling like a jerk because she had hurt *him,* she backed up a step.

"No, don't go yet," he murmured, reaching for her. "It's still pouring." His hands slid slowly up and down her arms, warming her. "I've got an idea. Let's see where this attraction leads."

She knew where it would lead, straight to bed, if they even got as far as a bedroom. "No." But because it sounded weak and maybe like she wanted to be convinced, she said it again, stronger. "No." Since she wanted to mean it, she stepped back, crossed her arms over her chest and added a glare for good measure. She had to because he was a man who attracted her in a way she hadn't been attracted before.

He sighed but let her go. And go she did, turning and running out into the storm as if an entire family of wild bears were on her heels.

It wasn't a bear. Just a man. One tough, intelligent, passionate man who had the unique ability to hurt her.

She couldn't allow it.

Chapter 8

The chores were easily divided. Zoe handled the business aspect and most outdoor duties, negligible as they were until they got stock. Maddie handled all meals and worked with Delia on the inside of the ranch house, trying to repair and clean up all the damage from neglect, which was extensive. And expensive.

Zoe reconciled the ranch's bank statements. They'd opened a new bank account to keep track of finances. Then she divided the bills into two: the pile that could wait a little bit longer, and the pile that could wait *a lot* longer.

She sighed and rubbed her forehead.

"That bad?" Delia came into the room, or rather flowed into it, looking beautiful and serene in a long silk pantsuit the color of a fresh, blooming lilac, despite how hard she'd worked all day removing ancient wallpaper, which had been rough, relentless, messy work.

Zoe could ignore the fact that her own T-shirt was wrinkled and her jeans ripped at the knee, because how often had Delia offered—begged, actually—to make her some new clothes? But it was hard to ignore how tired and discouraged she felt. "Not too bad," she lied, hesitant to say more.

Relations between her sisters never changed. They loved and supported one another through thick and thin, no holds barred. But Delia and Maddie didn't quite understand her obsession with being the true owner of Triple M and she knew it. She knew, too, that they would bury their hurt rather than press her about it.

It was a disgusting little truth about herself that shamed Zoe. It was wrong, this burning need to belong above all else, including her sisters' happiness. She hated that about herself.

Delia's mouth tightened, even as her eyes warmed. "Don't lie to protect me, hon. I know how tight the money situation is. Just tell me." Gracefully she sank onto the only other chair in the bedroom they'd converted to an office. "Are we going to make it?"

Lying would be good here, but Zoe just couldn't look into Delia's face and do it. Instead she studied the small room and what they'd done to it. The house had been cleaned and put into amazing shape in just the short time they'd been here, but all that effort had to be credited to Delia and Maddie, since Zoe had spent most of her time and efforts outside.

Even so, the large ranch house was now clean, and because it was, the treasure of the house shone through. Rustic wooden ceilings. Terrific wooden floors. Large hallways and breezy rooms. Of course most of that loveliness needed work, badly. Windows needed replacing. The outside needed new siding, trim and painting. The plumbing was pretty much shot. And Zoe was convinced that one good wind would take the roof right off.

The overall effect was shabby but clean, and full of character. And since it was theirs, all theirs, Zoe had never loved anything more in her life.

And she didn't intend to lose it.

Still, nothing could disguise the fact that they had a lot of house, more than three thousand square feet, but they had no idea what to do with it all.

Delia leaned back and studied her latest manicure, silver nails with gold sparkles. "I guess your silence answers my question pretty well."

"I could lie."

"And I'd know it," Delia pointed out calmly. "I always know when you're lying, I have since we were five and you dipped my hair in the red paint and tried to tell me Kenny Harkins did it."

"Well, how was I supposed to know you had eyes in the back of your head?" But the memory brought a smile to Zoe's lips, and they sat in companionable silence a moment.

"Is it that bad?" Delia asked softly. "Are we in that deep?"

"I don't know." Zoe shook back her hair and sighed. "I didn't count on spending nearly all of our nest egg on getting the buildings ready to house animals. I also thought there would *be* some animals."

"What are we going to do?"

Zoe thought about hedging, but in the end she had to say the rest, because if she didn't unload she was going to burst. "I don't know," she admitted. "Even if we had enough to stock the place with animals, not to mention hire the help to care for them, which we don't, we wouldn't have any extra for mistakes. Or even to allow for a bad season."

Maddie came into the office bearing a tray of tea and cookies. "You both look worried. Maybe this will help a little."

Zoe didn't have the heart to tell her sister that food

wasn't going to cut it this time. But then her nose kicked into gear, going into overdrive at the scent of vanilla and chocolate. "Oh Lord. Are they warm?" she asked hopefully, leaning forward, her mouth watering, her fingers already reaching for a handful of fresh, still-hot chocolate-chip cookies.

"Of course they're warm." With a small smile, Maddie handed Zoe a napkin. "Help yourself. I'll pour you some tea."

Zoe moaned at the first bite as chocolate melted down her throat. "Okay, this will definitely help."

She didn't try to continue her conversation with Delia until she'd put away three more cookies and an entire mug of steaming tea with tons of lemon.

Delia restrained herself to a single cookie, watching disdainfully as Zoe stuffed herself. "God. How do you do that?"

"Easy." Zoe eyed the tray and decided she could have just one more. "I open my mouth and shovel. Chewing's optional."

"And you don't gain a pound. That's disgusting." Delia slid an elegant hand down her trim figure. "I'd pay for that binge for weeks."

"Well, maybe you oughta give up Oprah and bonbons and work harder," she suggested, ducking when without losing an ounce of her cool calm Delia flung a manila file with deadly accuracy at her head.

Zoe straightened and grinned. "Hey, don't hate me because I can pig out."

Delia sniffed. "Well, at least I'm beautiful. I can always diet. You on the other hand…"

Maddie sighed at the familiar bickering. "Girls…please. Here, Zoe—" she handed her another cookie "—put this in your mouth."

Delia laughed. "Yeah, Zoe, stuff that trap shut."

"Delia," Maddie said mildly. "Drink your tea."

Her tummy comfortably full, Zoe sat back, watching Delia carefully to make sure she didn't get clobbered again.

Delia watched Zoe with equal attention.

Maddie sighed, but the sound was full of affection. "Now, tell me what's up."

"We've got money trouble," Zoe admitted.

"So?"

"*So?*" Zoe laughed. "Didn't you hear me?"

Maddie shrugged. "We've got money trouble. What's new?"

Zoe stared at her and then laughed again. "Well, that's putting it into perspective."

"It should," Maddie said. "Don't tell me you've forgotten all those nights we sustained ourselves on nothing but a twenty-nine-cent box of macaroni and cheese."

"With water instead of milk," Delia added. She laughed fondly, then groaned. "Yuck. We might be back to that soon."

Zoe's stomach growled at just the memory. There'd been plenty of tight times after they'd left their group home together, determined to remain a family despite all the insurmountable odds.

Three eighteen-year-olds, innocent yet toughened by life. Eventually Delia had found her niche working in a beauty salon, catering to the rich who so fascinated her. Maddie had always cooked, first at Hamburger Palace, true, but she'd worked her way up to much fancier establishments.

And Zoe...she'd had the hardest time finding her place. She hadn't known what she wanted out of life other than she wanted *more*. Finally she'd ended up at a city college, then the university at night. She was the only one of the three with a degree.

Business management.

She nearly laughed. What would she do with it on a ranch out in the wilds of Idaho?

Hopefully she'd pull this off, that's what.

Delia stretched. "It sure is getting old, being poor. I want the good life, dammit. I want someone else to give *me* a manicure for a change. And believe me, when I do, I'm going to tip really good."

"You'd *never* let anyone give you a manicure," Zoe pointed out with a laugh. "No one would ever do it just right and you know it."

"Well, that's because no one is as good as I am."

Zoe rolled her eyes and turned to Maddie. "If we've always struggled, why am I so stressed-out over this one?"

"Because it's different this time," her sister said wisely. "It means more."

"It does, doesn't it," Zoe murmured, staring off into space. "Because it's ours." She straightened, determined. "And we won't lose it."

"No, we won't lose it," Maddie said, equally determined.

"No failing allowed," Delia agreed. "But I have to say here, if you'd just let up a little with the whole Ty situation, you could have it much easier."

Here it was, Zoe had known she wouldn't be able to avoid it forever. "You want to let him in, don't you. You want him as a partner."

"Would it be so bad?"

"Yes."

"Why?" Maddie asked, and Zoe didn't have an answer.

"I mean, have you seen how that man fills out a pair of jeans?" Delia asked her incredulously. "Good Lord. He's got the greatest—"

"Delia!" Maddie broke in, horrified, laughing. "How his bottom looks is absolutely irrelevant here."

"How did you know I meant his butt?" Delia lifted eyebrows so high they disappeared into her perfectly aligned bangs. "You've been noticing, too, Maddie, haven't you? Admit it."

Maddie blushed to her roots. "Knock it off."

"You *have*." Delia laughed. "It's okay. I mean, he's gorgeous. You'd have to be dead to—"

"Got it." Zoe gritted her teeth at this candid discussion of the center of her nightly fantasies. "I don't care how he looks in jeans—"

"Oh, yes you do," Delia said calmly, smiling in a way that made Zoe want to smack her. "I've seen you drooling with lust."

"It was anger! That man is annoying as hell."

"Uh-huh."

Zoe looked to Maddie for help, but Maddie was giving her a small, knowing smile. "You know," her supposedly shy sister said slowly, "the way you lose it around him is very telling. I think maybe you protest too much."

Delia grinned and nodded. "Yes. Yes, she does."

Maddie's eyes weren't teasing but serious when they landed on Zoe again. "Did you know that Ty grew up on the streets of Chicago, without any supervision or attention or money or anything?"

Zoe blinked at Maddie, unsettled by the quick shift between lust and life. "What? He told you this?"

"Sure." Maddie poured more tea for herself. "He seemed to really understand the bond between us. So I asked him why and that's when I found out how hard it was for him. His parents didn't take care of him. He grew up pretty rough."

That day in the truck, when Zoe had blurted out how guilty she felt about losing Constance before she'd gotten to know her, she'd sensed Ty's deep understanding, his deep grief about something she didn't understand.

And she hadn't pressed for answers, not wanting to pry.

No, that wasn't quite true, she admitted. She hadn't pressed because she didn't want to get to know him well.

If she got to know him, she might care. And she didn't want that.

Only problem—it was far too late, she did care.

And now she yearned on top of that caring. Ached for the boy he'd been, all alone, just as she had been.

But at least she'd had her sisters.

Who had Ty had? She didn't want to know, didn't want to picture Ty as a lonely, frightened boy. "Let's leave Ty out of this," she suggested.

Delia gave her a knowing look. "Can you?"

"Of course I can."

"Uh-huh."

"Look, can we just get back to the fact that we're drowning here and I'd like to make this work? *Without* a partner?" Zoe let out a breath at both Delia's and Maddie's faces, which reflected both amusement and doubt. "I know you guys like and trust him, and I know it would be far easier if we let him in, but I just think we can do this alone."

There was a moment of thoughtful silence. Then Maddie reached across the desk for Zoe's hand. "I *do* like him, but I won't force you to do something you don't want."

Delia held back another minute and let loose a disgusted sigh. "Hell, hon, if you want to pass that fantastic man up, I think you're a fool. But I'm with you. We do this alone."

Zoe blinked, for the first time considering that maybe Delia wanted Ty. It wasn't a silly thought, both Ty and Delia were adults. Human ones. But clearly Delia sensed the attraction between Ty and Zoe, and she'd never jeopardize that. Zoe opened her mouth to tell Delia to feel free to make a move on Ty, but something held her back—a sort of strange ping to her midsection.

Too many cookies, she told herself. Yeah, that was it, too many cookies.

Ty relaxed and bit back a grin, taking a moment to enjoy his view.

It consisted of three shapely female rear ends, each wiggling enticingly.

Maddie, Delia and Zoe all stood in varied positions, painting the front of the main house. Ty could have told them it was hopeless, that some of the siding needed to be replaced first and the trim was all but shot.

But it would have been useless and heartless since he doubted they could afford to have the place fixed properly, anyway. If a cosmetic upgrade was what they wanted, they were doing a fine job.

So he held his tongue and soaked up the interesting sight.

Zoe saw him first, when she backed down from her stepladder. Surprise registered, then annoyance, then the expected temper. "You were staring at us," she accused him, dipping her roller into the paint. The sun lit her hair like fire. Her eyes were lit the same way, but it wasn't from the sun.

He rocked back on his heels, enjoying himself. "Yep."

Zoe's eyes narrowed at him, then she turned as if to confirm what he'd been looking at. Delia and Maddie were still painting, which meant their nice rears were still rocking and rolling.

Zoe's teeth were grinding together when she looked at him again. "Get a nice show?"

For weeks now Ty had been struggling to break through Zoe's barriers. He'd tried sweet-talking, he'd tried humor and sharp wit. He'd even tried seduction, and all it had gotten him was a bellyful of Zoe's fist.

Her indifference remained, except for when he infuriated

her, which was surprisingly easy. Then he got a full range of emotions, mostly anger.

He'd take what he could get. Besides, he loved the spark that rage brought to her usually pale cheeks. Loved the heat in her eyes and the way her body reacted, whether she was aware of it or not. "Very nice show, thanks." He grinned. "Don't stop on my account."

"Was there something you wanted?" she asked from a clenched jaw.

"You know, you have a bad habit of talking like that, all tightened up. You're going to have jaw problems later on in life."

"Thanks for the tip. Now, if you'll excuse us..."

Delia and Maddie put down their rollers. It was late afternoon, and each of them had pink noses from being out in the sun. Delia still looked predictably put together, signaling she'd taken plenty of breaks. So did Maddie.

But Zoe had a streak of paint across one cheek and exhausted eyes.

Ty had already put in a full day training horses. More than a full day, actually, since one of his trainers had been sick. He'd been up since before dawn and was as exhausted as Zoe looked. All he wanted was a hot shower, lots of food and some sleep, and not necessarily in that order.

Zoe, still glaring at him, swiped at a strand of hair blowing in her eyes. In the process she streaked more paint across her face and hair. Her shoulders drooped imperceptibly.

From too much work? Or the prospect of what she still had to do?

Either way, dammit, he was stuck.

Hell. "Give me a roller," he muttered.

"Here," Delia said quickly, handing her roller over without a qualm. "You don't have to ask me twice." She winked at Zoe and brushed her hands together. "Darn, now I don't have anything to do. Guess I'll head inside..."

Zoe shook her head in disgust and watched her sister leave. She turned to Maddie. "Go ahead," she said. "You take a break, too, you've been at this all day."

"So have you." Maddie swiped at her forehead, dipped her roller and started to lift it to the wood.

"It's okay, we've got it," Zoe insisted. "Go on, Mad, rest it. Okay?"

"Okay, but I'm making dinner, then." Slowly Maddie set down the roller, then looked at Ty. "You won't let her chase you off, will you?"

He smiled at her. "If you're cooking? Not a chance."

"All right, good. Stay and eat with us."

His smile spread, and it was genuine. "I'm not arguing."

Zoe was silent until Maddie had gone into the house. "We don't need any charity help."

"You've been feeding me for several weeks now, so we'll just call it even."

"I doubt a little food can compare to the work you've put into this place."

"I'm still manager, Zoe."

Her movements as she painted were jerky and it wasn't from inexperience. He'd caused it. He wondered if their close proximity disturbed her as much as it did him.

"I've had enough people in my life who've tried to manage me," she grated, rolling paint. More rolling, almost violent now. "And I don't intend to ever have another."

"I'm not trying to 'manage' you, Zoe. Just doing my job."

"Same thing."

He watched her paint and wondered how to break through to her. "Have I ever asked you to do something you don't want to?"

She ignored him, which stirred his own temper. He took

her wrist, held it still to stop her movements and leaned close. "Have I?"

"No," she admitted, tugging at the wrist he refused to loosen.

"Stop holding on to your painful past like a shield, Zoe. I'm not the enemy."

Silence. Her mouth tightened and that was it, he was tired of fighting her. "Zoe?"

She stopped struggling but didn't look at him, so he simply yanked her closer. "It's time to *live*," he said, not very kindly. "Live for yourself. And dammit, why don't you try to enjoy it for a change?"

Chapter 9

The fire in Zoe's eyes defied description. "I *am* enjoying myself!"

He let out a little laugh but didn't release her. "I can see that."

"I am!"

"You're a liar."

"That's it," she fumed, dropping her roller and shoving him back. Paint splattered over both of their feet. "Oh, great, just great." She lifted a tennis shoe for inspection. "I'll never get these clean now."

"You should be wearing boots out here, I've told you that. And gloves, too, dammit, to protect your hands. I thought you got some new gloves. Where are they?"

With a guilty gesture, she reached into her back pocket and he saw the new gloves tucked there. Fresh and unused, when her hands were red and chafed. He didn't want to think about that strange bursting thing that happened to his insides, knowing that the gloves were a novelty and she didn't want to get them dirty.

"Boots, at least," he said gruffly.

"Yeah, well, boots cost money."

"You know how to remedy the money problem, Zoe. The offer stands."

Which was apparently *not* the right thing to say. She rounded on him with fresh fury. "Can't you just leave?"

"Maddie invited me to dinner."

"I want you to go."

"That would suit you just fine, wouldn't it? Then you wouldn't have to face this."

"Face what?"

"Us."

She shook her head and backed up a step, eyes wide with what he would have sworn was panic. "No," she said unevenly. "There's no *us*. You've gotten the wrong idea, that's all."

He pulled her back so that they were face-to-face. "From the very first moment I saw you, we've been sparking off each other. Tell me you haven't felt it— Careful," he warned when she started to shake her head in denial. "I watch the pulse leap in your neck when I come close. I hear your breath catch when I look at you, and when I touch you…" His voice thickened as his own words made him hot. "And when I put my hands on you, I feel you quiver."

"Sounds like the flu to me." But her voice shook. So did her smile. "I think it's passing now. You should go…you know, before you catch it."

"I'm not budging, Zoe. It's time to have this out."

"Look, Ty, don't take this personally. But I don't have it out with anyone."

"You have a terrible habit of hiding your feelings, Zoe."

"That's a little like the pot calling the kettle black, don't you think?"

"No. I have feelings and I show them. For instance, in case you haven't noticed, I'm turned on right now."

"I've noticed," she muttered, avoiding his gaze.

He cupped her jaw so she had no choice but to look at him. "For weeks I've been trying to break through to you, struggling to get past that damn block wall you keep putting up. I'm tired of being patient."

Incredulous, she stared at him. "Has it ever occurred to you that maybe I don't want you to 'break through'? That I'm just perfectly fine and don't need you?"

"No."

She let out a little laugh and gripped the front of his shirt in fistfuls, though whether to keep him at bay or hold him close he had no idea and suspected she didn't, either. "I've been trying for weeks, too—to *ignore* you."

"I know. And I'm tired of that, too, tired of you pretending you don't care when I can see the passion burning in your eyes—passion for me!"

She tried to laugh again, then tried to scoff at him, but failed at both. Instead, she clamped her mouth tight, looking suddenly vulnerable and nervous. "You're mistaken," she told him, pale now. "I'm not a…passionate sort. I'm not the kind of woman to have it burning in her eyes, much less—" She bit her lip.

"Much less what, Zoe?"

"Much less cause it in you."

He could see she wasn't kidding, so he held back his startled laugh. God, could she really believe that about herself? "Zoe, I don't even have to *see* you to feel it. I just think about you and it happens. You're one of the most passionate people I know."

Dropping her head back, she stared up at the sky. "Why won't you just go away? I really don't want to talk about this."

She'd been hurt, that was obvious. At least one person had taught her that to feel hurts, and at the moment he wanted badly to hurt that someone. Instead he gentled both his hold and his voice. "It's time to let go, Zoe. Let go of what has hurt you. The past is over."

"I feel, you know. I feel for this place."

"Feel for *me*."

Her eyes widened at the bold dare and she took a step back. "I...can't do that."

"Why not?"

"I just can't!"

She was miserable, but he couldn't let her hide, not from this. "Tell me you feel nothing and I'll walk away right now," he said rashly. "Tell me."

"I—" She closed her eyes. "I want to tell you that. God, I really want to tell you I feel nothing."

"Then do it."

Her eyes opened and she licked her lips with a nervous little dart of her tongue. With just that small movement he became aware of their position and how close they stood. Her breasts brushed his chest. Her thighs met his. And between them was a heat that made him dizzy. "Tell me," he urged quietly. "I have to hear it."

They looked at each other, the air charged, and she said nothing.

"Zoe."

"When you kissed me," she whispered, staring at his mouth, "I saw fireworks. That's never happened before."

A smile crossed his lips before he could stop himself. "Did you like it?"

"Yes." She smiled, too. "That's why I punched you."

"If we try it again, just started with a little kiss, what would happen?"

"I'd probably still like it," she admitted.

His smile widened as he leaned close. "Don't slug me again." And he came closer still, brushing his mouth lightly over hers once, then twice. "No biting, either," he whispered.

A soft sound came from deep in her throat, and the soft, mewling neediness was irresistible. His hands slid down her arms to link his fingers with hers, and he took her mouth one more time, deeper, hotter. She met him, straining for even more. Then, when his brain was exploding with pleasure, she pulled back, put a hand to his chest and drew in a ragged breath. "Not good."

In his highly aroused state, he could hardly place together a coherent thought. "Felt good to me."

"You want something from me I can't give."

"Believe me, what I want, you can give."

"No, you want me to admit feelings that I...just can't. And..." She let out a little sound. "And never mind the rest."

He stared at her. He knew the rest suddenly, sharply, as if she'd spoken. She wanted something from him, too, something he wasn't sure he was any more prepared to give then she was.

The front door to the house opened and Zoe jerked back guiltily, even though they weren't in direct sight. But Zoe didn't want to get caught in Ty's arms and have to explain it to a curious, meddling sister when she couldn't even explain it to herself. She bent for the roller she'd dropped and let out an oath at the dirt clumped to it.

Maddie called to them from the front steps. "Dinner's on. You guys hungry?"

Ty hadn't moved an inch of his big, tensed body. He turned just his head and met Zoe's gaze. Something inside her chest tightened at his expression.

His slate eyes held lingering heat and frustration, equally mixed. That long, rangy body of his was tight with anticipation and irritation, also equally mixed. He was so...so overwhelmingly male.

In fact, he looked like trouble personified, and suddenly

it struck her as poetic justice. He was aroused and angry about it, and that made two of them.

"Not funny," he groaned quietly, reading her mind. "A guy could die of this, you know."

"So could a woman," she told him, then regretted it when his eyes smoldered.

"I'll take that as an admission," he told her bluntly. "And it's a start."

With that, he walked around her and headed toward the front door, where Maddie stood watching them both with clear curiosity.

Ty smiled at her, and when he got close enough for Maddie to hear, he murmured something that made her smile back at him in return.

Zoe drew in a deep breath, then let it out slowly. Another kiss like that, she thought, and she was going to go right up in flames.

How did he do it? How did he draw her so completely out of herself? It was startling, and once again she used anger to ward off fear.

He had some nerve, demanding she stop hiding and live. She did *live*. She did *feel*. Yes, maybe she did both of those things conservatively, but he had no right to criticize.

Not when he'd so neatly neglected to tell her how *he* felt about *her*.

She watched him set a gentle hand on Maddie's shoulder and lead her into the house. Maddie's soft laughter drifted to her and Zoe shook her head in disgust.

He couldn't care, not really. Right? All he wanted was the land. But the uncertainty had Zoe's head spinning. He seemed sincere with Delia and Maddie. Then there was the way he treated *her*. He'd held her as if she were important and meaningful, with no intentions of fooling her in those eyes. The only thing shining there had been hunger and yearning.

Apparently he'd grown up with even less love and affection than she'd had. Could he be just as reluctant as herself? She supposed it was possible, but it was so much easier to think the worst of him.

Easier and far more simple.

Momentarily forgetting he had as much reason as she to fear entanglement, Zoe vowed to put a stop to this insanity now. She would regain control of herself. That's all there was to it.

Zoe stalked off toward the house, determined to do just that.

The gloves she'd tucked into her back pocket flapped against her. Stopping, she reached back and jammed them in farther. She'd told Ty she'd gotten new gloves; what she hadn't told him was that they had appeared mysteriously wrapped in a brown sack in her bedroom the other night.

Zoe knew they'd come from Delia. It was just like her sister to buy them secretly, simply because Zoe's hands were cracking from the unaccustomed hard work. Delia loved to give presents, and strangely enough hated to be thanked or acknowledged, which always made Christmas fairly interesting.

Maddie and Zoe had long ago accepted Delia's inexplicable embarrassment, but now the gift meant even more. Shopping was a prized commodity out here in the boondocks. It was inconvenient, not to mention their precarious financial situation. Still, Delia had thought of her, and that was a thrill Zoe would never get used to.

A funny sensation burst in Zoe's chest. Love? Most definitely. Easy to define, not nearly as easy to express.

But that's what the gloves represented to her, a deep, abiding love. Maybe that's why she didn't want to ruin them by actually using them for work. It was her small, silly way of showing Delia that she loved her back.

Showing was much easier than actually spelling it out.

She wasn't proud of the fact she rarely told Delia and Maddie how she felt, when they told her often and easily.

Old habits were hard to break. Ty might have made the mistake in thinking she could easily define how she felt about him, but Zoe could never make that same mistake.

If she couldn't easily put to words her feelings for Delia and Maddie, then describing the wild and unpredictable feelings she had for Ty were all but impossible.

Her solution—avoid him at all costs.

Zoe's plan backfired.

There was no need to ignore Ty, not when he'd so effectively ignored her first.

And he hadn't just ignored her, Zoe was forced to admit, he'd completely avoided her.

On Monday he'd brought Maddie wildflowers for the table, disappearing before Zoe had come in for dinner. Tuesday he'd brought plans for the hot tub he'd promised Delia, once again doing the vanishing act before Zoe had set eyes on him.

The week had continued like that, until by Friday she was alternately telling herself how much she enjoyed her peace and quiet, and chewing her nails into stubs wondering if she'd kissed so awful he'd decided she wasn't worth any effort at all.

Friday night the three sisters had their weekly financial meeting, which had pretty much revolved around how bad that financial situation was.

Fact was, they needed to get the ranch going *now*, if they had any hope of making this work. The problem was, none of them knew anything about ranching. So far the only thing they'd agreed on was that animals seemed easier than raising crops. Zoe had spent much of her childhood fantasizing about horses, but her practical experience was nil.

Delia had suggested they utilize their manager—namely

Ty—and let him take over the technical aspect of the ranch, but Zoe didn't want to lean on him. She didn't want to lean on anyone.

But if she let her stubbornness have rein, she was going to lead them all to bankruptcy. She couldn't be that stupid, or selfish. The stress of it had started to keep her awake. She was hurting both Delia and Maddie with her hard head. It had to stop. She spent Saturday dwelling on it.

Sunday morning she woke up and without thinking about it, because then she might change her mind, she hopped into one of the old trucks and drove the short distance to Ty's house. The most difficult part of the ride was craning her neck to catch the view. It was limited only by the horizon. It was impossible not to be touched by the spectacular scenery as she bounced along on the rough excuse for a road. The land was rugged, untamed.

Serenity and serendipity, she thought. Both abounded here. Still, the closer she got, the more nerves danced in her belly. She hadn't been to Ty's house before, so she shouldn't have been surprised at the lovely, one-story ranch-style home, which was obviously well-cared for. The windows opened to the early sun, and flowers grew in a series of pots on the wraparound porch.

Flowers?

Frowning, Zoe hopped out of the truck, then didn't move as she digested the fact she was staring at yet another layer of the mysterious Ty Jackson.

She was here for a purpose, she reminded herself. And nothing would detract her from that purpose: no bickering, no teasing, and most definitely no kissing.

He didn't answer her knock.

Deflated, Zoe turned around, taking in the property. It was much smaller than theirs, and every bit of it looked to be wisely used. There were pastures, each occupied with horses. The barn was red against the green forest behind it.

The river cut close here, splashing even more color. It was such a perfect day she almost expected the colors to run together.

Then she heard sounds coming from the barn, strange sounds that were almost like loud groans...as if an animal were in horrible pain. She walked down the path and toward the building, slowing when the unusual noises became louder, then louder still.

It sounded like a horse in great pain, and when that horse screamed, a spine-tingling, ear-splitting whinny, Zoe started running. She burst into the barn, and when she did, someone let out a shout.

She recognized that shout—it was Ty's—and Zoe's heart stopped. Blinking uselessly in the dim barn, Zoe was forced to waste precious seconds as her eyes became adjusted.

"Zoe," Ty barked while she was still struggling to see. "Come here!"

She could make out the shadows in the stall now. A horse down on its side, its flanks rising and falling rapidly as the animal grunted and breathed as though she'd been running a race.

It was Abby, the pregnant mare.

Ty was on his knees behind her, face tense with strain. His shirt was plastered to him, covered in muck that Zoe didn't want to think about.

Immediately she realized the problem—the horse was in labor, and given Ty's face, she was not doing well. Just days ago she'd melted at the thought of a new foal, but being here, in the midst of the controlled chaos, watching Abby writhe in pain, was another thing entirely.

Suddenly she was sorry she'd followed the sounds.

When she didn't move, Ty swore and lifted his head, piercing her with his intense gaze. "You're going to have to help."

"Me?" The word came out like a squeak. As a true city

girl, she'd never even seen a dog have puppies. The thought suddenly made her feel light-headed. "Are you alone?" she asked in horror.

"Not anymore." He nodded curtly to the other end of the stall. "Hold her head still and talk to her when the next contraction comes. She's getting too tired to push, so I'm going to have to help."

"Oh God." She could see blood on the floor, in the straw beneath the whimpering horse, and on Ty. Her own blood roared in her ears. Her stomach did somersaults.

"Zoe."

She looked up at the low, terse command. Ty's eyes were lined with strain and determination. "I've had Abby since she was born. I'm not going to lose her now, dammit, because you're squeamish. If you're going to faint or throw up, then get the hell out."

"I'll be fine."

"This is ranch life," he told her harshly when she flinched at the strong smell of blood and sweat and birth. "This is life, period. And it's now a part of *your* life."

She got the picture. If she couldn't do this, she had no business being in ranching. But she resented him for pointing it out and resented even more his doubting her, when she had enough of her own.

The horse whinnied again, weaker now, her eyes rolling back in her head.

"Not much longer," he crooned softly. Abby immediately responded to his gentle voice, but she was still suffering, and it no longer mattered that she wasn't human—Zoe's body ached in sympathy.

She tried to imagine her own mother giving birth. Had she suffered? Cried? Rejoiced?

Zoe had no way of knowing and no one to ask, and the injustice of that was hard to take. Had she been a good baby or a sickly one?

Had she been loved?

"Zoe, touch her."

She did, whispering soft, inane words of encouragement as she fought emotions she didn't know she had. Time passed, could have been a moment, maybe an hour, but Zoe was so attuned to Abby and her pain it didn't matter. Abby's struggle became her own, so that when Abby made a horrible straining cry, so did Zoe.

Ty's jaw tightened, his hands spread wide on the horse's belly. The muscles in his shoulder and back rippled through the cloth of his T-shirt as he moved over the horse. "Another contraction," he clipped, his hands smoothing over Abby's bulging belly. Then they disappeared and Zoe held her breath as he checked the foal's position.

"Come on, baby, come on. Help me," he muttered, sweat beaded on his forehead. His face was tight with worry and fear, his voice perfectly calm as he let Abby know how much he cared in every breath he took.

What would it be like to have a man like that on his knees, desperate to relieve her pain? To have him care for her above all else?

"Talk to her, dammit" came Ty's low command.

Zoe, stroking Abby's face gently, did just that while the horse strained and pushed. "You can do this," she whispered, wondering if Abby really could. "I know it's awful, but women go through this all the time. Of course human babies don't have four legs and weigh...how much does a foal weigh, I wonder?"

Abby quivered and Zoe's heart constricted. She stroked some more and whispered more silly comments, anything to help calm her down. "You know what I wish? That the stallion that did this to you had to deliver the baby. Now, *that* would be justice."

"It's coming," Ty called. "Come on, Abby, you can do it."

Abby lifted her head and screamed—and it sounded so real, so utterly human, and so full of suffering, Zoe's throat closed. Her heart tightened in her chest. "Oh God," she whispered. "Oh God. Abby, honey, hang on, it'll be over soon! Ty is doing everything he can."

Abby screamed again, shivered once, then fell so still Zoe shot up to her knees. "Ty?" she cried, desperately afraid for the horse. "Ty!"

His wide shoulders were hunched over Abby, his face contorted into a grimace born of fear and stress. Sweat ran down his face. "I've got a hoof!"

A hoof? Just one? Zoe groaned and sat back down, leaning close to Abby. "Come on, Abby, almost there. Push. Do it for me. Do it for Ty."

Then suddenly Ty was shouting with triumph, his face split into a grin as he quickly helped clear the mucus and birth sac from the foal. He rose over Abby to see Zoe. "He's perfect!"

Abby lifted her head, saw her baby sprawled out wet and shivering, half in Ty's lap and half between her back legs, and struggled to get up.

"Let her," Ty said quietly when Zoe tried to hold her back. "She has to get to him."

Abby managed, though it was painful to watch her as she was so shaky. She whinnied softly, and the baby lifted its head, still and hopeful, its little nose sniffing.

Abby reached down and licked her new baby, awe and love in her warm, intelligent eyes, and Zoe watched, amazed as her baby responded instinctively, nuzzling close.

Zoe had never come close to seeing anything like this, though she'd dreamed of it often. A surge of yearning and excitement filled her unexpectedly. This was real life. And it was beautiful. Messy but beautiful. Deep inside, some part of her wanted more of this, wanted it so badly she had to blink back hot tears as she became overwhelmed with emotion.

She hadn't made a sound, but Ty's head whipped up and their gazes collided. Everything she felt, everything that had so awed and overwhelmed her, she saw mirrored in his own eyes.

New life. New beginnings. They'd just experienced it, and with all her heart Zoe knew she wanted more.

But "more" meant reaching out and taking it. As she stood there, locked in time, staring at Ty, she knew she couldn't do it. She couldn't face the pain it would bring.

Better to not feel anything than to allow herself to feel and lose.

As if he could read her mind and the cowardly thoughts in it, Ty looked away, breaking eye contact.

Zoe felt the loss more keenly than she'd felt anything, but the moment was gone. Whatever had passed between them was over.

The foal struggled awkwardly to his feet and went instinctively for Abby's milk.

Ty had risen and moved out of her vision, but now he was back, handing her a towel. She realized tears were streaming down her face, which she wiped at, horrified at the weakness.

"You okay?"

She would be if he'd wrap her in his arms. But he didn't, and she didn't ask. She forced her usual unfeeling mask into place with huge effort.

For a moment he only stared at her. "Thanks," he said stiffly. "I couldn't have done it without you."

He turned and walked away, without a cocky smile, without the teasing she'd grown to count on, without so much as a single sexual innuendo.

It had been exactly how she wanted things between the two of them. Casual. No strings attached.

PLAY...

"ROLL A DOUBLE!"

PEEL OFF LABEL AND PLACE INSIDE

GET 2 BOOKS
AND A
FABULOUS MYSTERY BONUS GIFT

ABSOLUTELY FREE!

SEE INSIDE...

(S-IM-07/99)

NO RISK, NO OBLIGATION TO BUY...NOW OR EVER!

GUARANTEED

PLAY "ROLL A DOUBLE" AND YOU GET FREE GIFTS! HERE'S HOW TO PLAY:

1. Peel off label from front cover. Place it in space provided at right. With a coin, carefully scratch off the silver dice. Then check the claim chart to see what we have for you – TWO FREE BOOKS and a mystery gift – ALL YOURS! ALL FREE!

2. Send back this card and you'll receive brand-new Silhouette Intimate Moments® novels. These books have a cover price of $4.25 each in the U.S. and $4.75 each in Canada, but they are yours to keep absolutely free.

3. There's no catch. You're under no obligation to buy anything. We charge nothing – ZERO – for your first shipment. And you don't have to make any minimum number of purchases – not even one!

4. The fact is, thousands of readers enjoy receiving books by mail from the Silhouette Reader Service™. They like the convenience of home delivery...they like getting the best new novels BEFORE they're available in stores...and they love our discount prices!

5. We hope that after receiving your free books you'll want to remain a subscriber. But the choice is yours – to continue or cancel any time at all! So why not take us up on our invitation, with no risk of any kind. You'll be glad you did!

THIS MYSTERY BONUS GIFT
WILL BE YOURS __FREE__ WHEN
YOU PLAY "ROLL A DOUBLE"

"ROLL A DOUBLE!"

place label here

SCRATCH HERE

?

SEE CLAIM CHART BELOW

345 SDL CQWV

245 SDL CQWK
(S-IM-07/99)

YES! I have placed my label from the front cover into the space provided above and scratched off the silver dice to reveal a double. Please send me all the gifts for which I qualify. I understand that I am under no obligation to purchase any books, as explained on the back and on the opposite page.

Name: _____
(PLEASE PRINT)

Address: _____ Apt.#: _____

City: _____ State/Prov.: _____ Zip/ Postal Code: _____

CLAIM CHART

🎲 🎲	**2 FREE BOOKS PLUS MYSTERY BONUS GIFT**
🎲 🎲	**2 FREE BOOKS**
🎲 🎲	**1 FREE BOOK**

CLAIM NO.37-829

PRINTED IN U.S.A.

The Silhouette Reader Service™ — Here's how it works:

Accepting your 2 free books and mystery gift places you under no obligation to buy anything. You may keep the books and gift and return the shipping statement marked "cancel." If you do not cancel, about a month later we'll send you 6 additional novels and bill you just $3.57 each in the U.S., or $3.96 each in Canada, plus 25¢ delivery per book and applicable taxes if any.* That's the complete price and — compared to the cover price of $4.25 in the U.S. and $4.75 in Canada — it's quite a bargain! You may cancel at any time, but if you choose to continue, every month we'll send you 6 more books, which you may either purchase at the discount price or return to us and cancel your subscription.

*Terms and prices subject to change without notice. Sales tax applicable in N.Y. Canadian residents will be charged applicable provincial taxes and GST.

BUSINESS REPLY MAIL
FIRST-CLASS MAIL   PERMIT NO. 717   BUFFALO, NY

POSTAGE WILL BE PAID BY ADDRESSEE

SILHOUETTE READER SERVICE
3010 WALDEN AVE
PO BOX 1867
BUFFALO NY 14240-9952

NO POSTAGE
NECESSARY
IF MAILED
IN THE
UNITED STATES

If offer card is missing write to: Silhouette Reader Service, 3010 Walden Ave., P.O. Box 1867, Buffalo NY 14240-1867

It was exactly as she would have done in reverse, if she'd been on the receiving end of that distancing look.

But as he left her standing there in the stall staring after him, she wondered why she felt suddenly so empty.

Chapter 10

Why had she come, Zoe wondered, alone in Ty's barn. Had she really imagined she'd be able to swallow her pride and ask him for help?

Yes. For her sisters she would.

Anything for them, including facing the one man with the ability to rock her world.

The bright sun felt good on her face when she left the barn, and she tipped it up, standing still for a moment.

Ty looked up from the water hose where he'd been washing up, and froze at the sight. Zoe faced the sun, her long neck exposed, her lips curved in a half smile as she soaked up the heat.

From where he stood he could see the rise and fall of her chest as she breathed, could see the tension from her body slowly drain as she grappled with, then won some of her annoying self-control.

Why he found that so arousing, he hadn't a clue. Always before he had preferred his women mild-tempered. No sharp tongue. A much softer appeal. And if they were blond and long-legged, so much the better.

So why he was drinking in the sight of this petite, fire-tempered little wildcat? She made him furious and hot at the same time, and never had he encountered such a woman.

He was still hurt at her cool and easy rejection of him, so he turned his attention away from her and continued to wash up. A shower would have suited him better than splashing icy water on his chest and arms, but he didn't have time. It was Sunday and he was alone. There was too much to do.

But even with his back turned, the image of Zoe was imprinted on his mind, the way she'd looked when Abby had given birth—elated, sweet, loving, touched. To dispel the picture, he dunked his head, ignoring the iciness of the water as it dripped off him. When he was as clean as he was going to get, he turned off the hose and shook it off. He lifted his head and his gaze hit Zoe's.

She'd not moved, not a muscle except her face, which was now turned directly toward him. Her mouth was open a little, as if she couldn't breathe.

Frowning, he took a step toward her, instantly forgetting his promise to stay clear of Ms. Trouble. It wasn't something he did consciously, for he wasn't a man used to caring about others, but caring about this woman and her sisters seemed to be something he would have to live with.

He reached her and she was still in that strange state of not breathing. "Zoe? You okay?"

Her mouth fell open a bit more, then she swallowed audibly. "Uh...yeah. Sure."

She sounded so...distraught. No, that wasn't right. Her eyes had gone wide, but there was no fear in them. "What is it?"

Her gaze was glued to his chest now. "Ah...nothing. I

mean, I've gotta go hard—er, *home* now and..." Her face flushed. "And get something to chest. I mean to drink. *Drink!*"

And with that, she whirled and ran toward her truck.

And get something to chest?

Baffled, Ty glanced down at his own bare, dripping chest, wondering what had gotten into her.

Something to chest.

Suddenly a smile split his face. His temper and frustration didn't vanish but rather settled in line behind amusement. He easily caught up to her since she'd dropped her keys three times, then fumbled with the door handle.

"Going to get something to chest?" he asked casually, coming to a halt behind her.

Her shoulders stiffened. Her fingers went still.

When he peered around to see her face, her eyes were closed, her mouth tight.

And her face was a most definite shade of red.

"It sure is warm today," he finished conversationally. "Never know when you're going to need something...to chest."

Something escaped her throat, it sounded suspiciously like a groan.

He laughed then, he just couldn't help it. Reaching for her, he turned her toward him, a feat in itself because she'd gone rigid as a corpse.

"Hello." It wasn't kind to torment her, but she had the ability to single-handedly drive him crazy. He figured it was his God-given right to drive her crazy right back. "Come clean, Zoe, gig's up." He grinned and rubbed his chest. "You want me."

She stared with great interest over his shoulder at nothing. "I have to go now."

"I can see that." He laughed again, he couldn't help it;

he suddenly felt lighter than he had in weeks. "Need another look at me first?"

Her face went even redder.

"Tongue-shy?" He bent closer, but she still wouldn't meet his gaze. "Wow, this is a first. Listen—you weren't by any chance back there…lusting after me, were you?"

"Shut up."

"You *were.*" He laughed again, earning himself a cold glare.

"All right!" she fumed, raising her hands. "All right! I *might* have been staring at you."

"Might have been?" He roared at this. "Slim, you were drooling." He had the satisfaction of seeing her gaze slip for a moment and run over his body. He went instantly hard, surprising himself, for up until that point he'd only been teasing.

She lifted her chin in that endearing yet annoying gesture of hers. "I have no idea why you're so amused about this," she snapped. "Just a moment ago you couldn't wait to get away from me."

"No, just a moment ago we were kneeling over a miracle," he reminded her, his smile fading. "Over Abby and her new colt, and nothing is more real or grounding than that. It's precious, Zoe. Seeing life start before your very eyes, and you know it, too, I saw you. I saw your face. God, the way you looked at me… It made me feel that something was between us. Something amazing. I know you felt it, too, Zoe, don't even try to deny it."

She said nothing, which was typical and frustrating, and suddenly he wasn't going to take it. "That's when you remembered you didn't like me, or that you didn't like the man you think I am, and it was over. Just like that, click, and you're back to unfeeling Zoe Martin. Even your eyes shuttered against me."

She drew an uneven breath, but to her credit, she didn't run as he'd half expected.

"We bring out the worst in each other," she said quietly.

"And also the best." Hell, he had no idea where that statement came from. He didn't even know what it meant. He didn't want this thing between them any more than she did, so why then did he constantly push her for more?

If he was falling, he was falling hard, and for a woman who had clearly been so hurt in her past she couldn't possibly return the feeling. But Ty had a will of iron. If falling for her was a mistake—which it was—then he simply wouldn't fall.

No problem. He was unfallen. That easy.

Straightening, he dropped his hands to his sides and turned from her, bone-weary. He'd been putting in long days at his ranch, then more hours at hers. And for the past two nights he'd been up sitting with Abby, waiting.

"Where are you going?" She sounded startled that he was walking away from her.

"I won't fight for your damn affection, Zoe. I won't even fight for your friendship anymore, I'm too tired. I have other things to spend my energies on—including saving your selfish pride over that ranch."

Now she looked a little frightened. He hesitated, thinking she would stop him, but she didn't speak. Disgusted with the both of them, he shook his head and strode away.

She followed him.

He gave her a look that would have any of his hired hands quivering in their boots as he walked. "What?"

"I…" Zoe couldn't form the words as she struggled to keep up with his fast pace. "We…we, ah, had a meeting last night. My sisters and I."

"Did you?"

"About the ranch."

"Okay." Now he stopped, halfway between the house

and his barn. The sun beat down on them. The water still beaded on his tanned chest, glistening, but it was all hard to enjoy when his face and voice were so distant.

She felt as though she were on an emotional roller coaster ride, one she was completely unequipped for. She knew nothing of these matters, she'd avoided exactly this kind of attachment most of her life.

Walking away would be so easy, but she had no choice. For her sisters, she had to do this. And really, just how bad could pride taste, anyway? "We figured we could fix up the barn," she said. "The cabins on the edge of the property aren't needed right now, so they can stay the way they are."

"We've discussed this."

"There's more."

He crossed his arms, his legs spread and steady. An aggressive male stance that screamed dangerously annoyed, tired male. She spoke quickly. "Then maybe we could get some animals, you know. Nothing too complicated at first. Maybe start out with some chickens."

"Uh-huh."

"And a cow or something."

No response. And agonized over what she had to ask, Zoe held her breath. "Only we need some…"

"Some…?" he repeated, ever so helpfully.

She sighed loudly. "We need some help, dammit. Okay?"

He looked disbelieving. "To handle a single cow and a few chickens?"

"I want more than that. Ty…I'm trying to ask you for help."

"Why is it so hard?"

"I don't know."

He didn't soften in the least, keeping his arms crossed

over the still-bare, still-magnificent chest she was trying her best to ignore.

"For the record," he asked finally, "are we talking technical help or financial help?"

"Technical."

"I'm already—"

"Yes, yes, I know. Manager," Zoe said, finishing for him impatiently. "This is different. I need more than a general manager. I need to be taught everything."

He didn't comment on the fact they'd be working together, closely. "Where is the money going to come from?" he asked instead.

"I'm going to get a loan."

"You?"

"Yes, me." Zoe forced herself to relax or she was going to split in two. "Delia has a…well, let's just say she got in trouble with credit cards and shopping a few years back."

"Bad credit, huh?" he asked, showing his first signs of sympathy.

For her sister! She was baring her guts here and he felt sorry for Delia.

"Maddie can't get a loan, either. She's never established any credit at all." And she tended to get suckered by every male she met as well, Zoe thought with a burst of worry that never faded, but she kept that to herself. "So that leaves me."

He looked unimpressed. "You have any credit?"

"Sure." Maybe.

He studied her seriously, his face impassive, his eyes still that startling ice.

It frightened her, this distant Ty, as nothing else could have. But why, when it was what she'd wanted all along? "We're…we're helpless without you," she said quietly.

"You're many things, Zoe," he said dryly. "But helpless is not one of them."

She was positive that was *not* a compliment. "I'm thinking of Maddie and Delia." Here was the swallowing-pride part. "I want this badly," she said with as much dignity as she could muster. "Will you do it?"

"I must be an idiot," he said wearily. "But yes. I'll help you. For Maddie and Delia, I'll help."

It was an effort to keep her voice even. "But not for me."

His eyes held hers, and for one moment they warmed and showed her a glimpse of what she'd seen before. Then it was gone, replaced by that frightening chilliness she'd caused. "How you'd resent that," he said softly. "If I dared do anything to help the independent Zoe Martin."

With that cryptic statement, he turned on his heels and walked away.

And this time, she let him go.

It was dessert time when Cliff showed up and asked if they needed anything done.

"Where's Ty?" Zoe asked casually as she let Cliff in. Usually Ty would be here sniffing out the goods.

Cliff smiled and removed his hat. "He went mountain climbing."

"Mountain climbing."

Cliff looked surprised at her shocked tone. "He always goes, especially when he's mad or unsettled." Cliff grinned and shrugged. "Which happens a lot with Ty. He's a dark sort of guy."

"Mountain climbing is dangerous."

"Especially the way he does it."

Zoe schooled her face into impassivity, but still Cliff's grin faded slowly. "Anyway..." He cleared his throat. "He takes off for a day here and there when he can. He loves it, though you wouldn't catch me dead doing half of the crazy climbs he does.''

Zoe's stomach dropped. She pictured Ty hanging off an edge of a cliff, reaching for another, and because of his state of mind—the state of mind *she'd* put him in—imagined him missing and falling.

Imagined his body broken and bleeding on the valley floor.

Ty Jackson was a big boy, she reminded herself all that night and into the dawn. He could take care of himself, he'd been doing just that for a long time.

She could take care of herself, too. And would.

The next morning, Zoe made excuses to her sisters and got into one of the ancient trucks.

She drove the long, windy road into the closest town. Lewiston. She was going to get a loan, it was the only way. All of Ty's expertise wouldn't help if she couldn't get the money.

She knew Ty would have loaned her money, but she had no intention of doing any such thing. It was bad enough she needed him at all. She'd been reading her library books late at night, soaking up the information she needed on ranching. But even Zoe wasn't *that* stubborn.

She still needed Ty.

And the money. But five minutes later, she was miserable.

Mr. Jacobs was everything Zoe imagined a loan officer being—impersonal expression and impossibly disapproving. He'd listened with polite disinterest, quickly becoming more disinterested, adamantly refusing to consider a loan. ''It's out of the question,'' he repeated. With a deliberate movement, he pushed his glasses up on his nose and looked down its long, thin length at her. He spoke through his nose. ''It's a bad investment.''

He might as well have said "*You're* the bad invest-ment," that's how personally she took his statement.

All her life she'd been told *no*. All her life she'd been struggling against feeling inferior. It should have been an easy swallow, but it wasn't. "I haven't even filled out a single form," she said calmly, though her heart raced and her palms were damp. She wiped them on the cotton pants she'd changed into for the occasion, when she'd stupidly believed she could dress for this part.

Truth was, it didn't matter what she wore, she had *Poor* stamped across her forehead. The bank officer had probably taken one look at her when she'd walked in and had de-cided before she'd even opened her mouth.

"Not necessary to fill out forms in this case." Mr. Jacobs looked past her, clearly hoping his next client was waiting. "Giving money to three women to start a ranch, when not one of you has ever even worked on one before, would be a grave error in judgment."

Zoe refused to be dismissed so easily. "We're hard workers, we won't give up. This can work."

Just as stubborn, Mr. Jacobs shook his head, completely without remorse. "Sorry, no can do. The ranch is not a good bet. Good day." He picked up his pencil, bent his head and proceeded to start on another project, rudely ig-noring her.

Head high as she could manage, Zoe left the bank, her stomach burning with shame and fury. She managed to make it home on autopilot, only to be ambushed by Delia at the door of Triple M.

Her sister took one look at her face and called for Mad-die. The two of them promptly dragged Zoe into the kitchen, where Maddie plied her with iced tea and home-made chocolate truffles.

Maddie nodded to Delia, and they each sat on either side

of her, faces worried and serious. They waited until she was full before attacking.

"Spill it," Delia demanded.

Zoe put down her tea slowly. How to tell them? She honestly didn't know. Thinking she had to protect them, she forced a smile. "I went to see about a loan."

"By yourself?" Maddie asked, concern wrinkling her brow. "Oh, honey, we should have been with you."

"Yes, we should have been," Delia said. "Dammit, Zoe, stop taking everything on yourself. We're a team."

Because there was a note of uncertainty in Delia's usually confident voice, Zoe mentally kicked herself and tried to smooth over the tension. "Yes, we're a team. I just thought I could handle this for all of us. It's such a pain."

"It's in the works?" Delia asked, surprised.

There'd been so much disappointment in their lives, Zoe refused to add to it. With the best smile she could muster, she nodded. "It's in the works," she repeated, thinking she'd try every damn bank in the state before disappointing them again.

Chapter 11

But there was no bank that would take them, and Zoe became insane with worry. To her shame, it had taken several days before she realized both Delia and Maddie had been uncharacteristically quiet.

"Your turn to spill it, guys," she demanded over breakfast two days later. She was dressed for work, as she and Cliff were going to tackle the barn and finish getting it ready for the animals she hadn't yet figured out how to afford.

But there was plenty of time to be stressed-out over that. "What is it?"

Maddie bit her lip and looked down at her plate filled with steaming pigs in a blanket. The pancakes were fluffy and light, the scent of the sausage causing Zoe's mouth to water.

Delia coolly drank tea.

"I've never known you to pass up a reason for telling me what you think of me," Zoe said, trying to tease them into answering.

A flash of humor hit Delia's serious eyes. "It's not easy to figure out where to start."

"That good, huh?"

"That bad." Delia's lips curved as she sipped tea.

It was impossible to be calm about this. She couldn't handle it if she'd finally caused them to turn away from her. "Please tell me," Zoe found herself saying hoarsely. "Are you both mad at me for keeping us here? Is that it?"

"Hon, don't be stupid," Delia said kindly, ignoring Zoe's dangerously narrowed eyes. "Come on, Zoe. Do you see me tied here, kept against my will? Do I even look like the kind of woman you could hold to a spot she didn't want to be in?"

"You know what I mean." But already Zoe felt a relief she didn't want to think about. She looked at both of them, unconsciously holding her breath. "Are you…happy here?"

"Happy is a relative term," Maddie said quietly. "I'm with both of you, that's all that matters to me."

"But you could be in Los Angeles, cooking in some fancy restaurant."

"Yes, and fighting off a boss who thinks he can sexually harass me because I look like a victim." Maddie shook her head. "I love the air here. The space. And the freedom." She reached across and took Zoe's hand. "Zoe, sweetie, I can cook wherever I am and be happy, as long as we're together. I just want to be with my family."

"Dee?" Zoe looked at Delia. "How about you? Miss shopping?"

"Oh, I miss shopping," Delia assured her. She dipped her fork into her bowl of fruit, shuddering in distaste when Zoe poured butter and syrup in excess over her own plate. "I miss freeways and gorgeous men jogging on the streets. But you're purposely missing Maddie's point."

"Well, if someone would tell me the point, I couldn't miss it, could I?"

"Don't get defensive, it gives you wrinkles."

"I'm getting pretty tired of people telling me I'm acting defensive."

"Then stop doing it," Maddie suggested, reaching for Zoe's hand.

"Tell me what's wrong," Zoe begged. "Oh God." She nearly choked on a bit of pancake. "Cade called, didn't he? This is all a mistake and we have to leave—"

"No!" Delia laughed and shook her head. "Relax, Zoe, this place is still ours."

"Then for God's sake, tell me what is wrong."

"Look, the truth is we're worried about you," Delia said bluntly.

"Me?" Zoe laughed. "I'm fine."

"You're not. You're taking this all on yourself, the success of the ranch, the money, even our happiness. And that's just dumb. Okay? We're in this together. We fail together, we succeed together. And we're happy together. Got it?"

"Well, we're going to be happy going bankrupt together." Horrified, she covered her mouth. "I'm sorry." She rubbed her head, stress pounding through it. "Oh, hell. I'm so sorry. I'm just so worried about this. We can't get a loan."

"Zoe." Delia took a deep breath. "We know how bad it is. And we don't want to give up, but you have to let us take on some of the stress or you're going to blow up. Stop protecting us."

"But—"

"But nothing. You have options. It's just for some reason, you're too stubborn to take them."

"There are no options," Zoe said flatly.

"We could borrow the money from Ty," Maddie said quietly. "I don't understand why you won't let us do that."

"Haven't we had enough of charity to last us a lifetime?" She regretted the words as soon as they left her mouth, as both sisters paled, but she wouldn't take them back. *She'd* had enough to last a lifetime.

How could they not feel the same way?

Delia made a noise of frustration. "It's a *loan,* Zoe. Just like you would have from the bank. This place means freedom to us. It's our inheritance and we won't lose it. What's a little pride, hon, when it comes to that?"

Zoe drew a ragged breath. "I just... You make me feel so stupid. Don't—" she said quickly when Delia grinned and opened her mouth. "Don't say it." Her fingers dove into her hair as her thoughts raced in tune to her pumping heart. "I hate needing money. I hate that we have to ask for it. And those banks..." She slumped. "I would have begged, that's what's so disgusting. If I thought it would have done any good, I would have gotten on my knees and begged for the money."

"Zoe." Maddie's eyes were dark and warm. "Ty would never make us beg. He's already offered."

"*I* could ask him," Delia suggested. "So you wouldn't have to, though why you can't be nice to that man is beyond me. He's—"

"I know," Zoe broke in quickly, knowing exactly what Ty was. "He's generous."

"He's *gorgeous,*" Delia countered.

"Delia."

"And smart."

"Delia—"

"He's also the most open, sincere, compassionate, sweet human being I've met in a long time."

"*Ty?*" Zoe gasped with laughter over that one. "*Sweet?*"

"He is," Maddie insisted.

"He's *sharp,* I'll give you that," Zoe admitted. "He's also fierce, intense, dangerous...and altogether a pain in my you-know-what."

Delia shook her head in disgust. "You wear blinders with that man, and if I didn't know better, I'd think you were falling for him. But you're impervious that way, men never seem to penetrate through that shield you wear."

Insulted now, Zoe sniffed. "I'm sure not falling for him."

"Then *you're* the idiot," Delia said. "Because I'm telling you, he's just about perfect—"

"Please," Zoe complained. "I'm trying to eat."

Maddie watched the exchange with a mixture of amusement and affection. As usual, when she spoke, she went right to the heart of the matter. "We don't want to leave. We need the money. The banks won't give it. There's only one thing to do."

They were right, but God, she didn't want them to be.

"So...who's going to tell him?" Delia asked.

Two pairs of eyes turned to Zoe and she let out a groan. "Fine. But I'll do it in my own good time."

"Fine," Delia said.

"Fine!"

"And don't shelter us any more," Delia ordered. "We're in this equally."

"Fine," Zoe snapped again. "And I hope you get a gray hair over this."

Maddie smiled. "She'll just dye it. We love you, Zoe," she said softly. "The sooner you get that through your thick skull, the better."

"I hear the thick skull part" said a familiar deep voice.

Zoe took an uneven breath and turned. Ty's wide shoulders propped up the doorjamb, and though the day had hardly begun, he looked as though he didn't have a care in the world. He looked…oh, boy. He looked gorgeous, just like Delia had so helpfully pointed out.

Who besides Ty could stand there so early and look so sexy? His hair was slicked back as if he'd just showered. Soap and clean male scent floated in the air. His expression was carefully masked as he met her gaze.

It was a forcible reminder that they hadn't had a decent conversation since the day she'd help deliver his new foal.

Obviously he was safe and sound and in one piece, and she'd wasted time worrying herself sick over him.

As if he could read her mind, a very annoying habit he seemed to enjoy, his eyes heated. No smile, no words, just hot, hungry eyes.

Instantly her nerves went on overdrive. "Didn't anyone ever teach you it was rude to eavesdrop?"

"Nope," he replied in that voice that never failed to give her the shivers. He grinned slowly, his face tanned, his teeth white and even. "Missed that lesson."

Maddie had gotten up, happily filling a plate with food. Ty took it and bent to kiss her on the cheek. Sitting down, he leaned over and gave Delia a quick hug.

He didn't touch Zoe.

She rolled her eyes and got up, storming over to the sink to drop in her plate.

"Zoe, hon, you heading out?" Delia asked, surprised. "You didn't finish eating."

And that alone was clearly so unlike her, both Delia and Maddie were staring at her wide-eyed. Great. Not only was she a jerk, she was a pig, too. She sighed. "I've got to go. I'm meeting Cliff in the barn."

Ty didn't so much as pause in his eating. "Cliff isn't coming," he said casually, continuing to pour food into that lean body with a speed that amazed her.

"Yes, he is. We're working on—"

"I know what you're working on," he said, wiping his

mouth with a napkin and looking at her with a smile she didn't trust. "But you're going to work on it with me instead."

Her pulse danced. "What happened to Cliff?"

"He's...busy."

"You mean you made him busy."

Ty shrugged, that annoying little knowing smile firmly in place. "You don't have a problem, do you? Working with me?"

Everyone stared at her and Zoe gritted her teeth. Oh, he was smooth. "No problem," she said sweetly, adding a sticky smile to the words as she swished by him and out the door.

But it *was* a problem, a big one. She'd have to work all day with the street-smart, smart-ass, gorgeous cowboy she'd been trying not to think about for days.

Five minutes later, Zoe stalked into the dark, dingy barn. Energy pulsed through her, as did the need to do something—anything—to put Ty out of her head. He was like a drug in her bloodstream and she didn't understand the addiction. It had been a good choice to come here, the place was a disaster and it cleared her head.

"The logical choice is to just give up." Zoe told this to the wood she started methodically stacking. She wore her surprise gloves, intending to clear out the piles of debris.

Deserted.

God, how she knew that feeling, and slowly she straightened, her troubles with Ty forgotten as she took a good look around her. Deserted. Yeah, she knew the feeling alright. Her animosity toward the barn faded at that thought. So it had seen better days, so what? With considerably more warmth now, she sighed fondly.

It might be dirty and in need of help, but it was theirs.

"I'll never leave you," she whispered to the empty

building, meaning it with all her heart. She'd been fighting all her life, and she wouldn't stop now. "I'm not a quitter."

It was her one strength, she allowed in a rare moment of self-discovery. Around her, the barn creaked, as if acknowledging her promise.

"We'll be fine." With or without money, yet another worry. There wasn't enough room in her brain for it all. "I've gone hungry before," she huffed as she struggled with a heavy scrap of wood. She paused and blew hair out of her face. "And there's certainly nothing new about being the underdog."

Watching her from the door, Ty felt his heart constrict painfully. "I hear you on that one," he said softly.

She whipped around to face him. "I hate when you do that."

What she hated, he thought, was the fact that he'd caught her in a moment of extreme vulnerability.

He sympathized, but was thankful.

Without these little moments of watching her unguarded, he might not understand her nearly so well. And he did understand her, whether she wanted to believe that or not. They were very much alike in many ways.

"I've been fighting all my life, too," he said, stepping farther into the barn. "And I've been hungry more times than I care to remember."

"A child should never be hungry," she said, her voice sad. "Or afraid."

"Or alone," he agreed easily. "But we both know it's not that simple."

"Is that why you want this land so badly?" she asked. "So that you will never be hungry or in need again?"

"I'm not hungry or in need now."

"So why, then? Why does the land mean so much to you?"

He couldn't talk about Ben, he'd never been able to. But

for a moment, he wished he could. Wished he could unburden his very real fear that he'd failed his brother. "It's complicated."

She made a discouraged noise. "Everything is when it comes to you."

"It doesn't have to be complicated between us."

"Complicated seems to suit me." In an unusually nervous gesture, she shifted her weight back and forth. "Ty...we need to talk."

"About?"

"Us."

That shocked him. "Don't tell me you've decided to admit the truth. You're crazy about me."

Her face was comical. "Ah...not quite."

"You're telling me you feel nothing?"

"I'm telling you I didn't mean *that* kind of us."

He sighed. "Zoe, then just say whatever the hell's on your mind. I'm tired of guessing."

"Well..." She bit her lip, glanced at him from beneath her out-of-control hair, then took off her gloves and shoved them in her back pocket. Then she pulled them out of her pocket and put them back on. "It's about the ranch."

She was nervous, he realized. "It's not a ranch yet."

"I know. It's that..." A muffled oath escaped her as she turned in a slow circle, encompassing the bedraggled barn. "I really want it to be."

"You have your loan yet?"

"I'm getting to that." Misery spilled over her expression. "That's one of those complicated things."

And he suddenly understood her misery. "You want to borrow the money from me."

"Yes," she whispered, her eyes filled with uncertainty and defiance and hope and dread all at once, and they were sparkling with unshed tears, which she blinked furiously at. "The bank wasn't very interested."

Hell, he thought as his heart constricted. He could only imagine what she'd been through that she'd admit to having trouble. "I'm sorry. Can't you try another bank?"

"Ah…no." Her head bowed. "I tried every bank around. I'm a bad investment." Her voice broke and so did his heart.

"God, don't cry. It's okay, the money is yours."

"We'll pay you back, you know." Her voice wobbled.

"I know," he said quickly, slapping his pockets for a damn handkerchief, which of course he didn't have.

"With *interest.*" She wiped her nose on her sleeve. "We always pay our debts." Her breath hitched funny, sounding like a hiccuping sob.

Damn. "It's no problem." He stepped toward her, dying to ease her pain, but she backed away, hand up to hold him off.

"I want to draw that up in a contract," she insisted. "We won't screw you, Ty."

He stood an inch from her, watching her struggle with pride and dignity. He'd never felt so helpless in his life. "I never thought you would," he said quietly. "I trust you, all of you."

"Still, it's important to us that we do this legally. On the record." Her eyes went hot and filled again. "This is not charity."

His helplessness doubled. *Tripled.* "Of course it's not."

"Well, okay, then," she whispered.

Afraid to come within ten feet of her substantially aching pride when she'd made it clear his comfort wouldn't be welcome, he slammed his hands in his pockets, but he really wanted them on her, pulling her close, holding her against him. While he was dealing with those shocking possessive thoughts, she turned on her heels and walked over to yet another pile of long-forgotten debris.

"Let's get to work," she called out, voice gruff. "There's a lot of it."

"Yeah." He heard her sniff and his heart squeezed again. "Let's get to work."

One week later, with summer in full bloom, Zoe was poring over the financial records for Triple M.

Maddie and Delia were painting the inside of the house, and she was putting her business degree to good use after all. A burst of uncontainable excitement hit her.

Yes, her calculator was small and ineffectual and there was too much to do. Yes, she still thought of her mother's abandonment far too often. And yes, she still dwelled every second or so on one Ty Jackson, but other than that, things were looking pretty darn good.

"Daydreaming, Slim?"

"Go away," she said, keeping her eyes glued to her work, because if she looked at him she might make a fool out of herself and throw herself in those capable arms.

"You say the nicest things."

She'd like to stop thinking about him, dwelling over the strange but unaccountable attraction that wouldn't go away. But he was around, nearly every day, and it was hard to forget someone whose face she had to constantly see. More than that, it was getting hard to forget the man who'd done nothing but help her.

He walked into the room and around her desk. He was behind her now, she could feel him with every ounce of her being. His body heat seeped into her back, and before she could stop herself, she peeked at him over her shoulder.

A corner of his mouth curved. "Well, hello."

He hadn't said a word about the loan, for which she was both grateful and suspicious. He hadn't said a thing about their last conversation before that, either, the one where he'd had the nerve to demand she admit she felt something for him.

"I'm working," she said unevenly.

"I can see that," he said, humor heavily laced in his voice. One work-roughened finger reached out and traced over her doodlings.

She stared at that finger. Unbidden came the erotically shattering image of what that callused finger could do to her skin. Goose bumps rose on her arm, which he promptly made all the bigger when he slowly ran his fingers over them.

"Cold?"

How could a voice be rough as sand and smooth as silk at the same time? And why did he affect her this way? He did it again, that little tingly thing with his fingers and she shivered violently. "Stop that!"

"Stop looking at you?" he asked innocently.

"Stop touching me."

"Are you sure?" He leaned close, a corded, tanned forearm on either side of her as he planted his hands on her desk. His chest snugged up to her back, his face came close to hers. "Because while your mouth is saying one thing, Zoe," he whispered, "your body is telling me another entirely."

She realized she'd pressed back against him, and that her nipples had hardened at his first touch and were straining eagerly against her white T-shirt. She groaned, closed her eyes and spun in her chair away from him.

He laughed, low and husky, a sound that she reacted to with her entire body. "Guess this means you're not ready to give up the fight and jump me."

"Not quite." But her body yearned to do just that. "Please, Ty, I need to work."

He whistled on his way out the door, grinning broadly.

"And just for the record," she told him haughtily, "it's cold in here."

He laughed and shut the door.

Leaving her alone. Again.

Cade called with no news. He was still waiting for the judge to open their records. Delia and Maddie took the news as due course, but Zoe nearly burst with tension.

She had to get out for a while and walk or she thought she might go crazy. So many unanswered questions. Where was her mother now?

Why hadn't her father and mother been together?

Were her parents ever married?

And why hadn't Ty kissed her again?

She walked and walked, until she was no longer even on their own land, but Ty's. Wearing black jeans, black sneakers and a black jacket against an even blacker night, Zoe crept into his barn with a singular purpose.

And found the colt.

He was every bit as precious as he'd been the day he'd been born, and her heart melted as she moved close, drawn by life, drawn by hope and love. Some of her terrible inner turmoil eased, and leaning on the stall to get a better look, Zoe found herself smiling for the first time all day.

The baby horse lifted his head and sniffed. Then, after butting gently against his momma for freedom, he bounced toward Zoe, but just as she would have been able to touch him, he bolted away.

"He's skittish."

Zoe gasped and whirled, blinking in the semidarkness.

"Just me," Ty said, lifting his hands. "Seems Danny isn't the only skittish one tonight."

"Danny?"

Ty shrugged and reached into the stall. Danny leaped right up to him for a scratch behind his ears, which Ty obliged. Danny had been the name of Ben's stuffed horse, and from as early as he could remember, Ben had dragged that dirty, old, bedraggled horse around everywhere they'd gone. Ty had taken one look at Abby's foal and had known what his name would be. "It fit," he said, turning his attention back to Zoe. He looked down at her feet and sighed. "Tennis shoes. Again."

"Yeah, well, boots are—"

"Expensive, I know." His expression was grim. "You're not going to use any of the loan for yourself, are you."

"No. I want a ranch, Ty. I know that sounds like a dumb thing for a city girl to say, but that's what I want."

"And you want Triple M to be yours."

She froze, shocked. Was she as transparent as that? Or did he just know her better than anyone else ever had? She recovered with effort. "Delia and Maddie deserve it every bit as much as I do," she said carefully.

"Yes, they do." He was closer now, and she could feel the very heat and power of him, so easily and carefully restrained.

"I understand, you know," he told her. "I feel that need to belong somewhere, too."

In the dim light of the barn their eyes met. His were surprisingly open and warm and caring. "It doesn't make you a bad person, Zoe. Don't add guilt to your already-loaded burden."

Did he really understand? The pain in his gaze told her he did. She'd seen flashes of his inner anguish before. What made him hurt so? Was it his past? "How do you know what it's like?"

"I know because I came from nowhere." He let out a breath, then spoke, his reply low and harsh. "Belonged nowhere and to no one."

She hadn't expected an answer, for he guarded his privacy as strongly as she. "What about your parents?"

"My mother was a hooker, my father a thief." He paused. "He liked to hurt people. She liked to watch."

Zoe hadn't known she could feel so much pain over words, simple words, but she did.

Abby shifted, nuzzled Danny. Danny made a sound of warm contentment and pushed closer.

Mother and baby as it should be.

Zoe sighed. "Life sucks sometimes, doesn't it?"

A small, humorless smile crossed his face. "Yeah, it does."

Yet he hadn't let life get him down for long, she thought. Maybe she could understand his drive now, his need for control. He would do anything it took in order to be different from his parents, and she could respect that.

She had to touch him more than she needed her next breath, so she took his hand, which he squeezed lightly. His eyes warmed, and she knew he realized this was the first time she had touched him first.

"Is there anyone else in your family?" she asked.

"No."

There was a great, encompassing hurt in his voice now instead of anger, and she knew there was more he wasn't telling. "Did anyone help you?"

He let out a harsh laugh. "You know what people expect of a kid like that."

"Nothing." How well she knew.

"Exactly." He looked at her solemnly, standing straight and tall and proud. "I wanted more than nothing, Zoe."

She thought she could see him as a kid now, still standing straight and tall and proud, with bruises and torn clothing and nothing to eat. Her throat closed. "So here you are."

"So here I am." His lips curved, easing his tight expression. "And here you are, too."

She nodded and looked again at Danny, feeling wistful.

"Why did you sneak in here like a thief in the night?" he asked as they turned side by side to watch his horses. She would have pulled her hand free but he held it tight in his. When their gazes met, he said, "You know you can come in here any time you want."

She nodded. She knew.

With a sigh, he turned her to face him. "You helped bring him into this world. You feel a bond with him."

"I feel a bond with you," she admitted. "And I'm pretty sure I don't like it too much."

"*I* like it. I like it a lot."

At the unmistakable heat in his expression, she stepped back.

He let out a soft, frustrated growl. "There," he accused, lifting a finger. "You just did it again. Blocked yourself off from me. You just admitted we have a bond, so what is it? Why can't you just…feel?"

His body was close, nearly cocooning hers. Instead of intimidating, it beckoned. But she had to make one thing very clear. "Just because I took money from you doesn't mean I have to…act on what's between us."

"This has nothing to do with the money," he assured her. "It has to do with this."

Dragging her closer, he sandwiched her between the stall and his powerful body, then took her mouth with his.

Chapter 12

Zoe was braced for a powerful, hot, demanding kiss, which she could have ignored. But when Ty's mouth met hers, it was slow, thorough and devastatingly gentle.

Time stopped. The smells of hay and horse faded. So did the sounds of impatient hooves and the night wind. Everything faded in comparison to the sound and feel of Ty. He nibbled at the corner of her lips, outlined them with his tongue, then lightly sucked on her bottom lip until she moaned.

Lifting his head, he cupped her face in his big hands. "Don't hide from me, Zoe. Don't fight this."

"Fighting…is second nature." Her voice was breathless, and she realized she had plastered her body to his.

"I know. It's a defense. I know that, too. I just want you to be honest. You act so tough, so unfeeling." He traced her jawbone with an achingly soft touch. "But it's just an act. I can see the true Zoe in your eyes, and that Zoe I see feels, laughs…loves."

He was so close to the truth, she couldn't stand it. He was the only one to ever have cracked her emotional block wall, and it so terrified her she couldn't speak, couldn't do anything but watch him with wide eyes as he carefully soothed her, his voice low and soft in a way she'd heard him use on his horses, on Maddie and even Delia, but never with her.

"Let me have *that* Zoe," he whispered, his arms warm and caring and oh-so-comforting as they slowly surrounded her. She could happily have drowned in them.

Oh, why couldn't he be his usual gruff and rough self? That direct, demanding, bossy man she could have resisted. But this Ty, and the emotion he was drawing out of her, was new. It wasn't the dark, thrilling excitement she'd grown to expect, but a genuine, undeniable, irresistible affection.

And it terrified her.

"I won't be rushed," she said quietly. She hated the expression that crossed his face before he managed to guard it. *Disappointment.*

"Why is it so hard for you?" he wondered, letting her move away from him.

Because you never tell me how you *feel.* She leaned on the stables, watching the horses. *Because I hate the way I feel when you touch me, completely out of control. Because I worry how I'll handle it when you decide we're done.* "I just don't choose to constantly put my heart out on the line for something that's not a sure thing," she said.

"There are no sure things." He moved beside her, restless. "But unless you try, you'll never know what might have been."

She stared at him and he turned his head, meeting her stare unflinchingly. Waiting…waiting. But when she said nothing, *could* say nothing, he shook his head. "Fine, feel nothing," he said roughly. "You'll never know what you're missing."

Oh, she knew. She knew all too well, but she didn't have the strength to reach out and get it. Didn't know how, even if she'd wanted to.

And a little part of her really, really wanted to.

"Zoe," he whispered, just that. Just her name in a voice thick with yearning, and even in her panic she recognized it wasn't a physical yearning, but something much, much deeper. "Don't miss this. Don't turn away from the best thing that's ever happened to either of us."

Her eyes filled but she didn't speak, didn't have the words.

He waited for an eternally long moment, but when she didn't say a word, he opened Abby and Danny's stall and slipped inside.

Abby nickered softly and Ty bent his head close, stroking her face. Abby blew at him.

Ty stood there with his back to Zoe, a tall, powerful man and an equally powerful horse, easily showing their affection for each other.

Zoe nearly broke down.

Then Ty hunkered low, speaking softly to Danny, who tossed his head, drawing a quiet chuckle from his owner. Zoe watched him put his arms around the foal, watched Ty's lean strength shelter Danny in a way that made her ache all the more.

She wished she were in Danny's position, being securely held safe.

Ty would never desert them, and the horses knew it. They were more secure than she, and that was pathetic. That's what she hated most of all, that in spite of her bravado she wanted promises, too. Once upon a time she'd waited years and years and years for her mother's return, finally accepting it would never happen.

She had vowed never to put herself in that position again. She would renew that vow now, instead of moping around the gorgeous man murmuring with love to his horses.

At the sound of the barn door quietly shutting behind her, Ty swore in frustration. Danny pushed at him with his head to Ty's stomach, clearly wondering why he'd stopped being stroked.

Ty hugged Danny close, feeling more lost and alone than he had since Ben had first died.

Zoe walked through the night, just as alone, just as full of grief. The house was dark and silent, and it suited her mood.

On her bed was a big brown bag, just like the one her gloves had come in, and in it was a new pair of boots in her exact size.

Overwhelmed, Zoe sank to the mattress and fingered the good, expensive leather. The thought of Delia hoarding her pennies and spending them on such a necessity had the tears she'd been struggling with rise back to the surface.

With the precious boots in her lap, she sat down, kicking off her beat-up tennis shoes.

What was the matter with her? She never cried.

Crying was a useless emotion, hadn't she learned that well? As a child, she'd often plastered herself up against the window of the group home, tears rolling silently down her face as she'd waited for her mother to come back.

She never had.

And eventually Zoe had stopped crying.

But as she laced up the new boots, affection for her sisters causing her chest to be tight and uncomfortable, she cried now.

One week later, Cade came to Triple M. He sat at the table with the three women, inhaling another of Maddie's meals, and making everyone laugh.

It was a nice change from the stress, Zoe admitted to herself. Thanks to Ty, they had money to start the ranch, and indeed they'd been looking into specific plans to acquire horses and a small herd of cattle, but it had been far more difficult than she'd ever imagined.

She loved it. They *all* loved it, but there wasn't much time for fun and relaxation in the face of all that had to be done. Zoe eyed the last muffin, considering. Her jeans would be too tight all day if she succumbed, but a girl needed her energy, didn't she?

With that ready excuse, she reached for it, freezing when Ty walked in.

He had on his climbing gear, and a dark scowl.

She knew that scowl, knew its origin. He'd been wild and cranky and unapproachable all week, even since that night in the barn where she'd nearly bared her soul.

At the sight of him now, and his clear-cut plans to go climb a mountain to relieve his tension—tension that *she'd* caused—she felt her stomach tighten with unease.

She hated fearing for his life, hated worrying that she'd never see him alive again.

"Going climbing?" Cade asked Ty.

Ty nodded curtly, his gaze still on Zoe. His gaze ran slowly over her, from her unbound hair all the way down to her new boots, which given the way his jaw relaxed, seemed to give him great pleasure.

Maddie handed Ty a bag bulging at the seams. "Take this," she insisted, pressing it into his hand. "It's food."

His face softened as he looked at her. "I have food, Maddie."

"I made it just for you."

Touching surprise flitted across Ty's face first, then pleasure at the gentle but inexorable sisterly pressure. "Thank you,'' he said, looking down at the package in his hands as if it were made of the finest bone china.

"Don't stay out there too long," Maddie said.

Delia wasn't nearly as subtle. "If you're gone more than two days, I'm going to send for search and rescue. So don't get embarrassed, because I've warned you." She grinned and kissed him goodbye. "Take care," she whispered.

Ty accepted the embrace with the same quiet surprise, clearly unused to someone thinking of him, and Zoe felt a strange stirring watching his struggle. Was he also unused to someone worrying about him? Too bad if he was, she couldn't help it. "Be careful," she said softly.

His head came up and their gazes met yet again, all of the heat still very much there but much of the animosity drained. "I always am."

She nodded, and bit her tongue before she could beg him not to go. Before she could tell him how much he'd started to mean to her, and how much that frightened her.

When he was gone, when those wide shoulders had disappeared out the kitchen door, Zoe sagged and sentenced herself to a long day of worrying.

"He'll be okay," Cade said, touching her arm.

"I'm not concerned." Because that sounded awful, and was so blatantly untrue, she gave in. "Much."

Delia was watching her with frank curiosity. "What's going on with you two, anyway? Whenever you guys are in the same room it's like watching a fireworks display."

"There's nothing going on."

"Right."

"There's not!" Zoe tossed up her hands when everyone just stared at her. "Jeez, can't a person just plain not get along with another person without drawing all sorts of suspicion to themselves?"

"A normal person maybe," Delia conceded. "But since you dislike everyone equally, you don't count."

"It's unlike you, Zoe, to be so hard on someone," Maddie said. "What's wrong?"

"We just don't get along, okay?"

Delia shook her head in disgust. "That's a sin, hon. To be at odds with a man like that."

Cade grinned and looked at Delia hopefully. "If it's such a sin…you ought to be far nicer to me."

"Don't count on it."

The two of them started their typical verbal sparring, and Zoe breathed a sigh of relief. Her little fantasy was safe. Even more shameful was how that dream of hers had grown. No longer was it a harmless little sexual escapade involving Ty's incredible mouth and body. It had become deeper, and therefore a darker secret. A ridiculous one.

She wanted him to fall in love with her.

But how could he when she didn't even know who Zoe the woman was? She knew nothing about herself, about her heritage, and while it shouldn't matter, it did.

Too much.

Later Zoe was alone, standing in one of the arenas she'd recently weeded. It was exciting to stand there in the center of the property and look at the land, even if it was empty of animals.

It was breathtaking, so different from where they'd come from. Here, no one ever asked for the time of day. Here, a desk job was a four-letter word. Here was, no matter what happened, an exhilarating, unforgettable, one-of-a-kind adventure.

Hopefully, they'd soon have cattle. Ty had been checking prices for them. But if it didn't work out, Zoe had a backup plan. They could raise cattle for other ranchers who didn't have enough land. Which could work out, especially since Delia wouldn't even consider raising cattle specifically for beef.

Zoe grinned at this. It was okay to raise the cattle for other ranchers who would eventually sell for beef. As long as *they* themselves didn't.

The plan was to start small, which was the reason they'd taken less money from Ty than he'd wanted to loan them.

The equipment and repairs had been costly, far more so than she had estimated, though Ty had warned her.

And she still had to hire several ranch hands because she needed help.

So much work, and yet all she could do was look at the mountains and think of the tall, powerful, intensely passionate man who'd turned her world upside down. A man she'd chased away yet again with words and actions while her heart had secretly cried in protest.

She wanted him, she admitted, and it wasn't for the physical attraction, but for the way he made her feel. Special. So why did she keep pushing him away?

Easy. It was her past, and wrong as it was, she couldn't help it. Until she knew who she was and why she'd been left in the group home, she wasn't free to follow her dreams.

The mountains were every bit as wild and fierce as Ty, she fretted as she stared at the triple peaks. Even now, in late June, the tops of them were still covered with snow. Unforgiving, unrelenting. Lethal.

People died on those mountains.

"He'll be back." Cade stopped at her side, turned his gaze from the mountains and smiled at her.

She brushed her dusty hands on her jeans. "I'm not really worried."

"Is that right?"

She shrugged. "Well, maybe I am. A little, sort of. In the same context as I worry about the wolf spiders eating all the mosquito hawks."

Cade laughed. "You sure you and Delia aren't blood relations? You're both stubborn."

"Cade…" Zoe took a deep breath and plunged. "I need you to find my mother."

"I've been trying, Zoe, believe me. For Constance—"

"Not for Constance. For *me*." She turned to him, her new boots crunching in the dirt. "I know you've been looking at all three of our pasts, but you've been searching for our fathers."

"Mostly."

"I want to know about my mother. I *need* to know. Why she left, why she never came back, why—" Her voice cracked, horrifying her. "Why she didn't love me enough to want me."

He grimaced and reached for her. "Zoe—"

"No, don't. I'm fine." She forced back all emotion, not quite meeting Cade's gaze because she couldn't stand the sympathy she found there. "Can you help or not?"

Her sharp voice didn't chase him off. He merely smiled at her. "I can help."

"But so far you've found nothing?"

"Only that she disappeared the day she dropped you off."

Zoe looked to the mountains and again felt that inexplicable yearning to see a tall, dark, gorgeous man mysteriously appear. She didn't even care if he gave her that crooked, cocky smile, she just wanted to know he was safe, damn him.

Cade followed her gaze. "Probably much cooler up there."

"What does he think about when he's climbing? It looks horrifying."

"He probably thinks of you," Cade said casually.

"No," she said firmly. "It's not like that between us." Ty wanted her, she knew that. But as for anything else, anything deeper, he'd been closemouthed. Was it any wonder she doubted his motives?

No, that wasn't fair, she allowed. He'd made no secret of wanting their land, and still, he'd done everything in his power to make sure they didn't lose it.

"I've known Ty since Constance first hired me, Zoe. We both came from a big city, we're both relatively new to the country. I understand him. He's not always so…well…" Cade looked at her with true compassion. "Let's just say only a man who cares deeply would have such a hard time controlling his emotions."

After a while, he left her alone to stare at the wilderness of peaks, at the canyons and the river, and wonder if she wasn't fooling herself.

If she and Ty both didn't care far more than either of them wanted to admit.

Late the next night, Zoe couldn't sleep. She was thinking too much, and while she was at it, she was feeling too much, as well. It made her angry.

And being angry was hungry business. She headed for the kitchen, walking through a dark house so she wouldn't wake anyone up. Not that she minded sharing her snack, but Maddie would worry and Delia would tease, then they'd fight and Maddie would worry some more.

It just seemed easier to deal with her stress alone tonight. Gathering up a bag of chips and a Coke, she crept into her office.

The books were there and she opened them up, happily munching as she studied the numbers. There was plenty of room for failure, but Zoe couldn't help but smile even though they hovered firmly in the red. She was accustomed to hard work, they could do this. They'd never been closer.

She was home, for the first time in her life.

When her bag of chips was empty, she tossed it in the

trash and sighed. It was then that she noticed a small brown paper bag on the corner of her desk. Inside was a brand new compact adding machine, equipped with an electrical cord and a roll of adding paper. A small thing, really, not an expensive one, but Zoe clutched it to her chest, eyes bright.

Delia.

Had anyone ever had such a thoughtful, caring, smart-ass sister? She didn't deserve either of them, Zoe thought. Didn't deserve the love they showered on her constantly; Delia with her tough concern and secret gifts, and Maddie always plying her with motherly affection and really great fattening food.

Love bubbled and overflowed, but so did guilt, for Zoe didn't tell them nearly enough how she felt.

That would change, she vowed then and there.

Then she plugged in her new machine and happily balanced their dangerously low checking account.

It was early, he was tired, and he was an idiot to boot. For the first time since Ty had come to Idaho, he ignored the spectacular sunrise, which was the highest-rated show for three hundred miles in all directions.

Shaking his head at himself, he got out of his truck, then reached in for his little, squirming burden.

"Mew."

"Shh," he told the kitten, who popped its little red head out from beneath the blanket. "You're supposed to be a surprise, dammit."

He had no idea what he was doing, only knew when he'd found the deserted kitten crying in his barn, with no brothers or sisters or momma in sight, that his insides had gone to mush.

Immediately he'd thought of Zoe, and how she continued to sneak into his barn to watch Danny grow. She loved babies almost as much as she loved to hide herself from him.

His entire body was tense at the prospect of seeing her again. Little of his frustrated fury over her inability to accept what was between them had faded.

It probably wasn't a good time to come here, when he was still aroused and aching from last night's dreams about her, but he'd punished his body good over the past few days in the mountains. What was the difference if now he punished his mind as well?

Tucking the kitten under his arm, he strode to the side door of Triple M Ranch, intending to quietly enter the kitchen and leave his surprise.

But the surprise was on him. In formfitting stretch pants and a T-shirt, her hair loosely tied back, Zoe opened the door, looking rumpled and sleepy.

Her eyes came fully awake at the sight of him. "What do you want?" she asked warily.

"Such a sweet greeting," he mocked. "You really need to restrain yourself, Zoe. Someone's going to get ideas."

She stepped back, probably intending to slam the door on his face, but then she caught a glimpse of what he carried in his arms.

Abruptly her face softened, her eyes warmed. "A kitten," she breathed. "Oh, Ty, what are you doing with such an adorable kitten?"

"It's for you, dammit," he said gruffly, shoving the tiny thing at her. He stepped back, far back.

She just stood there, staring down at the kitten. "You brought it here...to give to me?"

"Yes, dammit, if you want it."

When her eyes went suspiciously bright, he let out a concise oath. "Oh, no. God. *No.* It's just a cat. You're *not* going to cry. Don't even think about it."

She shook her head but still looked...damp.

"Stop it. Stop it now. If you don't," he told her desperately, "I'll...I'll take the thing back."

Sniffing, she shook her head and clutched it closer. "I'm not crying. The sun is bright is all."

The kitten mewled again, a small, pathetic little sound. Zoe's face crumbled adorably, and she held it close, bending her face close to the kitten's.

He had no idea what he was doing, bringing a kitten to a woman, trying to worm his way into her heart. God, he wanted to be gone from here, far gone.

Zoe kissed the kitten's nose, laughed in delight, then lifted her face. And gasped as she caught her first good look at him. "You're hurt!"

He touched the long gash on his cheek that he'd gotten while rock climbing and doing the ridiculous—thinking of her. "No big deal," he said.

"No big deal," she repeated, still staring at him, looking at him so deeply and openly, so much that for the first time he felt he was really seeing her. She was looking at him as if it was good to see him home safe and sound, as if she was relieved and happy. As if she'd missed him. And she proved it when she reached out with a light finger and touched his face gently.

He couldn't believe it and was afraid to move, afraid to speak and ruin the moment. She looked so beautiful standing there, so right, so...happy.

Had he done that?

The kitten cried out once more and Zoe blinked, dropping her gaze to her precious burden. She nuzzled it close, tucking it into her neck.

And suddenly, quite savagely, he wanted to be held in her arms like that, as if he meant the world to her, too.

"Thank you," she said quietly.

He nodded, not knowing what to do, feeling awkward and inept with a woman for the first time since puberty.

Then she really shocked him. She stepped toward him and with her free arm she pulled him close, drawing him into a gentle embrace that meant more than all their previous almost-violent ones had meant put together.

He held himself rigid a moment, his pent-up frustration dictating that he not give in and yank her against him as he wanted, because it would be a weakness to show how much he needed her when she didn't need him back.

But maybe she did need him back, just a little. She placed one arm around him now, her face open and for once free of shadows. And her eyes, God, those eyes, they pulled him right in. "Thank you," she whispered again, the soft skin of her cheek against his rough one.

Then in her first show of trust since he'd known her, she laid her head on his shoulder and snuggled close, the kitten between them.

God. And he was supposed to resist this? Her breath stirred gently against his neck.

Hell, he was a goner, and with a shuddering sigh, he gave in and returned the embrace.

He could do nothing else.

Chapter 13

Ty had never felt quite this way before, as if he held the world—his world—in his arms. He was cold and hot at the same time, and a little dizzy, too.

He buried his face in Zoe's sweet-scented hair and held on tight, letting out a little laugh when the kitten meowed at him. They stayed that way for a long moment, swaying gently with the morning sun warming them.

Around them, the early dew lit up the yard like a thousand sunbeams. The air stirred lightly, reminding them that another hot summer day was on its way.

All the problems seemed so far away.

"Meow."

Zoe was hesitant to let go of Ty, of this moment, even as sharp claws dug into her chest. But this incredible, nearly overwhelming feeling of being held so tight, so protectively, so carefully…she didn't want it to end.

"Mew."

Ty let out another little chuckle and lifted his head. "Noisy little thing."

"He's perfect." Pretending as if being held by a strong, warm, sexy man was the norm, Zoe leaned back in his arms and stroked the kitten's head. "And I can't wait to show him to Maddie and Delia. This is exactly what they need...they've been working so hard."

He dipped his head, ran his jaw along hers, and she savored the feel of him. "So have you," he said in her ear.

"But it's harder on them."

"Why is that?"

"They're..." Well, she didn't know exactly, she just innately felt more suited to this life. She worried about that and dealt with the guilt, which was becoming harder to do with him making thinking so difficult. "It just seems to be easier for me out here. They'll just melt over the kitten, though."

Ty remained silent, and finally she looked up into warm eyes the color of a summer storm. They were filled with things that made her feel weak and strong at the same time, things she wanted to hear him say. One big hand came up to stroke her jaw; his skin rough, his touch gentle. "Do you have any idea how much it means to me to see you like this?" he asked. "To see you let loose with a show of love for your sisters?"

His words startled her. "You've seen that before."

"No, I've seen you bicker with them, tease them. Show worry and anxiety over them." He never stopped touching her. "Nothing like this."

He put a finger over her lips when she would have retorted and smiled at her. "Don't blow it, Zoe, I'm proud of you. Just let me have this moment, okay?"

"But I *do* show them how I feel," she said stubbornly.

He cocked a brow. "Do you *tell* them?"

She felt the flush cover her face and pushed back from him because suddenly she needed breathing space. "This is really none of your business."

"Don't get defensive."

"Why does everyone always say that?" She glared at him. "Why don't I list off *your* faults and see how you feel?" She hitched the kitten up in one arm and lifted her other hand, one finger for each adjective. "For your information, you're demanding, bossy, arrogant, a know-it-all, temperamental—"

"Careful, you're going to run out of fingers."

She paused in mid-insult, then shook her head, perilously close to laughter, which had her all the more confused. Within a few moments' time, he'd brought her the full gamut of emotions. From yearning to happiness to laughter…to more yearning.

And it occurred to her in that shocking moment of clarity that somewhere along the way, she had no idea when, she'd lost the last of her protective barriers with him. He'd torn down her brick wall, the one protecting her heart, one brick at a time.

She was bare. Vulnerable.

No. No, she wouldn't allow it, not when he wasn't the same way. She backed to the door, reaching blindly for it.

He blinked and whistled low and long, and shook his head. "The way you do that, switch gears so fast, is positively frightening." He leaned close, so close she could see specks of blue light dancing in his gray eyes, and they were no longer light and happy. "Go on, run inside. Run away from this, from me."

"I'm not running."

"Yeah? Then tell me how you feel about me."

His challenging voice wasn't what penetrated, but his eyes. They weren't sharp and daring, but…needy? Wait a minute…the tough, unshakable Ty Jackson needy?

"Know what I think?" he asked, his voice low and taunting. "I think you're crazy about me, about your sisters, too. But you can't even say so."

She cuddled the kitten close, unwilling to expose her emotions when he hadn't done so first. "What do you know about love, Ty?"

His eyes shuttered and he stepped back, alarmingly distant. "We're not talking about me."

But suddenly she wanted to be. "No, tell me. What makes you such an expert on this subject? You're alone, too."

He stared at her, then looked at the sky for a moment, then at the kitten, and finally, back to her. "I used to be an expert," he said, his voice rough. "I loved my brother." He swore softly, shoved his fingers through his dark hair and abruptly turned away. "I'm behind on chores."

"Ty, wait—" He didn't stop and she let out a despairing sound, knowing his temper now was spurred by pain, pain she'd brought to the surface. "Ty!"

His long legs churned up the distance to his truck. His wide shoulders were hunched, his hands stuffed in his pockets, as if he carried the weight of the world. But somewhere under all that bunched muscle and frustration beat a wonderful, caring heart.

She was holding proof of that heart. "Dammit." She snuggled the kitten and ran after him.

He had the truck running when she caught him. "Go inside," he said wearily, looking straight ahead, even when she leaned in his opened window.

"I want to talk."

"You want to be real sure about that, Zoe." He turned then and searched her gaze with his tortured one. "Because when we talk it's going to go both ways, and there won't be any holding back."

Involuntarily she stepped away and he let out a laugh completely void of amusement. Anguish settled in his eyes. "Go away, Zoe."

And he drove off.

* * *

The truth was hard to deny when it was staring her in the face. Zoe pushed back the set of books she'd been working on, bent her weary head on her arms and sighed.

"Mew."

"Hey, Socks." Not exactly an original name for a red kitten with white paws, but it worked for them. Socks butted his head gently against Zoe's hand until she relented and petted him.

He dropped to her papers, sprawled spread-eagled on his back and started to purr, making her smile. Her sisters loved him. And seeing their happy, laughing faces had been a great reward. Their happiness meant everything to her.

But what about yours?

She was happy, wasn't she? Even if they were still drowning in financial woes. They had fixed up the bare minimum on the house. They'd put the barn in shape, ignoring for now the series of cottages on the edge of the property. They continued to lease part of the land to Ty, which, at the moment, was the only solvent part of the ranch.

The problem was the price of stock was high this year, higher than anticipated. They couldn't afford both livestock and crew. One or the other, yet they needed both.

Bottom line—they were still short money.

It was so frustrating, she wanted to scream. Grim and bleak, with energy pulsing through her, Zoe got up. She scooped up Socks and gently set him in Maddie's dark, silent bedroom, where she knew the kitten would find a warm, welcome bed.

The night was complete, the moon just a sliver against the black sky. Long silver clouds streaked across, blanketing the stars from view.

Zoe passed her truck—too much blood pumping through

her veins for a sedentary ride. Instead, she started running, letting the cool night take her.

Ten minutes later, breath puffing, she stopped at the end of Ty's drive, uncertain.

Why had she come here?

Telling herself it was to see Danny, not his owner, she walked toward Ty's barn.

A shadow emerged in front of her, shifting into the shape of a man. Ty. He wore black jeans, a black shirt and a black expression to match, and as he stood there watching her, his face impassive and stoic, something passed between them, belying that very distance.

He felt it to his toes, then cursed himself for it.

"I wanted to see Danny," she said defiantly.

"Zoe," he said wearily, slipping his hands in his pockets to keep them off her. "Truth."

"Okay, truth." Her jaw tightened. "I don't have what it takes to get the ranch going."

The admission startled him, and her misery tore at something deep inside. Despite his resolve to stay the hell away, he took a step toward her. "Of course you do."

"No." Impatient, she shook her head. "I mean, we don't have enough money. Something has to give, only there's nothing left. I've checked the numbers a hundred times."

Her frustration felt like his own. "I tried to make your loan bigger."

"You gave us enough."

"Your pride doesn't belong here." He got angry because her grim eyes were too hard to take. The last time he'd seen eyes so despairing, he'd been looking into Ben's dying face. And into that dying face he'd made a promise that haunted him to this very day. "You could let me buy—"

"No." She whirled around in a circle, staring into the dark at his small spread. "I want to make it work. I want…'' Her shoulders sagged and her voice broke. ''I want it all. Dammit, is that so wrong?''

She covered her face and her suffering was too much for him to bear. ''It's okay,'' he whispered, coming close and setting his hands on her shoulders. Gently he drew her close, cursing himself as he did. ''It's going to be okay.''

''How can I be so close and fail?''

Same reason he could be so close to her, could see her for what she was—a woman determined to never need another soul—and still so desperately want her for himself. ''You won't fail, Zoe. It's not in you.''

Determination filled her fierce expression, but she hugged him back, her body willing to trust him for comfort even if her mind wasn't.

''It seems obvious to me.'' Cade took another bite, moaned with pleasure, winked at Maddie and spoke again. ''A guest ranch.''

Zoe sputtered, nearly choking on her iced tea. ''A what?''

''You know…bring in rich vacationing people to do all the work for you. They used to call them dude ranches.''

Maddie, Delia and Zoe just stared at him.

''On top of that,'' he said around another bite, ''they pay for the privilege of doing all your chores. It's great.''

Delia looked speculative. ''Rich people? Such as…rich *men?*''

Cade was disgusted. ''Hey, baby, *I'm* rich. Why don't you fall over me?''

''I'm looking for personality, Slick.''

Maddie gave Delia an admonishing look, then turned back to Cade. ''A guest ranch would be like an inn, right?''

''Sort of.''

Her eyes lit with speculation. ''It would need a really

great kitchen, wouldn't it? With fabulous meals for lots of hungry guests.''

"Hungry, *rich* guests," Delia said with growing interest.

Zoe could see her sisters caving. "You're all crazy."

"Zoe, *think* of it." Maddie's eyes were shining. "These people *pay*."

"Yeah, as in cash money," Delia added. "Can't believe we didn't think of it before. We're in the best spot in the world. People love Idaho."

"*Capital*," Zoe reminded her sister. "We'd need capital. And someone with the know-how."

"We already have a manager who'd be willing to help," Maddie said quietly.

The man who'd held her last night, the man who'd helped her believe in herself. Ty.

Zoe pushed away her dinner plate, suddenly no longer hungry. She was feeling a lot of things, *too* many things, most of it owing to the private conversation she'd just had with Cade where she'd learned there was no news on the inheritance front.

Her mother had disappeared off the face of the planet twenty years ago and not a word from her had been heard since.

Fine. She could deal with that. With being deserted. She could deal with anything, and had. "We can do better than this," she declared. "I mean, come on...a guest ranch? Triple M Guest Ranch?"

But as she walked along the river that night, after an exhausting run, contemplating her failures, Zoe kept coming back to the thought...a guest ranch.

How bad could it be?

She smiled, thinking her sisters were going to enjoy being right.

"Well, isn't that something? A smile." Ty dismounted

his horse, let it loose to graze in the wild grass and leaned negligently against a tree. "Can't say I've seen that too often." He waited a beat. "Did it hurt?"

"Very funny. Why are you following me?"

"I came to the house for dessert. Maddie told me where you were. You shouldn't be out here alone."

"Ty, you climb rock monoliths sixty stories high for fun. I think I can handle a little tame walk along the river."

"I meant because you're lonely."

Her heart stopped, then started a heavy pumping that was louder than the roar of the river.

Ty stepped closer. "Being alone makes loneliness worse, Zoe."

"Well, I'm not alone now, am I?" She speculated, then gave him a sideways glance. He certainly looked the part of the cowboy tonight, dressed in jeans so faded the stress points were white, and oh boy, did he have stress points. She dragged her eyes upward to his plain T-shirt, partially covered by an unbuttoned blue chambray shirt.

She'd missed him, but he'd been so busy they'd hardly spoken. Not that she would have known what to say. He wanted something from her she wasn't ready to give.

And where did that leave him? He still wanted her land. What would he think of this latest idea? Only one way to find out. "What do you think of guest ranches?" she asked suddenly.

Ty laughed, then sobered when she glared at him. "You're serious?"

She spread her hands. "What choice do we have at this point? The big house could be a lodge, the cottages individual cabins for families to stay. We're smack-dab in the middle of thousands of acres of wild, unexplored federal park land, all of it ready to play in. Day hikes. Rides. Big-game hunting. It's a four-season playground. Just think…it could be a hot, exclusive place to go."

"You've really thought about this."

"Better than selling out."

He went grim. "Yeah. You'll still need more money." He bent, picked up a stone and tossed it into the river.

"Yes." She bit her lip. Considered. "But a guest ranch has potential for earning money back much faster than a working ranch if done correctly."

"It will also take much more capital than a working ranch."

"I know. I was thinking we could take on a partner for the venture…one who knew what he was doing."

His head whipped toward hers, eyes narrowed. The moon peeked out from beneath a cloud, lighting up the small clearing where they stood, casting everything in a dreamy glow.

"Know anyone who'd be interested?" she wondered.

"You know damn straight I'm interested, but it involves trust, Zoe." He shifted closer until she could feel the heat of him. "Ready for that?"

"No more than you are."

"What does that mean? I trust you."

"Tell me about your brother, Ty."

A long, pent-up breath escaped him. "Where did that come from?"

"Is it such a surprise that I want to know more about you?"

"That you're admitting it is." But she was staring at him, waiting. And he suddenly wanted to tell her. "He was…Ben." He lifted a shoulder, struggling for words. He'd never talked about his brother before, and suddenly it didn't seem right to be burying Ben's memory, not when Ty wanted to remember him always. Ben deserved to be remembered, to be talked about. "He was wonderful, funny. Smart." He smiled as memories, good ones, washed over him. "And he kept me in line."

She smiled, too. "You were close."

"We survived." He looked at his own big hands and knew he could never be like his father, could never use violence against another.

"He's...gone?"

"He died." God, it was hard to say it aloud, to put the images back into his head. "In my arms, after a fight with a gang member on the streets of Chicago where we lived. He was sixteen."

"Oh God, Ty." She reached for him, the ground crunching beneath her as she moved, her soft warm body pressing close. It wasn't in any way a sexual embrace, it was different, and it was somehow far better.

There was no sound except for the soothing rush of the river, and he urged her even closer, folding her tight to him, soaking up the affection he'd been starving for since that day he'd given her the kitten.

"I'm sorry," she whispered after a time. "You were left alone. It was so unfair."

It wasn't a question, but a statement, from someone who knew just how unfair life could be. "He made me promise to keep our dream," he said. He lifted his head and met her gaze steadily. "To raise horses. Lots and lots of horses. We knew little about them then, other than the ranch life represented a freedom we'd never experienced."

She smiled sadly. "That's why you want Constance's land. Because yours isn't big enough. Oh, Ty, I wish I'd known. I thought...I thought..."

"I know." She'd thought the worst, believing it had been nothing more than selfish greed motivating him.

But what did this change?

He touched her face softly, and for the first time in a long while he felt a surge of hope. "I don't think a guest ranch occurred to Ben, but somehow I believe he'd approve. Zoe..." He didn't know how to finish the sentence, didn't know what he wanted to say, only knew the moment was special, that they were jumping yet another hurdle…directly into the unknown. "I would love to be a partner in Triple M."

She stepped back with a little, touchingly nervous smile. "I'm glad." She bit her lip. "There's so much to do. We have to get advertising together, permits, and there's still so much to fix up in the cottages and the other barn…." She laughed and he smiled at her, loving the sound of her joy.

"You ought to do that more," he said, touching her lower lip with his thumb. "Laugh."

She reached up and held his hand to her face, lowering her eyes.

"I don't imagine there's been much to laugh about in your life, has there?" he asked quietly.

"No more than yours. But life is good right now."

"Yes," he agreed. "It is."

A small, satisfied smile came back to her lips. "There's a long way to go, but at least we're on the road now."

"I like the *we* part."

She studied him carefully. "I don't do the 'we' thing very well. I'm basically a loner."

"I don't believe that."

"It's true, I don't let people in very well."

"You let your sisters in."

"Yes, but even with them I hold back," she admitted, cringing a little at the thought. "You have this way of pushing my safety barriers and I like to be alone. I have been ever since…"

"Ever since what, Zoe?"

"My mother left me." She closed her eyes, her skin pale in the glow of the night. And he'd never seen her look more vulnerable or beautiful. "I was three and she promised to come back for me, only she never did. I didn't understand then, but I do now.''

"What do you understand?''

"That it's better to be alone than get hurt.''

"I don't believe that.''

Her eyes heated. "Well, I do. Look, by the time I was five, I was making up excuses for my mother. She'd found her prince, she was living in a castle far away, stuff like that.'' She sighed. "And when I was ten and everyone in my class was writing about their past and their families, I made mine up because I didn't know anything about myself or where I'd come from. I knew her last name, that's it. Not my father's, though.'' She shook her head. "By the time I was eighteen and on my own I knew the truth. I'd been deserted, and no amount of wishing and dreaming and hoping was going to change that. I'm an orphan because no one wanted me, and I have to live with that every day of my life.'' She let out a short, harsh laugh and turned away. "That was probably far more than you wanted to know.''

Turning her around, he slid his hands over her stiff, proud shoulders, down her arms until he could grasp her hands and link their fingers. "It was *exactly* what I wanted to know,'' he assured her. He wanted to ease her pain as she'd eased his, he wanted to let her know he was there for her, but Zoe was a woman for which words didn't mean much. It had to be action.

Action was fine with him.

He bent and kissed her softly, lightly. Then again, and when he pulled away, she made a soft sound of protest. "I hope we'll share more of ourselves,'' he said. "Like we did tonight.''

"Ty—''

"Shh.'' He kissed her again. Then lifted his lips and smiled when she moaned at the break of contact. "I just

realized you need 'slow.' I'm not a patient man, but I think
this just might be worth giving it a shot." He squeezed her
hands and let go. "Now. About hiring a staff."

Her delicious lips parted in surprise at the quick change
of subject. Relief filled her gaze, and he knew he'd done
the right thing by backing off in a moment when she burned
for more.

Maybe with a little more of that patience he wasn't so
good at, she'd continue to open up and let him in.

All the way in.

Chapter 14

For one solid week, everyone worked like crazy. The inside of the ranch house got its second coat of paint. The cottages were cleaned out and also painted, the arena and corral fences repaired, the barn finished, and they had daily meetings on all that their guest ranch would entail.

Advertising went out for their first season, which normally wouldn't start until next spring, but they couldn't survive without income through the winter. So they would open in the fall, have one very short season, then start again in the spring. For now, they would probably take winters off, until they were more comfortable with all that an incredibly heavy snow load would bring. They needed to hire a handful of experienced staff since it had become clear they would need help immediately.

Maddie wanted to create a first-class kitchen that would rival any five-star restaurant. Delia, always the social one, wanted to handle the decorating of the cottages and main lodge, then also the housekeeping, reservations and front-desk activities. Zoe would handle the financial aspect, manage the staff and also learn the outside duties. Ranch hands would take on the animals and the daily guided rides, overseen by Ty. They hoped to also provide hiking, rafting and big-game hunting.

At the end of an exhausting week, the weather turned unusually chilly. At dark one night everyone gathered around a hot, crackling bonfire. Cade was in town, and the five of them sat on fallen logs, relaxing for the first time in weeks.

Maddie provided hot chocolate, which Cade had liberally doctored with brandy, insisting it was necessary for warmth.

Unused to the alcohol, Zoe watched with fuzzy eyes as everyone's tongue loosened. She struggled with a dark mood, brought on by Cade's unhappy news.

Now news on her mother. The need to know continued to gnaw at her, eating at her insides.

Cade helpfully refilled her drink often as she sat there and listened to the wood crackle pleasantly, the occasional cry of a coyote, a hoot of an owl. The scent of the outdoors was strong, too, of pine and fire and water. Easy to lose herself in her own world while the others talked and laughed around her.

"Truth or dare," Cade said suddenly, grinning broadly in the dark. "Let's play."

"That game is for the very young or the very drunk," Delia said haughtily, and Zoe smiled at the tone. Cade could have suggested a full shopping spree on him at Saks Fifth Avenue and still Delia would have scoffed.

"You first, Delia," Cade decided. "Seeing as you fit both the criteria. Truth…or dare?"

Delia lifted her nose and ignored him. To everyone's

surprise, Maddie laughed. "Chicken," she chided, and Delia gaped at her.

"I'm no such thing!" She whirled on Cade. "I'm not chicken."

"Then play." He raised his eyebrows comically, daring her.

"Fine. Dare then, you idiot."

"Okay." Even in the dark he looked mischievous. "I dare you to kiss me."

Delia's jaw dropped. *"What?"*

Maybe it was the brandy, but Zoe burst out laughing at Delia's expression as all composure escaped her usually so-composed sister. It was just absolutely priceless.

As she laughed, she caught Ty's eye. He smiled slowly at her, an approving, warm smile that made her feel all the more fuzzy and dizzy, all the way to her toes, and her laughter faded.

Her warm, fuzzy feeling did not. She almost fell off her log staring at him as her bones melted away, and in return his smile turned hot and knowing.

Delia folded her arms over her chest, looking prim and proper in spite of how she weaved back and forth from too much spiked hot chocolate. *"Truth,"* she said, lifting her chin. "Because all the brandy in the world couldn't make me desperate enough to kiss you."

Cade grinned, uninsulted. "Okay. Your most memorable sexual experience, then."

"What about it?"

"Tell us the details."

And if Zoe had laughed at Delia's expression before, she roared now, holding her aching sides as she let go.

Delia, horrified, just glared at her.

"You know what a forfeit is, dear Delia?" Cade asked

sweetly, and they all roared again when Delia eloquently told Cade where to put his suggestion.

"Okay, never mind. I'll start," Cade relented, still grinning. "Um, let's see…most memorable sexual experience… In an elevator."

"An elevator?" Shocked, Zoe pictured the short distance between any two floors. How did that work? she wondered. "Wow, Cade."

"Oh, don't encourage him!" Delia tried to hold on to her frown, but gave in with a laugh and a quick swig of her laced drink. "Fine, then," she said, refortified with courage and brandy. "Started in an open field, blanketed by wildflowers." She lifted a saucy brow at Cade. "Satisfied?"

Of course he wasn't, he was full of trouble, and it shone from his eyes. "*Started?*" he said, wanting clarification. "Or *finished?* It makes all the difference, you know."

"Bees. Lots of bees," Delia said with a remembered shudder. "Ruined the mood."

As they laughed and drank more hot chocolate, everyone turned to Maddie, who went beet-red. "I can't think of anything," she said quickly, so obviously embarrassed that no one had the heart to press her.

"Zoe?" Cade asked, and all heads swiveled to her expectantly.

Her amusement quickly faded. "This is *so* immature."

"But wicked fun," Cade encouraged. "Come on. Your turn. Most memorable sexual experience."

"Um…" With brandy buzzing her veins and everyone looking at her, it was hard to think, but she felt no one's gaze as much as Ty's, and suddenly she couldn't come up with anything.

It might have been the fact she had consumed far more alcohol than she was used to.

It might have been that she had only one experience in her life to even discuss, and that had been pathetically short and completely unsatisfying.

Or it might have been that she didn't want to talk about it in front of the one man in her entire life she'd actually fantasized about. Other than Mel Gibson, that is.

"I can help you out here, I think," Ty said kindly.

"You can?" Relief was so great, Zoe beamed at him, thinking he was pretty darn nice as well as gorgeous. Maybe even as gorgeous as Mel.

"Uh-huh." His smile spread, causing her stomach to do little flip-flops that had nothing to do with the brandy. "Let's see…" He considered her seriously as he stroked his chin. "I'd have to say in the barn."

Wait, Zoe thought, befuddled. Wait a minute. He was talking about him and *her!* Ty laughed, a low, sexy sound that had heat and longing spearing Zoe's skin.

"Alas, also unconsummated," he added regretfully.

Delia's eyes widened. "Zoe? With…*you.* In the barn?"

Zoe decided Ty wasn't nearly so cute anymore. And not nice at all. In fact, she was going to kill him, just as soon as her vision cleared and she could figure out which one of his two heads was the right one.

"Oh, boy," Maddie whispered. Then she giggled, slapped her hand over her mouth and started to shake with laughter. "Oh, boy."

Delia bit her bottom lip, but couldn't hold back. Soon the two of them were screaming with laughter, tears spilling down their faces as they struggled not to fall off their log.

"I don't see what's so funny!" Zoe stood, wavered on her feet, than glared down at her sisters. "And you didn't ask him *why* it was unconsummated. For your information, I punched his lights out!"

"Uh, Zoe? Actually, you slugged me only the first

time," Ty corrected her helpfully. "The second and third time we made out, you kissed me back. A lot."

Zoe stalked off into the night then, in tune to Maddie and Delia's shrieks of laughter. Face hot, heart racing, she stormed, her legs churning up the rough ground.

Definitely going to kill him, she thought, stumbling over her own two left feet. The nerve, the absolute nerve! That he had been correct didn't matter in the least. "I wish I could just forget the whole thing," she muttered, passing the barn in a huff.

"No, you don't."

At the sound of the man who had just given her sisters ammunition to tease her with for years to come, Zoe sped up her pace, refusing to even look at him. "Go away."

She didn't look at him, just kept going, needing a place to be alone where she could wallow in her mortification in peace.

Ty followed; she could hear his footsteps, much smoother than her own clumsy ones. Why had she drunk so much? She never drank. In the morning she was going to kill Cade, too, just on principle.

Her own breathing rang sharp in her ears as she passed the cottages, and on the cold night, her breath fogged in front of her face. Behind her, Ty wasn't even laboring, which only infuriated her all the more.

Before she knew it, she had come to the edge of Triple M and stood staring down at Ty's much smaller spread. He'd left the lights on in his house. It looked warm and inviting, and confusion welled as she wavered.

"You're the only one," she whispered, facing the night but talking to the silent man behind her. "The only one I've ever let see me. You know, the *real* me."

His voice was just as hushed. "Have you asked yourself why?"

She hesitated, feeling emotionally stripped. "I don't know why. I don't understand. No one else...ever," she trailed off lamely. She shivered and he made a low sound of...regret?

"Come on," he said, touching her hand with his. "You're cold. I'll make more hot chocolate—*without* the brandy."

"I'm not drunk." But she went meekly with him, suddenly realizing she had to concentrate on each footstep, one at a time, because walking had never been quite so difficult.

"How many times did you let Cade fill your mug?"

"At least one too many."

He laughed softly in agreement. They went down the hill, into the most beautiful wilderness she'd ever seen. Of course she couldn't see much now, not in the dark. But she didn't have to see, she could remember. It was forever imprinted on her soul, this new home of hers. The wildflowers, which were so abundant they were show-offs in the day's breeze. The trees, which outnumbered the trout in the river, but not by much. She knew Lewis and Clark had called this land Paradise, and she thought they were right. It *was* paradise. Her paradise.

The night seemed to swallow them. Zoe shivered again. Ty let go of her hand and wrapped a strong arm around her, and never in her life could she remember feeling so safe.

"I want to be able to forget our kisses, but you keep reminding me," she said, bewildered. Definitely too much brandy. It loosened her tongue.

"Why would you want to forget?"

Now he was breathing heavily and she realized it was because he was supporting her weight as well as his. Good, served him right. "Because they felt so good. Why is that, Ty? Do you practice a lot?"

"No." But he was grinning, she could heard it in his voice when he spoke. "Man, are you going to be mad at yourself tomorrow."

"It's not my fault, really, that I melt when you kiss me. It's because I haven't been kissed like that in…" *Forever.* "Well, a long time," she said defensively. "You can't blame me for turning into Jell-O when you touch me."

"Can't blame you one bit," he agreed, hoisting her closer when she threatened to slide down to the ground.

She waved her hand when she talked, nearly slapping him in the face. "And now Maddie and Delia will never let me forget that I've kissed you, not when I've been pretending to hate you."

He tucked his tongue into his cheek and vowed to get her drunk more often.

Finally they made it to his front door. When he got her inside, he headed toward his fireplace, wanting to get her warmed before he drove her home.

"Your house. It's…lovely." She craned her neck, looking around. He knew what she saw—high wood-beamed ceilings, rustic interior, sparse but comfortable furniture.

She met his gaze as he hunkered by the fireplace, match in hand. "It's a home," she said with some surprise. "A real one."

"Yes." He knew exactly what she meant, for their backgrounds weren't all that different. Neither of them had belonged before, had ever had a true home. The ranch house was his first, and it gave him one of his few good pleasures because it was warm and cozy and everything he imagined a real home should be.

"But…" Distress filled her expression. "I don't want to know this about you," she whispered, suddenly looking stone-cold sober. She wrapped her arms around herself, confused. "I don't want to know you're capable of this, that you can…"

He lit the kindling, then rose to his feet in one movement, suddenly restless. "You don't want to know I'm a real man with real needs like warmth and comfort and love and affection?" Anger was a slow, inexorable burn in the pit of his belly. "A man who maybe isn't just after your land, but maybe something much, much more important?"

"Yes, that," she agreed softly, backing up as he took a step toward her.

The fire crackled, the night outside the windows was complete. Inside was close and toasty and soothing. It absolutely terrified the woman in front of him in a way he understood better than anyone else would.

"You said we'd go slow," she whispered hoarsely as he came close.

"Yeah, well, I think I've just ran out of 'slow.'" He tossed aside the matches and reached for her. "Face it, Zoe. You're not mad because I told your sisters we kissed. You're mad because you liked it, because you know you want more. But mostly you're mad because you know that those kisses meant more than just sexual tension—which, by the way, is running between us so hot I can no longer even function."

She swallowed and took another step away from him, her gaze glued to his lips, which made him instantly hard.

"Tell me, Zoe," he said quietly, stalking her in the living room, unable to handle her distance. "Tell me now, when you're staring at my mouth as if you could devour it, tell me, dammit, the *truth*. That those kisses meant more than anything, more than even your wildest dreams."

"I…I don't want them to."

"It's too late."

"No! Don't you understand?" she cried. "I can't give myself when I don't even know who that is!"

That stopped him. "You know who you are."

"No, I don't, I know *nothing* about myself. *Nothing!* Not what kind of place I came from. Not my heritage, my culture." Slowly she shook her head, staring off into space. "I don't know if my father ever held me. Hell, I don't even know if he knows I exist! It drives me crazy that I can't remember."

"You were only three," he said softly. "Just a baby, Zoe. It's not your fault."

She wanted to believe that. "I just wish I knew why my mother left me."

"You could try to find her," he suggested quietly.

"I've tried. Cade's working on it, but there's nothing. She's gone and I have no idea who I am."

He was shaking his head. "*You* decide who Zoe is, no one else can do that. It doesn't matter if you were born in the gutter, no one can take *you* away from *you.*"

He was talking from experience, they both knew that.

"And then there's you," she whispered. "You make me feel things…things I don't want to feel. You want to know me, you want me to let you in…." She let out a pained laugh. "You want me to let you in when I can't find the door to open. I mean, I can't even tell you what my father's name was, Ty."

"Zoe." There was compassion in his voice and something that sounded very much like pity, which she couldn't take. She was going to break down right here in front of him if she so much as blinked.

"I'm sorry," he said so gently her eyes filled. She needed out. Now.

"I'm thirsty," she muttered, and dashed into the kitchen, swiping at her eyes.

When Ty followed her, he found her standing in front of his opened refrigerator.

"I need something to eat," she said with a hitched breath.

"I thought you were thirsty."

"Well, now I'm hungry."

He sighed. "I'll take you home."

"You...you want me to go?"

He looked at her, saw the fear and nerves, and cursed himself for pushing her. Cursed himself for caring so much. "Fine. You won't talk, but you want food." He yanked a tub of ice cream out of the freezer and dropped it on the counter. Grabbing a can of whipped cream from the refrigerator, he shoved it at her. "Go for it."

Reflexively she took the can, clutched it to her chest. "I don't know what you want from me."

"I want..." What *did* he want from her? "Hell," he muttered.

"See?" she cried. "It's not that easy, is it?"

"Yes, it is," he decided. "I want you to open up and talk to me."

"No, you want me to tell you how I feel about you."

"That, too," he agreed.

"But— But you've never told me how *you* feel."

No, he had to agree, he hadn't.

"Tell me, Ty."

Without warning, his heart started pumping, because she was right, it wasn't nearly as easy to define as he'd thought. He stared at her, struggling. "Zoe—"

"Oh, forget it." Turning from him, she touched the container of ice cream. "I don't want to know how you feel, anyway."

A blatant lie, but one he was willing to let her have at the moment, because for some reason he was frightened, truly frightened. Big, bad, tough Ty Jackson, scared to death by this woman. "I want you," he said to her back. "There's more, but I'm not sure I'm ready for the rest."

"Convenient."

"Honest," he corrected her. "I won't ever hurt you with lies, Zoe."

"So you want me. That's not really that big of a secret, Ty."

"Neither is the fact you want me back."

She stiffened and clammed up, which infuriated him. "Eat," he said, opening the carton. "Go on. Keep pretending you're not the least bit affected by me, that you feel nothing—"

She whirled around. "At the moment, I don't have to pretend a thing!"

"You're so full of—"

She popped the top off the whipped cream and sprayed it in his mouth and on his face, muffling the rest of his sentence.

Cold stickiness clouded his brain so that for a moment he could only gape at her, he was so shocked. She was shocked, too, if her wide eyes were any indication. Slowly those eyes blinked, then ran over his face, stopping at the sight of the cream around his mouth. Ty licked his lips to speak and her eyes were riveted to the action.

Heat spiraled through him irrationally. He didn't stop to think about the wisdom of his actions, he simply reached for her, but she was quicker. Backing up a step, she aimed the can at him and looked comically fierce. "Don't take another step," she warned.

No way was she going to squirt him again, he thought, taking another step.

She shot him in the chest and stomach, layering whipped cream over his shirt.

"You're going to be very sorry for that," he promised, grabbing her, wrestling the can from her hand and, without qualm, using his superior strength to wrap a long arm around her, holding her immobile against his side. He held up the can with a nasty smile.

"Don't you dare," she choked, wriggling against him in a way that had his blood boiling.

"*Never* dare me, Zoe." With that he deliberately and slowly shot whipped cream over her, ignoring her struggles and squeals. Or maybe using them as an excuse to shoot lower, across her front. Her outer plaid shirt, unbuttoned, had come off her shoulders in the struggle, pinning her arms to her sides. All the more perfect, he thought diabolically. It took only a couple of more squirts to have her T-shirt plastered to her breasts, the firm curves perfectly outlined for his enjoyment.

Her nipples were hard and straining against the thin cotton, and his mouth watered. His body tightened and he held her still, staring down at the sight he'd created, wondering how in the hell he was supposed to let her go now.

"I'm going to scream," she gasped, but her eyes told him something entirely different.

"Yeah?" he whispered thickly. "Do it." Still holding her, he bent her back over his arm and put his mouth to her throat, sucking the gooey stuff from her skin in little love bites, waiting to see if she made good on her threat.

She didn't scream at all, but moaned and clutched at him. He trailed his tongue down, licking as he went, and Zoe went wild in his arms, leaving no doubt in his mind as to what she wanted. He dragged openmouthed kisses down, down, then hovered over an aroused and waiting nipple.

She stopped breathing.

So did he.

He felt as though he were drowning in desire, needing

her beyond all sanity. His tongue darted out and licked at her through her cotton T-shirt and she did scream then, arching up so that he could suck her breast into his mouth.

When she was without reason, Ty lifted his head, gazing down into her flushed, damp face. "This is where you belong, Zoe. In my arms. I'm going to prove it to you."

Her eyes cleared and flashed, her mouth opened, surely to claim otherwise, and he took full advantage, swallowing her angry words with his lips. He could taste the lingering brandy, and her own sweet breath. Could taste her desire, and the fear of that very thing. Could taste the confusion and remembered pain of her past, and that hurt he tasted touched him as nothing else could have.

Gentling the kiss, he drew her even closer, sank his fingers into her glorious, now-sticky hair and deepened their connection. She responded immediately, pressing against him with an urgency he understood all too well. This had been too long in the coming, too much tension, and he had no idea if he could slow down enough to do it right.

But then he slid his hips against hers and she stiffened in his arms, inexperienced and uncertain. There was just something about her, so wise and yet innocent, and it tugged at his soul.

And he knew in that moment that for her, he *could* slow down.

He could do anything.

"Zoe."

She looked at him from beneath slumberous green eyes. Their bodies were glued together by the whipped cream, belly to belly, chest to chest. He wanted to make love with her, but he wanted so much more. And even more shocking, he wanted her to want those things, too. "I want—"

"Kiss me again, Ty."

"But—"

"Dammit, you started this, now kiss me!"

Taking matters into her own hands, she wriggled her hands free, grabbed his ears and pulled his head down to hers.

The kiss was wild, and he was weak, losing himself in the woman holding him as if she'd never experienced anything like it before. As if he were all she could ever want.

A nice fantasy, but he wanted it to be a reality. *His* reality. "Zoe—"

"You talk too much," she murmured against his lips. "Make love to me instead. Please, Ty. Make love to me."

Chapter 15

So much for him claiming this woman as his own. Zoe was doing that for him.

She reached for the hem of his sticky shirt. Pulled it over his head. Stared in wide wonder at his bared chest, letting out an appreciative breath that made him laugh shakily.

"You're so beautiful," she whispered.

He did the same, pulled off her shirt, and was equally awed. "Not like you." His voice was thick with need, and he was surprised he could speak at all. "I want you, Zoe. I want you skin to skin, beneath me. I want to hear you cry my name as I sink into you." Her eyes darkened to a forest green, her breath quickened. "I want you wild for me," he whispered. "Only me. Always only me."

Now fear flared in her again, mixing with her need, and he didn't care because this kind of fear he could assuage. Once again he drew her close, slipping his hands down her bare sides, his thumbs flirting with the curves of her breasts.

"I want you to want me back, to give me everything you have. One hundred percent of you, the real you."

Even in a haze of desire, she understood every word, which only increased her fear. She had hurt him by holding back and he needed to know, in this one area at least, that she would give all. But she herself was just beginning to know the real Zoe. How could she share that woman? "Ty—"

His fingers played with the front clasp of her bra.

"Um...Ty?"

The clasp fell open.

"I..."

"What, sweetheart?" His hands found her bare breasts and every thought danced right out of her head.

She wanted skin to skin, too. She wanted to be beneath him. She wanted to go wild, right here, right now, because in Ty's arms she was everything she wanted to be. He could make her feel loving, warm, wonderful...a somebody. In his arms she was a passionate, hungry, beautiful woman, and she liked it.

She surged forward and kissed him, and it wasn't sweet or tender. It was hot, deep and full of need. She jerked him closer, then closer still, until she could feel every sticky, powerful muscle of him. She could feel his hard length behind the buttons on his jeans, and when she slid against it as he had done to her earlier, he moaned low in his throat, a sound that thrilled her.

"Be sure." His voice was gritty, harsh.

He was barely holding on to his control, and Zoe's excitement surged. She'd never been more sure of anything in her life. "*Now,* Ty. Please, now."

He pressed her back against the counter. His expression was fierce, nearly violent. "All of you," he demanded. "This time, all of you."

He wasn't talking about her body now, but he'd take that, too. "Yes."

Her simple acquiescence fueled him. Lifting her left leg up and around his waist, he pressed himself intimately against her, making her gasp. His eyes flared as he slid himself against her slowly in a mimic of what he really wanted to do. His tongue teased hers, his hands streaked over her. The rhythm of his hips drove her to the very edge, making her dizzy and overwhelmingly out of control. Consumed by heat, crazed for more of this sampling of true passion and undeniable need, she dragged him down to the floor.

"Zoe." His voice was so rough and grainy she hardly recognized it. "Not here," he managed to say, pulling away. "God. Not on the floor, not the first time. Let me—"

"No." She couldn't let reason intrude, and it would if she let him stop now to take her to bed. She wrapped her jeans-clad legs around his waist, holding him, pressing herself against his rigid heat.

He went still, every muscle tense, his eyes glittering. And when he would have spoken again, she slid against that same spot. "Please, Ty."

He growled as his restraint broke. Reaching for her jeans, he nearly tore them off as he dragged them down her legs. His tongue blazed a trail from her jaw down over her neck, licking at any lingering cream he found, making a low sound of approval in his throat as he went. He found the sensitive spot behind her ear, at the hollow of her throat, at the edge of her collarbone. And finally, oh finally, the taut, aching tip of her nipple, which he took into his warm mouth, sucking deeply until she was arching and writhing and rolling her hips, unable to catch her breath.

His hands stroked her, soothed and tormented all at once, until she felt as though she were on fire, sensations and emotions ripping her apart as she'd never felt before. His fingers stroked her thighs, shifting them open to touch her moist, creamy center, which he purposely and slowly traced with his finger. "Please, please..." she gasped over and over, mindlessly unaware of what she was saying.

But Ty knew, and he understood the fire. He'd wanted her like this, consumed and beyond all reason. Only he hadn't expected that fire to be his, too.

She was wet, hot and all his, and it was all he could do to keep from sinking into her, burying himself deep and taking them over the edge with just one stroke.

Impatient with his pace, Zoe surged up and yanked on his jeans, tearing at them until he helped. "Tell me you replaced the condoms for new ones," she gasped.

He had, and she got yet another first that night—rolling one on, which was such a turn-on they were both sweating by the time she had finished. They rolled over the floor, kissing, stroking, nipping, licking...moaning.

He tucked her beneath him, holding her face in his hands as he looked down at her with a hungry tenderness. "Zoe...sweetheart...is this your first time?"

She laughed breathlessly, both exhilarated and embarrassed. "I'm not a virgin, but—I've never..."

"Had an orgasm?"

She reddened at his characteristic bluntness and nodded.

"You'll come for me," he promised in a thrilling whisper. "Soon."

He rolled again, taking her with him. On his back on the linoleum, Ty lifted her up to straddle him. She felt... exposed. "Bend down a little," he coaxed. "Yeah, like that. Just like that." And he took a breast into his mouth, teasing the aching peak with his nimble tongue. Her hips moved restlessly against his, brushing against him until he groaned her name. "Take me," he murmured, his hands on her hips, urging her. "Zoe, take me."

She hesitated a moment, which nearly killed him, then she was sinking, sliding down on him one slow inch at a time, until he was buried deep. They both let out a gratified sigh.

Gripping his shoulders, she dropped her head so that he was draped in her beautiful, wild hair. She stared at where they were joined, and she went utterly still.

She had changed her mind and he was going to die. Right here on the floor, still coated in whipped cream and covered by Zoe.

"It's...so..." Experimentally she shifted, staring at him now, her eyes so dark they were black. "It's...oh, Ty, it's amazing," She closed her eyes. Her head fell back now, her body arched, her breasts thrust out. "Don't stop."

"Never," he promised, but "never" came far too soon as she slowly rocked her hips on him. He was shaking with the urge to grab her hips and thrust deep, but he wanted the pace to be hers, wanted to see her shatter over him. With his thumb, he stroked her slowly. She gasped. Her breathing came in short, little pants. Her hips rocked faster, then faster. She whispered his name, her eyes flying open to gaze at him in wonder, in an open way that allowed him to see into her soul.

He lost it then, gripping her hips, plunging into her until she moaned his name again, until she convulsed and shuddered and came over him in a mind-shattering explosion that triggered his own.

His heart thundered beneath her ear. His skin stuck to her. Though it took every last bit of energy she had, she smiled.

"I'm not sure anything about that was amusing," Ty

managed to say, his hand caressing her back where she lay collapsed on him in a trembling, contented heap.

"I'm thinking it was the whipped cream that did it for me," Zoe said. "You know…the missing ingredient." Embarrassment hit her then, because her admission that what they'd just shared had beat anything in her experience seemed naive. "I mean—"

"I know what you mean." His hand came up to cup her cheek. His other arm snugged her closer against him, a protective, possessive gesture that somehow warmed her. All trace of humor was gone when he answered, "And it wasn't the whipped cream, Zoe. It's us."

Commitment terrified her, that hadn't changed with their little kitchen romp. No matter how wild, how hot, how soul-shattering it had been for her, she still couldn't find the words to tell him he was right.

She didn't make promises. They were meant to be broken. And he'd made none himself.

Beneath her, he sighed, stroked her back once more, then sat up with her still against him.

The kitchen light was suddenly harsh, and Zoe was far too naked.

Ty rose to his feet, jaw tight and eyes sad. He picked up her T-shirt, shook his head at the whipped cream clinging to it and reached for a soft plaid shirt that lay across the back of one of his kitchen chairs.

"Here." Gentle hands belied the gruffness of his voice as he dressed her, even buttoning the shirt for her. When the backs of his fingers brushed against her skin, she sucked in her breath in response, her nipples hardening yet again.

A muscle in his cheek twitched at the sight, but he didn't say a word, just handed over her jeans.

It was a shock to see him standing there completely, gloriously nude. Silly, after what they'd just shared, but she was completely unprepared for the "after," especially when he looked so casual—and magnificent—in the buff.

She'd known he was perfectly made, she'd spent many covert moments watching his tough, rugged body as he worked outside on the two ranches these past weeks.

But without clothes...wow. He was hard, lean, his shoulders broad, his torso long. Her eyes continued downward, then halted abruptly, startled.

He was aroused again.

Caught staring, she brought her gaze up to his wryly amused one. She thought of the other condom.

Behind his amusement was a wealth of hurt, hurt that *she'd* put there. She turned away to slip on her shoes. "I'm sorry."

"Regrets already." His voice was carefully blank, nothing like the husky one that only moments before had been whispering sexy promises in her ear.

The only regret she had at the moment was ruining this magical time with him, but she had no idea how to get that languid, deliciously relaxed feeling back. No idea what to do or say.

So she stood there, facing the back door with her arms wrapped around herself in growing misery.

"Safe to look," he said, and when she turned, she saw that he'd pulled on his jeans, leaving off his whipped-cream-covered T-shirt. He was holding his keys.

"I'll walk," she said quickly.

"No you won't." He opened the door for her.

The Idaho night was dark and unforgiving. Unrelenting. And for the first time since she'd arrived in this state, she resented it.

Ty needed to use his frustration and anger to his advantage, needed to turn it into energy. Energy worked for him, it allowed him to *do* instead of *think,* because if he started thinking he might go mad.

He had promised himself he'd be patient with Zoe, that he'd show her in actions how he felt, which were far better than promises she wouldn't believe, anyway.

But even those actions hadn't been enough.

He'd rushed her.

And even knowing that, he couldn't pull back. The more he was with her, the more he wanted, and the wanting was a burning, undeniable need.

But he was the only one wanting and needing, and that hurt.

It had to stop. He had a job to do, and for now it would be enough. It had to be.

Strangely enough, in the midst of all this turmoil over Zoe, he felt more in peace thinking about Ben than he ever had, and he knew that was because he'd talked about Ben and felt better. The dream that had haunted him would serve another purpose, one they hadn't intended, but a good one nevertheless. Ben would have loved the idea of the guest ranch.

The morning after the whipped cream fight he would never forget—and he doubted he'd ever look at whipped cream the same way again—Ty rose before dawn, completed some chores, got his ranch hands and trainers set up for a day's work. Then he headed over to Triple M.

He had a guest ranch to prepare.

He told himself it didn't matter what Zoe said or did this morning, he would act normal. If she wanted to pretend that the wildest, hottest, most soul-shattering lovemaking hadn't happened only hours before, fine.

He could pretend with the best of them.

He hoped she was as miserable as he. That she hadn't

slept any more than he had, which was all of about three minutes.

When he discovered Zoe was still in bed, his disposition didn't improve.

"What do you mean she's not up yet?" he asked Maddie, who handed him a mug of steaming coffee.

"She's...ah...pretty miserable." Maddie glanced upward and lifted a shoulder. "I think she's hungover, to tell you the truth. She's not used to drinking."

"Hmm." He set down his coffee and headed for the hallway door.

"Ty, where are you going?" Maddie called out, alarmed. "She's in a bear of a mood. Ty! Come back here, you'll get your head bitten off."

"Don't worry, Maddie," he called back over his shoulder. "She's crazy about me."

He found her in bed. She was a burrower, he thought. Not even an inch of her showed from beneath her covers. Just her thick auburn hair. The hair he'd thought to see spread across *his* pillow this morning.

God, just looking at her made his heart ache, and that really ticked him off. She should be in *his* bed, under *his* covers, burrowed up against *him*.

Shutting and locking her bedroom door behind him, he moved to the bed, intending to rudely rip the covers off and demand she get up and work.

So they could both suffer.

Instead, he found himself sinking to the mattress and dipping a hand beneath the covers, just to touch her. To feel her warm, soft, giving body, just once more.

He found her body, all right, and smooth, bare skin.

Beneath the quilt she was completely nude.

Groaning, he leaned over her, his mouth hovering close to her ear. "Get up, Zoe. There's work to do." In contrast to his rough words, his hand smoothed down over her shoulder, down her side to her hip, squeezing gently.

Zoe made a soft noise and turned onto her back. Which put his hand low on her belly. He glanced at her face, but she was still sleeping deeply, with her body warm and silky beneath his fingers. God. He inched down until his palm was filled with her and found her damp. He groaned again, sucking gently on her ear.

"Ty..." she mumbled. "Don't go."

"I won't," he said, thinking she'd woken.

But she hadn't, she was still out. "Don't desert me, too," she murmured.

In that moment, his heart shattered. So much for his resolve to stay away from her. "I won't, Zoe...I promise."

A promise. Oh Lord, he was in deep now.

Another sigh escaped her, a deeper one, and her legs opened as she pressed herself into his hand.

It was too much. He was just a man. A very weak, red-blooded man who was about ready to explode from just touching her. "Zoe," he whispered, half hoping she'd wake up and shove him away.

Instead she arched up, and he was a goner. Sliding one finger into her, he leaned closer and kissed her mouth, his tongue plunging in tune to his moving hand.

Making soft mewling noises that nearly undid him, Zoe gripped him tight, writhing against him, rocking her hips, gasping, melting...then shuddering, shuddering, shuddering.

Hot and dying, Ty kept on touching her until she quieted, thinking he hadn't felt so out of control without being touched himself since he'd been a teenager.

Her eyes flew open and she stared at him, her breathing harsh and uneven.

It took a moment for those eyes to clear completely, but

when they did, she shot straight up, clutching the blanket to herself. Mute, she stared at him, blinking uncertainly.

He wondered if she was hoping she'd dreamed the entire thing and he was just hot enough, just miserable enough to not be kind. "I don't suppose you'd think it was my turn now."

Her eyes closed. Her face went beet-red. And he felt marginally better, but his jeans were still far too tight.

Zoe's hands went up to her head. "I think my head is going to fall off."

Not exactly the romantic words he'd hoped for. But since her face had gone from red to green, he believed her.

She dropped her hands and looked at him. "I...I thought maybe I was dreaming...?"

Slowly he shook his head. "Not that last part, no."

She nodded, and her eyes fell to his lap and his very obvious arousal, then widened. Visibly, she swallowed. "Ty—"

"Get up, Zoe." His words were harsher than he'd intended as he rose, but dammit, he was frustrated beyond hell.

He tossed her a pair of jeans he found on the floor. "I'll be outside waiting. Hurry."

"I'll get there when I get there."

Seemed Sleeping Beauty had fully awoken and had sharpened her tongue. "Get there fast," he said calmly, meeting her gaze steadily. "Or I'll come back for you."

He shut her door behind him, grinning when he heard something hit the other side of the door, right about head-level.

It hit with the solid thunk of a brand-new boot.

Zoe showed up relatively quickly, which surprised Ty. He thought she might have stayed back dwelling on things, stalling, doing whatever it was a woman did while she pouted.

But she came outside in less than half an hour, not a sulk in sight. The sun lit her hair like fire as she walked toward him, looking more beautiful than any heartbreaker had a right to look. Her slim body was encased in jeans and yet another T-shirt, void of whipped cream. She was wearing her new boots and her gloves. She looked comfortable, confident and well suited for the beautiful but harsh environment of ranching.

Pride flowed through him at her versatility. At her resilience.

She came close, and he saw that her eyes were red.

Dammit. "You've been crying," he accused, tossing down his gloves and moving toward her with guilt and need and a million other things. "Not about what happened in your bed—"

"Don't be ridiculous."

"Zoe—"

She lifted her chin but didn't quite meet his gaze. "Back off, Ty. This is work. Where do we start?" She saw the cans of paint. "At the cottages?"

He lifted her chin in his cupped hand. "Tell me why you were crying."

Not surprisingly, she slapped his hand away. "It's nothing." When she whirled away from him, he saw the folded piece of paper sticking out her back pocket, and not knowing why, he grabbed it.

She went wild, leaping at him, tackling him down to the hard ground—which happened to be wet, dammit—clawing and reaching to get the paper he perversely held just out of reach.

"Gee, I guess it has something to do with this," he drawled from flat on his back. She was straddling him, leaning over his body so that her breasts just grazed his chest. Rather than groan and crush her to him, which he nearly did on instinct, he grinned up into her face. "You sure like to be on top."

"Give it back."

At her pale, drawn, panicked expression he lost all ability to tease her. Holding her firmly to him, he sat up and handed back the folded paper.

Startled at his compliance, she took it. Her legs were around his hips, her bottom snugged to his crotch. An erotically shattering position, and yet it was suddenly so much more than that. Gently he put his hands to her hips, lightly squeezing. "What is it, Slim? Can't you tell me?"

Her eyes filled but the tears didn't spill. She hesitated, then shoved the letter at him. Staring at her, he slowly took it, opened it, then scanned the letter.

It was a short note from Cade, and it had been faxed to the new machine they'd bought to make guest reservations easier.

Dear Zoe,
So sorry, I know all this waiting and wondering is difficult for you. I have some news, small as it is. Your mother was indeed allowed to come and get you for visitation as you thought. Why she never did is a mystery to all involved. She never called, as you'd suspected. And she never wrote. In fact, from the day you were dropped off, she never checked in. Not once.

I'll keep searching for her, Zoe, and I know I'll find something soon.

Your friend, Cade.

Ty read the words, his throat tightening on each word. Here it was in black and white for Zoe to see and deal with for the first time.

She'd indeed been orphaned, purposely and cruelly. And apparently, without the least bit of regret.

"Zoe, I'm sorry—"

She jerked off of him and to her feet. Crossing her arms over herself, she shrugged, refusing to look at him. "Don't be."

"But I am—"

"It doesn't matter."

"Yes, of course it does—"

"I already knew all that stuff, anyway. She dumped me. No big deal."

If he touched her, she was going to break. Normally he'd be running—hell, he'd be *flying*—as far from a crying female as he could get. His mother had used tears a lot; he'd long ago become immune to such things.

Yet Zoe's tears were different—she didn't do it to manipulate or twist or hurt. She hated crying, he knew she did. Watching her struggle now, trying to hide them from him as she swiped at her eyes, did something to him, made him want to slay beasts and hold back entire armies. But the only dragon was Zoe's mental block wall and he had no means to tear it down.

He reached out, needing to fix this for her somehow. "Zoe, sweetheart—"

"No." She held up a hand, backed another step and shook her head violently. "No. I'm fine. I…am just fine. I don't want to talk about it."

"Is there anything we *can* talk about?"

"Look, it's over, okay? My mother dumped me, and I know that. It was dumb to want to find her. Now, can we work?"

And for the rest of the day, she refused to speak about it. About anything that made her feel.

Chapter 16

"Hurry up, would you?" Ty knew he was being a jerk but he couldn't help himself. He had docked his jet boat in Lewiston and was waiting for Zoe.

Normally driving the high-powered aluminum-hulled craft gave him great pleasure. It was practical as well as fun, for in this rough territory he could ascend and maneuver the river safer and faster than the roads, and in a fraction of the time.

But today was different. He and Zoe were standing in town, just the two of them, ostensibly ordering tack and supplies for their prospective guests.

Ty could have done it alone. It certainly would have been easier, for Zoe hadn't wanted to come. But he'd insisted, saying that she hadn't been pulling her weight.

A lie.

One that even Delia had pointed out to him, reminding him that Zoe did indeed work desperately hard. But not even for Delia and Maddie could he relax about their troubled sister. God only knew how she continued to ignore what was between them, but she did. She had for an entire week now, and he was so full of explosive energy and longing he was going to burst.

It wasn't just that he wanted her in his bed, though he did desperately need to hold her. But he was so certain she was going to be able to walk away from what was between them.

Zoe walked next to him on the sidewalk, doing her best to ignore him. She was giving him the silent treatment now, which quite honestly, he probably deserved.

"If I said I'm sorry, will you speak to me?" he asked. He sighed when she didn't answer, and as annoying as that was, he could still remember how shattered and abandoned she'd looked when she'd read Cade's last note. Picturing it now, he thought maybe he could find the words to apologize after all. "Zoe—"

She came to such an abrupt stop, he nearly plowed her over. "What the—"

She pressed her nose to the display in the window.

Ty glanced up at the jewelry store. *A jewelry store?* Zoe never even wore earrings.

"Oh, it's beautiful," she breathed, her eyes glued to a small delicate gold bracelet. Then, catching him gaping at her moment of whimsy, she straightened and walked past him.

Ty stared at the bracelet in surprise. She'd never even hinted at a yearning for anything material before. Her longing to belong to the ranch was an entirely different thing. He watched her move on, chin tilted at a defiant angle.

If he thought she would accept it, he'd have bought the pretty chain for her in an instant, but all she wanted from him was his distance.

Sighing with frustration, he followed her. "Soon enough

you'll be able to buy yourself whatever you want,'' he said quietly as he walked next to her.

She let out a little smile and shook her head. "I hope the guest ranch is that successful, but I don't need anything."

"We all need something once in a while, Zoe."

"Really?" She met his gaze. "What do you need, Ty?"

"You," he said simply, stopping, putting a hand on her arm to stop her, too. "I need you."

There on the sidewalk, with the hot Idaho sun bearing down on them, Zoe closed her eyes.

He stepped closer, leaned in enough so that he could smell her soap, her shampoo, both far sexier than any perfume. "I need you so much I ache with it," he told her.

Her eyes flew open, and her gaze slowly ran over him, down to where his need was usually quite apparent.

He let out a laugh that held little mirth. "I'm not talking about that kind of need, Zoe. The need I'm talking about is greater than anything physical."

"Oh."

"You don't believe that."

"I don't know what I believe anymore." She started walking again.

They spent the rest of the day in tense, terse silence.

Zoe's office window drew her for the tenth time, where she peeked into the yard. Unable to get a really good view, she stretched farther, nearly falling out in the process, but then she could see and what she saw made her blood pump. "Oh Lord," she whispered.

"What's out there?"

Zoe jerked back as Delia and Maddie entered the room. They looked surprised to see her leaning out the window, twisted to see something just out of their vision, and she straightened quickly.

"Nothing," she said as casually as she could. "It's nothing." She shut the curtains nonchalantly.

"Hmm." With a lift of her smooth brow, Delia walked over and lifted a corner of the curtain, then tucked her tongue into her cheek. "Well if 'nothing' is the most gorgeous man I've ever seen, stripped to his tanned, toned waist, working in the sun, then you're right. There's nothing out there, and his name is Ty."

Maddie leaped for a view, and the two of them stood in awe for a moment, watching the man as he reinforced the wood railing on the arena. "Wow."

Muscles gleamed with a faint sheen of sweat as he pounded nails. "Double wow," Delia agreed.

"Oh, for God's sake, you're drooling," Zoe snapped, making them both laugh at her.

"You never did explain that kiss we didn't know about," Delia said lightly.

"*Kisses*," Maddie corrected her helpfully. "Remember at the bonfire? Ty specifically said 'kisses.' And they knocked his socks off. What kind of kiss knocks that kind of man's socks off, I wonder?"

"A damn hot one," Delia guessed, grinning as Zoe rolled her eyes.

"Do you really have nothing to do that you can come in here and drive me insane?" she wondered.

Delia smiled innocently. "What happened, hon? You were working outside, helping Ty. Did it get too…uh, *hot* for you out there?"

It was true, Zoe had been helping outside, in between covert glances at Ty's unbelievably sexy body, until he'd caught her.

He'd come straight to her, dropping his hat and hammer.

His gloves went next. "You keep looking at me like that," he'd vowed in a low whisper for her ears only, "and I'm going to take you into your office and remind you whose turn it is to be satisfied."

At the reminder of what he'd done to her in her bed, at how fast he'd driven her to climax with his mouth and fingers, she'd nearly moaned out loud.

He'd half groaned, half laughed. "Don't say I didn't warn you," he threatened softly. "Because I'll be happy to show you what that look on your face does to me."

Now, in her office with her two grinning, meddling sisters waiting for answers, Zoe cleared her throat and wished it was as easy to clear her mind. "For your information, I had to work on the books," she said primly. She reached for Socks, who was snoozing across her desk. He meowed a lazy greeting, rolled on his back and offered his belly for scratching.

"Coward," Delia said to her, moving back to the door with Maddie. "That man is crazy for you. And I think you're crazy for him." She paused and looked meaningfully into Zoe's eyes. "And you *do* deserve him, Zoe. You, more than anyone I know, deserves a chance at real happiness. At letting a man love her."

Love. Her stomach tightened. "No one said anything about love."

Delia smiled sadly. "No one had to."

"I'm fine, Delia."

"I hope so. This wouldn't by any chance have anything to do with thinking you don't know who you are, would it?"

Zoe sighed and rubbed her temples. "Delia—"

"It's so ridiculous, hon, I'm sorry. You are who you make yourself." She let out a little laugh. "No one knows that better than me. Except for maybe that man out there, the one who's trying not to pay any more attention to you than you are to him.''

"How did we get on this subject?'' Zoe asked, lifting her hands in exasperation. ''I don't want to talk about this.''

"You never do,'' Delia murmured.

"I *am* a coward,'' Zoe told Socks when she was alone, snuggling him closer. ''But God help me, I have no idea what to do. How do I tell him how I feel when I'm not even sure *I* know?''

But deep down, she knew that was a lie. She knew how she felt, she was just too afraid to admit it.

Triple M began to show promise. A few reservations trickled in for fall. Just enough to generate excitement and rejuvenate energies.

No one, least of all Zoe, was able to predict success, and everyone's pocket was stretched to the limit, even Ty's. Still, the feeling of such pride was immeasurable.

Ty was thankful for the long, busy, tireless days. It gave him something to do other than think.

But the truth was, he had finally come to terms with Ben's death, and he knew Ben would be happy with what Ty was doing for Triple M. The loss still hurt, but the mountains, the clear air, the utter peace the wilds gave him worked like a healing balm.

So did Zoe.

He wasn't sure why that was, when for every step he took forward, she shoved them back three, but he just accepted the fact. Zoe had changed his life. For the better.

He was on his horse, checking and retracing one of the day paths they intended to use for guests, when he came upon her. It surprised him, for she was on one of the horses they'd purchased, and she was by herself. A beginner, she'd taken to the saddle the way she took to everything. With utter concentration and conviction. She didn't ride often, she didn't have the time, but he hoped that would change simply because he loved the expression on her face right now. The quiet peace he saw there gave him hope.

Maybe he wasn't the only one the wilds of Idaho had helped to heal.

"You look good up there," he said, and she did, with her hair free and cheeks red from the outdoors. "Like you belong."

"It feels good," she admitted. Beneath her, Misty shifted, impatient to run. Just a moment before that impatience had been her own. She'd wanted to race into the hills, where the wildflowers lined the winding trails through deep woods, along spongy marshes and sagebrush flats. She'd wanted to go and never stop, until she could laugh aloud with the freedom of it all and not be heard.

"Are you happy?"

Ty's sudden question surprised her; the seriousness in his voice did not. He had a hat on today. His dark hair was getting long, his face tanned from the long summer days. He sat in the saddle as if he'd been born there, his broad shoulders relaxed, the reins light in his hand, looking like a man well fitted to his life. To *her* life.

He was a part of her, she realized with some surprise. She'd spent some part of every single day with him for months. He could make her laugh, he could make her cry. He could make her angry.

And he could make her weak with just one, dark, hungry look that tugged at something so elementary, so deep, she couldn't define it.

Truth was, he made her *feel*, and she could no longer envision her life without him in it. "I am happy here," she admitted, a little unnerved by her realization. *I'm happy when I'm with you.*

He shook his head. Sliding off his horse, he came closer, reaching up a hand so that she had no choice but to get down as well.

When they were face-to-face, with him still holding on to one of her hands, he said, "That's not what I asked. Are you happy, Zoe?"

Around them, birds chirped. Insects hummed. The trees blew in the slight breeze. Far above, majestic mountain peaks framed their valley, outlining their home. Staking their territory. It was easy, enjoyable, unspoiled, uncrowded, unhurried. Perfect.

It should be a simple thing, happiness. "I'm..." She blew out a breath, confused.

"You don't know, do you." He considered her with a tilted head and warm eyes. "Or maybe you don't even recognize it."

"Maybe I'm afraid to admit it."

He was startled briefly at her honestly. "It's okay, you know," he said. "You do deserve it, Zoe. Just reach out and grab it." His smile encouraged her. "No one else can do it for you but you." He touched her face, just a light, barely there touch, and Zoe found herself turning her cheek into his callused palm.

She sighed. "I'm happy right now."

His smile was slow in the coming, but worth the wait. Wide and sexy, his lips curved, his eyes smoldered. "What would make you happy all the time?"

"To know who I am."

She could see both compassion and temper mingle in his eyes. "You're Zoe Martin. You're a rancher in Idaho, a woman who loves her sisters. It's that simple."

"It's not," she argued, wishing it were. "I want to belong, and I know that's pathetic, but that's how I feel. I want the truth."

"The truth is right in front of your nose. No one is ever going to make you leave. I'd give you my last penny before that happened."

"I don't want your last penny! I want a birthright."

His eyes softened. "Your life starts now, Zoe, with each passing second." He gave her an endearing grin. "See? Just wasted two of them."

He was something. And he made her laugh. No man had ever done that before. "What do you see in me?" she wondered, amazed that this man could want her.

"Are you kidding?" He seemed stunned at the question. "From the beginning, I knew. I took one look at you that night on the porch. You were terrified then, lost and afraid and in a new place that wasn't half of what you'd expected, but hell if you'd let any of that show. You were so brave." He smiled fondly. "I saw an incredible woman I couldn't take my eyes off of. Your pride, your passion, your everything drew me like a moth to a flame, and I've been getting burned ever since." He let out a little laugh. "Don't you see? You stopped me in my tracks, brought me out of my too-driven goals. Reminded me as I haven't been reminded since Ben was alive that there is so much more to life than work, work, work. I'd gotten locked into that, trying to live my life for a dream that wasn't even mine."

"But Ben wanted—"

"My dreams are different from Ben's. It took me a while, but now I know that he would hate for me to be living my life for him." He reached for her. "I have to live it for *me*, Zoe. You taught me that, watching your joy over this place, watching you come alive…that's what showed me."

He meant it, she realized with surprise and hope and fear. He meant every word. And she understood that he meant it because she felt the same way.

"There can be no one else for me," he told her, his eyes steady and sure as he drew her closer. "No one but you, but until you realize and believe that, it does me no good."

Heart racing, she stared at him, absorbing the first verbal commitment she'd ever heard from him. "You...want me. *Just* me?"

"Hell, yes!" His fingers plowed into his hair, leaving it standing up in little spikes that should have been comic. Instead he looked fierce and wild and as if he could devour her on the spot.

Being devoured didn't seem such a bad thing, but before she could figure out how to make that move, another horse came up the trail. It was ridden by Maddie, and from the look in her eyes, Zoe knew it was going to be bad.

She dismounted and came immediately to Zoe, took her hands and stared into her eyes, her own filled with tears.

"Maddie, you're scaring me," Zoe said urgently. "What is it? Delia?"

"No. Zoe, honey...we just heard from Cade." She looked at Ty and some unspoken communication passed between them. Clearly Maddie decided Ty should stay. That or she figured it would be impossible to get him to go.

"Cade wanted to talk to you," Maddie said. "He's leaving for here now, but I think this will be...easier coming from me."

Zoe's legs felt weak. Maddie never overreacted. Never. "God, Maddie, what? What is it?"

Ty slipped an arm around her waist, silently offering her his support for which she was grateful when Maddie spoke.

"It's your parents, Zoe. Cade finally located them. The files were opened by the judge and Cade was able to trace an old address down."

Relief, fear, anger and then more fear ricocheted through

her. Cade had found them. After so many years she could contact them if she chose and...God. Why had she wanted so badly to find her mother? Obviously the woman wanted nothing to do with her. How pathetic that she'd spent so much time and energy. Pathetic and asinine and stupid.

"She's dead, Zoe. Oh, honey, I'm sorry. But your mother has been gone since the week after she left you at the home. She died from an aneurysm in Arizona, which was why Cade couldn't locate her. She was staying in a hotel where your father had once worked, and when she died, no one knew about you."

It seemed to Zoe that her world stopped. Abruptly. The buzzing insects went silent. The birds went quiet. Even the air stopped moving.

Her mother was dead.

She'd not been purposely deserted.

These realizations hit her at once. She'd spent so many years wasted on regrets and fears, all of it useless.

Maddie's anguish was clear. "Your father's name was Brian Willis."

Brian Willis. Both Ty and Maddie looked at her while she absorbed this. The name meant nothing, no matter how hard she strained to remember.

"He died only weeks before you were born, Zoe," Maddie said. "He was killed in a car accident."

The truth sunk in. They were both gone, both of her parents.

"According to what Cade learned from the owner of the hotel, your mother loved your father madly."

"The owner remembered?"

Maddie's smile was sad and haunted. "Yes, Zoe, he did. It's amazing, I know, but he said he never forgot your parents, the way they were deeply, madly in love. Your mother never recovered from his death. She left you so she could go to the hotel to be close to him in spirit. She was poor and had to work a lot, and couldn't bring you. She planned on coming back.''

"She didn't want to live without him," Zoe murmured, the memory coming from nowhere. She backed away from both Ty and Maddie so she could think. "She couldn't live without him."

And Constance was not her grandmother. The thought came from nowhere. The ranch was not hers.

And her life became fragmented, falling apart right in front of her eyes. All she'd ever wanted, *poof,* gone.

Her fingers came up to her mouth. No crying, she told herself firmly. No being selfish in front of Maddie or Ty, who had both suffered far more in their lives than she ever had.

"Zoe." It was Ty, speaking gently, with a warm, caring tone she couldn't handle. He'd come close and put a hand on her arm, but if she let him so much as touch her, she'd fall apart. And this time, she'd never be able to put herself back together. "No, I'm fine. Fine."

"Zoe, sweetheart, please. Let me—"

"No." It was the endearment that did it, for she suddenly knew the truth from the emotion blaring out of his eyes.

He loved her. God, what would she do now? Unable to stand it, she turned from him.

Her parents were dead, and they'd been dead all those years she'd harbored bitterness and resentment at them for deserting her. Guilt hit, stabbing at her for every negative, mean thought she'd ever had.

Ty was right behind her, not touching her, but she felt his presence in every fiber of her being as he silently gave her his strength. Maddie, too. "I just...need a moment," she said, staring into the lush meadow before her.

She was truly an orphan, always had been, but not because she'd been deserted on purpose.

She wasn't Constance's heir.

And Ty loved her, the real her.

But how was that possible when she didn't even know who that *her* was? Ty was still right there, so was Maddie, and they were clearly worried sick. "Please," she whispered. "I need a moment alone."

"No," Ty and Maddie said at the same time.

Ty reached for her, drew her slowly and steadily into the circle of his arms, undeterred when she struggled. "Shh," he said, holding her to his chest.

Maddie stroked her back.

"I want to be alone, you know." But she clung to him.

"Sorry," Ty murmured. "But not ever again."

She kept resisting, kept pushing, to no avail. And a small part of her was so very grateful.

With the sun overhead and Maddie and Ty holding her, Zoe stopped struggling and closed her eyes, absorbing their love.

Chapter 17

"All right, that about wraps it up, then," Zoe said, addressing the group in front of her. "Any questions?"

She sat on a log in front of the place they'd held their "truth or dare" bonfire a couple of weeks ago. Around her sat Maddie, Delia and the three ranch hands they'd hired for their fall season.

Cade was there, too, he'd come up twice in the past week, both times to offer Zoe as much support and information he could. He was still determined to figure out which of the two remaining sisters was Constance's heir.

Ty watched the informal staff meeting, both annoyed at and proud of the woman sitting there so stoically.

He wanted, as he'd wanted all week, ever since she had gotten the news of her parents, to shake the hell out of her. Shake her until she broke, until she started to deal with everything going on in her head. Until she let it all out.

Then he wanted to yank her close, bury his face in her hair and never let go.

He was losing it big time.

"So we work in twelve-hour shifts?" This from Cliff, who had practically begged Ty to be switched from Ty's ranch to Triple M. Not that he hadn't enjoyed his work at Ty's ranch, but he was excited at the prospect of working with people.

"Yes," Zoe said. "Long days, I know, but you'll only be on four days a week. Thursday through Sunday for now."

"What about if reservations pick up?" Red asked. He had come from a neighboring ranch, a huge man, with a loud, boisterous voice and a quick sense of humor to match his carrot-colored hair. He was also an excellent worker who came greatly recommended.

Zoe smiled at his question, though only Ty knew by its brittle edges that it didn't come from the heart. "Not *if*, Red. When." Laughter erupted. "And when we get too busy, we'll reevaluate the schedule. We'll decide whether to open more days or just be more picky about who we let in."

Ty would bet on the first. He knew Zoe's drive, knew she held high hopes for a booming, reputable guest ranch that people would talk about from all over the States.

Which was fine; he wanted that, too. But what he wanted even more was Zoe's joy back. Her zest for life, the one she had just been beginning to nurture.

"I don't know about you guys," Delia said dryly to everyone. "But I like that schedule. Three days off to play."

"I look at it the opposite." Maddie sighed with pleasure and clear joy. "Four days in which to be in that kitchen all day, concocting huge meals for people who will be starving."

Ty smiled in spite of himself. Delia and Maddie had dealt

with Zoe, mothering and fussing over her. He remembered when he had been part of a unit that tight. When Ben had guessed his every move, had anticipated his every word. When he'd been loved.

It was over now. Ben was gone, and Ty had accepted that. Finally.

But he wanted love again. Wanted to both give and receive it. And looking at the petite, auburn-haired beauty who had made him feel this way, he wished he could have it with her.

The small staff dispersed. Delia and Maddie and Zoe all hugged, then Delia and Maddie set off toward the house.

Zoe stood still, alone in the circle, staring off into the mountains.

Ty came up behind her, knowing he was giving her one more chance to shove him away, but unable to help himself. "That went well," he said.

She shrugged.

He swore.

She glanced at him over her shoulder, her expression frighteningly flat. "Something wrong?"

"Yes, something's wrong." Pain blazed out of her eyes and broke his heart. "You're what's wrong."

"Ty...not now." She walked away from him with a shake of her head, gasping in surprise when he hauled her back.

"That's it," he muttered, pulling her along, stirring dirt up as she dragged her heels, not stopping until they were at his truck. "Get in."

She crossed her arms over her chest. "I have work—"

His short oath told her what he thought of that. "Get in." Leaning past her, he opened the driver's door, not so gently pushing her in, climbing in after her before she could fight him.

"Where are we going?" The peal of the tires in the dirt and the quick acceleration of the truck had her leaning back in the seat, in a deceptive pose of acquiescence.

But Ty didn't let down his guard. He knew if he slowed down, she would be out of the truck in a flash and back out of his life.

He'd had enough of that. It was a gamble, a huge one, and if he lost, he'd lose everything. But he couldn't stand back and not take the chance.

"Ty—"

"Zip it for a moment, Zoe." Tense, he took the off-road path outside his ranch, the path intended for horses only. He knew exactly how far he could take the truck, knew exactly where he was going, and nothing was going to stop him.

Five minutes later he pulled off the trail into a small clearing. He got out of the truck, reached in and grabbed a small blanket, which he tucked under one arm. With the other, he pulled out Zoe, who came very reluctantly.

"Ty, please. I—"

"Come on." Tugging her not all that kindly, he led the way. They were minutes away from the deepest canyon on the North American continent, surrounded by the most amazing, spectacular scenery in the world, but Ty was blind to everything but the stubborn woman beside him. The path quickly became single-tracked, but he didn't let go of her hand, providing support when the nearly nonexistent path climbed sharply.

He heard Zoe huffing behind him and he smiled grimly. Good. An out-of-breath Zoe couldn't talk. Or complain.

Ten minutes later the terrain suddenly evened out. They were standing on a plateau.

"This is ridiculous," she grumbled. "I have a thousand things to do—"

"Look around you." Grimly he dropped the blanket and turned her, his hands firm on her shoulders when she would have jerked away. "Look, dammit. Look and then tell me what you see."

The glance she shot him was full of daggers, but she didn't waste any more breath. She looked.

And gasped.

Then raced to the edge of the cliff they stood on and let out a soft sigh. "Oh. Oh, it's beautiful."

Far below them was the valley where their ranches lay. Beyond that, greens meshed with golds, which meshed with more green. The view was spectacular. Oregon, Washington, Montana and Idaho, all four states visible in all their mind-boggling glory.

Awe-inspiring.

And, Ty hoped, irresistible. "What do you see?" he repeated.

She bit her lip and stared. Looking as if a good wind could knock her over. He backed off for a moment and spread out the blanket. "Come here."

She sank to the blanket beside him, her eyes riveted to the view. A huge, soul-shattering sigh escaped her.

"Well?"

"I see...a place I wanted to be mine. But it's not, not really." She hesitated, closing her eyes, hiding. "I wanted it be home, Ty. I wanted that so much."

"You still haven't figured out the truth. It's right before your eyes and you won't even see it."

"I don't know what you're talking about." She seemed to fold into herself, shoulders hunched as she knelt on the blanket as far from him as she could get.

It hurt, watching her hurt. "It's simple," he told her. "Open your eyes, Zoe, and face it." Unable to hold back, he grabbed her shoulders and made her do just that. "Look, dammit, and face the fact that you *are* home." He added a little shake for good measure, then whipped her around so he could see her pale face. "God, Zoe, get a clue. It doesn't matter whose name is on the deed of Triple M. It doesn't matter what your birth certificate says your last name is."

"Doesn't matter?" She tried to shove him away, but he wasn't going to budge. "Maybe to you, a man from nowhere and no one, it doesn't matter. You don't care about who and what your parents were, but I—"

"I never said I didn't care. My mother was a whore, and when she wasn't having men over behind my father's back she liked to drink. My father hated being tied down by his kids. He liked to use his belt to prove the point. He got himself killed in prison on his tenth visit and I was glad. *Glad*, Zoe. I lived in the streets with my brother for more years than I want to remember, starving and fighting and stealing to survive, so don't you ever tell me I don't care where I came from."

She'd stopped shoving at him at his first words, so it surprised him when he tried to pull away and she reversed their roles, gripping his shirt in two tight fists. "Ty—God, I'm sorry."

"I care where I came from, Zoe. It's molded me, maybe even dictated who I am today. But I don't use it as an excuse to waste away the life that was given to me. And it makes me sick to watch you do that very thing."

She held on to him with voracious strength, even when he tried again to pull away. Surprising him, she dropped her forehead to his chest and shook her head. "I feel so stupid when you put it like that."

"Not stupid." He caved in, wrapping his arms around her slight figure as he'd wanted to do for so long. "Muleheaded, most definitely."

With a little laugh, she snuggled closer, tucking her head beneath his chin as if she belonged there. As if she'd *always* belonged there. His heart surged in his chest so painfully he couldn't speak.

"I'm sorry, Ty."

"You scared me this week," he said when he could, his voice husky with emotion. "So stoic. I was unprepared for that, for what it would feel like to watch you calmly nod at the destruction of your dreams. To watch you refuse to talk about it, watch you continue to work, so silently destroyed."

Her arms tightened around his neck.

"I was so desperate I nearly begged Delia and Maddie to sell me the land just so I could give it to you."

She froze, then lifted her head. "That's crazy."

"Well, Slim, that's what I am. Crazy."

"For me." She stared at him, startled. "Why? I can't figure that out."

"Neither can I most of the time."

He was teasing her, and she didn't seem to know how to take that. So he dragged her onto his lap. "It's not really a logical thing, Zoe. It's more like a heart thing. A 'just because' thing. Because I can no longer picture my life without you. I love the way you look at me when you think I'm not looking back. Because I love the way you love your sisters with everything you've got, even though you doubt and mistrust that very love. And I think you're the smartest, sweetest, most passionate woman I've ever known." He paused. "Should I go on?"

She was baffled, touched, frightened. "I don't know what to do with you."

That deflated him a bit, for it seemed obvious to him. "Do whatever feels right," he finally said, weary.

"Anything?" She looked up at him, bit her lower lip, so

unsure she shook with it. She hated this, this self-consciousness that would not go away. But he'd bared his soul; the least she could do was try to show him how she felt in return.

He was looking at her with that dark, hungry look that always made her so weak. She knelt up before him, nearly losing her courage. "Anything at all?"

"Yes."

Slowly she pulled her T-shirt over her head, then at the look of shock on his face, she balled it up and pressed it to her breasts. "I—I'm sorry. I just wanted to show you how I felt— Forget it, I'm really bad at this." Fumbling, she tried to right her shirt again.

His hand covered hers, and when she could force herself to look at him, his stormy eyes were clear. And hot. His voice shook. "Let me get this straight. You wanted to show me how you felt because you couldn't tell me?"

Miserable and ashamed, she nodded.

"And to show me how you felt, you wanted to make love with me?"

"Yes," she whispered.

His smile was slow and sexy. "Then what are you waiting for?" He brought her fisted hands to his mouth and kissed her knuckles. Slid the wrinkled shirt out from between her fingers and tossed it aside. "Show me how you feel, then, Zoe. Show me before I die of wondering, of wanting and yearning."

Tears were in her eyes when she kicked off her boots and wrapped her arms around his neck. No one understood her as this man did, and some of the pain of the past week began to fade.

"Show me some more," he said in a raspy whisper, his mouth blazing a trail up her jaw to nibble on her ear, his hands sliding up her bare back.

With that encouragement, she wriggled out of her jeans, kneeling before him in nothing other than her white lacy bra and matching panties.

He traced the valley between her breasts with a finger, swallowing visibly at the sight of her body trembling for his. "I've been dying," he murmured. "Dying watching you push me away over and over again. Tell me you won't do it anymore, Zoe. Tell me that you're trying to show me how much you care in the only way you know how."

She wanted to, but the promises stuck in her throat. She wasn't sure she could ever tell him, even now. "I—" His hands, those wonderfully talented hands, skimmed down her sides, teasing, making her burn. Closing her eyes, she groaned. "I'm trying, Ty. Trying to show you what I can't tell you."

He was up on his knees now, sweeping her off hers, wrapping her legs around his waist and then sinking with her back down to the blanket.

Towering above her, he looked into her face. "Someday," he told her, sliding his hips slowly over the wisp of silk between her legs, making her arch up and gasp, "you're going to tell me instead of show me." And he moved on her again.

"Someday," she agreed mindlessly, nearly coming undone when he removed her bra and just looked down at her for a long moment. He let out a long, shaky breath as he admired what he'd uncovered, finally dipping his head down to slide his mouth over her. A finger hooked in her panties, drawing them slowly down, and he groaned at the sight spread out before him.

Her senses were swimming, her heart drumming. And she wanted him as she'd never wanted another. "Ty…one of us is overdressed. Way overdressed."

He got out of his clothes in five seconds flat, both of

them laughing breathlessly when a chipmunk scolded them, startling Ty into swearing. Then the laughter was gone and his powerful body was stretching out over hers as he linked their fingers. "Just the beginning," he vowed, then bent over her, taking her mouth as he plunged into her.

She arched up into his thrust, whimpering shamelessly for more. "Ty—"

"I'm here, Zoe." His voice was rough, his words low and thick with passion. He held her hips in his big hands, lifting her to meet him. "I'm right here."

She gasped his name again as he surged against her in a hard, even rhythm. Over and over.

"You've got me. All of me." Faster and faster. "Always," he assured her.

They soared together beneath the sun and the wide-open sky. And when it was over, when they were tangled together in a damp pile of trembling limbs and pounding pulses, their misty gazes met and held, each of them shattered apart by emotion, yet whole in a way they'd never been before.

Ty had meant to spend the entire day at his own ranch, working on some desperately needed chores. Instead he found himself riding to Triple M.

He had to see Zoe. See if yesterday in the woods had been a fluke. Hell, maybe she'd just had an itch and he'd been handy to scratch it.

Some scratch.

What had happened between him and Zoe was a once-in-a-lifetime thing. He knew that now, and knew he could never walk away, not from her.

His pensive mood vanished when he came over the ridge and looked ahead. Zoe and two of the ranch hands were painting the last of the cottages, though Zoe seemed to have more paint on her than the window edging she was working on.

He dismounted and moved close to Zoe, making sure no one was within hearing range. "Morning," he said, his voice unintentionally husky and full of promise.

She gave a little jump. Her nose was sunburned. So was her neck, and he wondered what other parts they'd sunburned yesterday. "How are you?"

"Um…" She glanced around, as if making sure no one could hear. "I'm fine."

He laughed. "There's nothing indecent about being fine, you know. No one is going to take one look at your face and realize you did it outside while screaming my name—"

She slapped a hand over his mouth and looked horrified. "Shh! Someone will hear you! I said I was fine! Fine! Fine! Fine!"

Fine. Great, she was fine and he was dying. He decided to go for the direct route. What the hell, he didn't have a doubt in his head. They belonged together, and as he saw it, she was just putting off the inevitable. "I love you, Zoe. Stay with me tonight."

"You…*tonight?*"

She looked so shocked. So unsure. He nodded but felt the sudden heaviness in his heart. "What's the matter? You turn into a pumpkin if you make love in a bed?"

Crossing her arms in that stubborn gesture he recognized all too well, she shook her head. "I…don't think it's a good idea to rush this."

"Rush this?" He laughed, but it was hollow. "Zoe, I fell for you the first day I saw you. It's too late to be rushed now."

Her face crumpled then and so did her composure. Her eyes, her huge, beautiful eyes, nearly killed him. "I need a little more time, Ty."

"Time," he repeated dully.

"Yes."

"You get naked with me, twice now, but you can't come over and sleep in my arms?"

She closed her eyes.

How was it that he was completely bowled over by what they had between them and she could still pretend it didn't exist? He turned away, needing distance if he was going to come up with any patience at all. He mounted his horse and was nearly out of earshot when she called after him.

Reluctantly he stopped, knowing everything he was, everything he felt, was on his face. So exposed, he thought with a grimace, but he couldn't help it, couldn't hold back what he felt, not even for her.

Slowly, he turned.

She stared at him, misty-eyed. "I'm sorry," she whispered, her words carrying on the breeze. Her hand rubbed absently at her heart, as if it hurt. "I'm so sorry."

That made two of them.

Everything he wanted, everything he thought about…his entire future stood there looking at him with eyes that proclaimed a love she couldn't admit to.

It was the hardest thing he'd ever done, but he had to let her go. Had to give her the space she needed.

Heart aching, he turned away and rode toward the harsh mountains. He needed to be alone, and high on the peaks was the only place to go to do that.

Chapter 18

Zoe felt as though she paced for two days. Two days, and not a word from Ty.

While he was gone doing only God knew what in those unforgiving mountains that she stared at a thousand times a day, Triple M received another reservation request for fall. And several for the following spring.

Their modest, hopeful success felt good.

And for Zoe, it also felt empty.

It was amazing that people wanted to come from all over and help run their ranch, and *pay* for the privilege. It was exciting to share with her sisters, to have a real future for the first time in her life.

But she wanted Ty. Wanted to see him, and tell him she knew she was home. Wanted to laugh with him and race their horses over their land. Wanted to spar with him and then make up.

She wanted to make love with him.

But he didn't come back, and she had no one to blame but herself.

On the third night Zoe went to bed early. There was a package there, lying on her quilt, wrapped in the familiar plain brown paper bag that signified her mysterious gift giver. Her throat tightened as she sank to the bed.

Delia had done so much for her over the years and somehow she always just knew when Zoe needed her the most.

She opened the bag, and a delicate gold bracelet fell into her hand. It was small, dainty, and her heart nearly burst at its beauty. It was the bracelet from town, the one she'd admired so many weeks ago. And now it was hers.

"Oh, my God," she breathed, because Delia hadn't known about the bracelet. No one knew how she'd coveted the beautiful gold chain.

No one but Ty.

Clearly he'd remembered how she'd yearned for it...but it meant so much more than that. It meant that all along it had been Ty leaving her the presents. The gloves, the boots, the adding machine. "Oh, Ty," she whispered, covering her mouth with shaking fingers as memories flashed.

Ty frowning over her cut fingers, and then the gloves mysteriously appearing. Ty pointing at her tennis shoes and demanding she better protect her feet, then the new boots that had shown up only days later. Ty telling her she worked too hard, that she needed help, and then the adding machine had appeared and had been such a welcome addition to her office.

Ty had done all of it.

As Zoe sat there alone on the bed, frightened sick about the man she couldn't stop thinking about, her heart warmed, really warmed, as maybe it never had before.

"Oh, Ty," she whispered, aching. "Where are you?"

She'd chased him away. He would come back eventually, sooner than later, because he'd have to for his horses, but things wouldn't be the same. Not when he'd declared his feelings for her and she'd cruelly pushed them away.

Zoe moaned, dropped her head into her hands. Ty had been through so much in his lifetime, and still he'd managed to recognize love when he felt it. He hadn't been afraid.

And neither should she. She'd been so terrified, so sure that keeping herself blocked off was the only way. She'd hidden behind her past to do it when she should have been looking to the future.

She'd gotten hurt, anyway, and it had been of her own doing. It couldn't be too late. Ty was gone, and she could only hope he came back soon, but there were other ways to express this newfound surging of hope and joy and…yes, love.

It didn't matter how late it was, this couldn't wait. Giddy, she dashed down the hall and flicked on the light in Delia's room.

With a string of impressive swearwords, the now-rudely awoken Delia covered her eyes. "You'd better be male, gorgeous and built to please," she declared in a voice rough with sleep.

Zoe laughed. "Sorry. Female, short and—"

Delia's pillow hit her in the mouth with deadly accuracy, and Zoe happily leaped on the bed to retaliate, but she was quickly pinned beneath her taller, stronger sister.

"You're dead," Delia swore, sitting on her, but before she could meet that threat, there was a gasp at the door.

Maddie stood there in a nightie holding Socks, eyes sleepy…and shocked as she gaped at her two wrestling sisters. "What are you two fighting about?"

"We're not fighting," Zoe managed to say breathlessly, squirming to get free to no avail.

"Zoe, she's on top of you with a pillow raised over your head," Maddie answered dryly. She kissed Socks on the top of his head and set him down. Hands on her hips, she said, "You're fighting. Delia, get off of her."

"She's insane," Delia complained, but got off Zoe, who took a deep, grateful breath.

"I'm not crazy," Zoe told them, and reached down to hug Delia. "I'm just really happy."

Delia froze, then frowned up into Zoe's face, feeling her forehead.

"And I'm not sick, either," Zoe assured her, holding out a hand to Maddie, who came quickly.

"Maybe she's had more laced hot chocolate," Maddie said worriedly to Delia, also feeling Zoe's forehead.

Zoe rolled her eyes. "Didn't you two hear me? I said I'm *happy*." At their shock, she sighed. "Look, I know I've never come right out and said that before. But it's true." Or it would be, as soon as Ty came back.

Delia scooted over on the bed, making room for them all to sit. She offered everyone covers, which they took, snuggling close like old times, when they'd sneak out of their beds at their foster home to be together. "You don't have to lie, Zoe," Delia said kindly. "We know how much you hurt over finding out about your parents. And we know how much you wanted this place to be yours. How much it meant to you." Delia's eyes filled, a shock because she never cried. "And I promise, hon, if I knew for certain this place was mine, I'd give it to you."

Maddie squeezed Zoe close. "Me, too," she whispered. "We just don't want you to go."

"Go?" Zoe choked, holding on to them so tight they each winced, but she didn't let go, couldn't. How could she have done this to them? "I could never leave you. Never. Ever. I swear. I can't believe you thought I would."

"You've been so unhappy." Maddie's smile was shaky. "We've been so worried."

"I'm just a slow idiot," Zoe said. "But I have it together now. I'm so sorry."

"Then we'll stay here," Delia said tremulously. "Together, forever. Right?"

"Right," Zoe vowed, still clutching them. Socks meowed gently, adding his vote as he came in to be part of the snuggle. "Forever."

"No matter whose name shows up on the deed when Cade learns the truth?"

Zoe looked at Maddie, saw the fears she'd been living with, and wanted to cry. Hell, she *did* cry. "No matter what, I promise. God, you guys."

They hugged tightly, content and soggy. Zoe was surrounded by them, just as she wanted to be. "I wasn't faking before," she said with a sniff. "I *am* happy. I just never gave it much thought before. We've always been…well, too busy to be happy. You know?"

"Yes," Maddie whispered, gently tucking a strand of Zoe's hair behind her ear. The three of them sat Indian-style under the quilt, holding hands. "But even while being busy, Zoe, you can still be happy."

"I know, but I didn't get it before. Not until now. Not until here. I'm sorry, I know I'm a pain in the ass. I'm a pessimist. I'm selfish. I'm a lot of things, but I'm trying to change here. And I wanted you guys to know something, it's why I woke you up." She swallowed because suddenly there was a lump in her throat the size of which couldn't be believed. "I…love you. I love you both so much."

She could feel their shock and didn't blame them. It had been far too long since they'd talked like this, too long since she'd told them. She laughed, delighted with them and herself, then hugged them again. "I do. I love you both so much."

"We love you, too," Delia cried, which made Zoe tear up again.

"We need stock in Kleenex if we're going to do this often," Zoe joked, swiping at her eyes.

Maddie cupped Zoe's face, eyes narrowed. "What's happened to bring that light to your pretty eyes?" she asked.

Zoe let out a little laugh and covered Maddie's hands with her own. "It's pretty unbelievable, Mad. Not even sure *I* believe it."

"Well, we're sitting down, aren't we? Tell us," Delia demanded. "Tell us what has such a grouch doing a one-eighty until she's spewing love all over the place."

"Well…" Zoe held her stomach. Butterflies leaped wildly. It was one thing to remind them that she loved them. It was another to tell them what she'd discovered about herself. That she had much more room in her heart than she'd ever believed possible. That she was actually standing on the very edge of a future that beckoned and enticed her. All she needed to do was leap.

She dragged in some air and plunged. "I love you both. I always will. But I also love—"

A shadow appeared in the dark doorway and she nearly swallowed her tongue. Standing there, looking positively, lethally gorgeous, was Ty, and he had eyes for only her.

"You love…?" he questioned in a voice made harsh by need.

"Ty," she breathed, her face lighting up with so much emotion it hurt him to look at her. God, he'd missed her so much, it was all he could do to stay there in the doorway and just look his fill. He'd come just to stare at her sleeping, wondering if she had liked the bracelet he'd left on her bed. He hadn't planned on seeing her, but he wasn't sorry, not when she was watching him with her heart in her eyes.

She let go of her sisters, shot them a little nervous grin and stood. Her hair was wild, her eyes bright, just as he'd imagined her over the past long days.

She wore a huge T-shirt that had seen better days. It came to her knees, baggy and shapeless, and it didn't matter.

He knew what was underneath, but more important, he knew what lay in her heart, even if she didn't. Inside and out, she was the most beautiful woman he'd ever seen.

Somewhere on the mountain he'd come to terms with the fact that she was going to be slower than him to accept the crazy, undeniable love between them. And he was going to be patient if it killed him, which it just might.

"I didn't know you were back," she said softly.

"I just got back." He'd come straight here, even though it'd been late. After three days of emptiness and anger and regrets, he'd missed her insanely. He'd had to see her.

Her eyes were huge and damp, her dark lashes spiked with tears. But her lips were curved as she came closer, stopping just before him.

"Ask me again," she said.

She was killing him, but he played along. "Who do you love?"

"You," she whispered. She let out a little laugh, then said it louder. "I love you, Ty Jackson."

Before he could even begin to absorb the words that had his heart lodged in his throat, she was reaching for him, sliding that body to his and wrapping her arms around his neck.

Catching her to him, he whirled her around, squeezing her tight as joy flowed through his veins.

A delicate cough reminded him they weren't alone, and

he lifted his head over Zoe's, smiling down into two pairs of misty, happy eyes without letting go of his future. He had two handfuls of shirt and skin and warm woman and he wasn't sure if he *could* let go, since Zoe had a viselike grip on his neck.

"I suppose you're hungry," Maddie said to him through her tears.

"Starved." He hugged Zoe closer.

"And I suppose you're going to want us to leave now," Delia said through a wet smile.

"Wait." Zoe pulled back to stare into Ty's eyes. He could swear he could see all the way into her soul, and his was mirrored there.

Then, so gently he felt his own eyes go damp, Zoe cupped his face, smiling with the tenderness and love he'd only dreamed about.

"All of you, all three of you love me," she said, her voice thick and husky. "I'm sorry I was so slow to understand that. I felt burdened by the weight instead of blessed, but I was wrong. I'm the luckiest woman on earth, because together you gave me the greatest gift of all, the gift of life." Her fingers stroked Ty's jaw and she smiled at him through her tears. "Much as I tried to throw that gift away, you persevered, and now I want to give something back."

"The only thing I want, Zoe, is you."

Maddie and Delia sighed dreamily.

Zoe's eyes filled again. "Then take me," she said. "I'm yours."

"For keeps?" He nudged her closer. "As in becoming my lover, my best friend, my soul mate...my wife?"

The tears fell. "Yes, I want to be Mrs. Jackson. For now and forever."

Epilogue

It wasn't until much later that night, after Maddie and Delia had finally stopped hugging and feeding them, that Ty was alone with Zoe.

"Finally," he said, coming slowly toward her. They were in his house now, in his bedroom, right where he'd wanted her for too long.

"Finally what?" She smiled, but it was a breathless one and he hadn't even touched her yet. Ty looked forward to making her much more breathless before the sun came up.

"Finally I get to see..." He slipped off her sweatshirt. Beneath was the loose T-shirt he'd been dying to get off her. "Kick off your shoes, sweetheart. Yeah, like that." Her sweat bottoms slid down her legs at his touch. Then he lifted her arms and slipped off the ragged T-shirt, leaving her bare and glorious.

"No sunburn," he whispered, gliding his hands over her smooth, creamy skin. "I was worried."

"You protected me well." Smiling up at him, she

wrapped her arms around his neck and brought that incredible body flush to his.

"I always will," he vowed, scooping her up. He was halfway to the bed with her when she laid a hand on his chest and looked at him steadily, love pouring from her gaze.

"Both our dreams have been met," she whispered, her voice thick with emotion.

Gently he set her down on his mattress and covered her with his body. He braced his weight on his arms as he looked down into her face. "The mystery wasn't solved," he reminded her gently. "You still don't know which of you is owner of Triple M."

"But I know something better." Tugging, she pulled him close, then closer still, kissing him with her entire heart and soul. "I know I'm loved. By Delia and Maddie. By you. And I know where I belong, Ty."

"With me." Capturing her head in his big hands, he kissed her back. "Forever and always," he reminded her.

"Forever and always," she repeated softly. And they let their love take them to ecstasy.

* * * * *

If you enjoyed what you just read,
then we've got an offer you can't resist!

Take 2 bestselling love stories FREE!

Plus get a FREE surprise gift!

Clip this page and mail it to Silhouette Reader Service™

IN U.S.A.	IN CANADA
3010 Walden Ave.	P.O. Box 609
P.O. Box 1867	Fort Erie, Ontario
Buffalo, N.Y. 14240-1867	L2A 5X3

YES! Please send me 2 free Silhouette Intimate Moments® novels and my free surprise gift. Then send me 6 brand-new novels every month, which I will receive months before they're available in stores. In the U.S.A., bill me at the bargain price of $3.57 plus 25¢ delivery per book and applicable sales tax, if any*. In Canada, bill me at the bargain price of $3.96 plus 25¢ delivery per book and applicable taxes**. That's the complete price and a savings of over 10% off the cover prices—what a great deal! I understand that accepting the 2 free books and gift places me under no obligation ever to buy any books. I can always return a shipment and cancel at any time. Even if I never buy another book from Silhouette, the 2 free books and gift are mine to keep forever. So why not take us up on our invitation. You'll be glad you did!

245 SEN CNFF

345 SEN CNFG

Name _____ (PLEASE PRINT)

Address _____ Apt.# _____

City _____ State/Prov. _____ Zip/Postal Code _____

* Terms and prices subject to change without notice. Sales tax applicable in N.Y.
** Canadian residents will be charged applicable provincial taxes and GST.
   All orders subject to approval. Offer limited to one per household.
   ® are registered trademarks of Harlequin Enterprises Limited.

INMOM99   ©1998 Harlequin Enterprises Limited

THE FORTUNES OF TEXAS

This BRAND-NEW program includes 12 incredible stories about a wealthy Texas family rocked by scandal and embedded in mystery.

It is based on the tremendously successful *Fortune's Children* continuity.

Membership in this family has its privileges…and its price.

But what a fortune can't buy, a true-bred Texas love is sure to bring!

This exciting program will start in September 1999!

Available at your favorite retail outlet.

Silhouette®

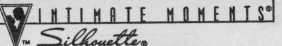

Available July 1999 from Silhouette Books...

AGENT OF THE BLACK WATCH
by BJ JAMES

The World's Most Eligible Bachelor:
Secret-agent lover Kieran O'Hara was on a desperate mission.
His objective: Anything but marriage!

Kieran's mission pitted him against a crafty killer...and
the prime suspect's beautiful sister. For the first time in his
career, Kieran's instincts as a man overwhelmed his lawman's
control...and he claimed Beau Anna Cahill as his lover. But
would this innocent remain in his bed once she learned his
secret agenda?

Each month, Silhouette Books brings you an
irresistible bachelor in these all-new, original
stories. Find out how the sexiest, most-sought-after men
are finally caught....

Available at your favorite retail outlet.

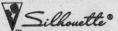

W J
Jm

THE MACGREGORS OF OLD...

#1 *New York Times* bestselling author

NORA ROBERTS

has won readers' hearts with her enormously popular
MacGregor family saga. Now read about the MacGregors'
proud and passionate Scottish forebears in this
romantic, tempestuous tale set against the bloody
background of the historic battle of Culloden.

Coming in July 1999

REBELLION

One look at the ravishing red-haired beauty and Brigham
Langston was captivated. But though Serena MacGregor
had the face of an angel, she was a wildcat who spurned
his advances with a rapier-sharp tongue. To hot-tempered
Serena, Brigham was just another Englishman to be
despised. But in the arms of the dashing and dangerous
English lord, the proud Scottish beauty felt her hatred
melting with the heat of their passion.

Available at your favorite retail outlet.

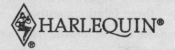

HARLEQUIN®